Squid Boy Raven Girl

R. R. DAVIS

A Blackwater Press book

First published in the United States of America by
Blackwater Press, LLC

Library of Congress Control Number: 2024952858

ISBN: 978-1-963614-06-0

Cover design by Eilidh Muldoon

Illustrations by Francesco Dabbicco
francescodabbiccoart.com

Blackwater Press
120 Capitol Street
Charleston, WV 25301
United States

blackwaterpress.com

Praise for
Squid Boy Raven Girl

In this engrossing novel R. R. Davis deftly immerses the reader in the atmospheric, enigmatic, and perilous inner and outer worlds inhabited by Robert, a preteen living in a coastal Canadian Inuit village. The atmosphere of this book lingers in the mind long after it is put down. A good read.

Patricia Vestal, author of *Passageways*

This book kept me a little off balance all the way through and it was precisely this which drove me forward to the ending. This is a tale of growing up and seeing things as they are. Or are they? Set on a remote island in Labrador, this story explores an Inuit community that is striking in its wisdom and resiliency, and at the same time suffering broadly from the impacts of colonialism. It's an engaging story wrapped in a shroud of mystery.

Iain MacDonald, author of
I Piped, That She Might Dance

Praise for *The Various Stages of a Garden Well-Kept*

All the more impressive when considering that *The Various Stages of a Garden Well Kept* is author R. R. Davis' debut as a novelist, this original and exceptionally well written collection of memorable characters and an inherently interesting and narrative driven story of the emigrant in America is especially and unreservedly recommended.

Midwest Book Review

Almost otherworldly ... a story of love and loss, but it is ultimately buoyed by the possibility of what fresh insights a new season might bring to light.

Bold Life

1

Summer Solstice

June 21, 1995

"I found another one!" Jacob screams in delight as he rips a blue six-armed starfish from the rock it had chosen to anchor itself to within the tide pool. With the sensitive ears of an eight-year-old, Jacob can hear the soft Velcro sound of each minute suctioned foot as it reluctantly releases its grip under his monstrous power. My younger brother puts the starfish on his face and looks up at me, yelling in mock terror, "Robert, it's attacking me. It's the monster from the dark sea!" He flails his arms, rolls his eyes, and makes cartoonish grimaces with his mouth as he laughs uncontrollably. His laughter is contagious, and I break out into laughter too.

I am the more serious and focused of the two of us. Jacob says I'm nerdy because I like reading and studying, which he really, really doesn't. We're very different in many ways, but the way I see it, we complement each other. While he plays his silly games, I turn back to my own aquatic world to find the elusive creatures that lay hidden within. Periwinkles and whelks move in slow motion, waving their antennae with the fluid grace of ballet dancers from the realm of mollusks. There are a number of sea urchins sitting like green pincushions on the pink-purple crusty algae growths, hidden within the Irish moss. The sea urchins seem never to move, but I know they do. The life of echinoderms – urchins and starfish. They live in such a timeless world that snails run as fast as fish compared to them. I continue looking through this particular pool until at last I find what I am looking for. A sea urchin marked with a wire bread tie fastened to its spikes. I placed this marker on the urchin yesterday during the low tide, about this same time, and promised myself I would return to it today to look for the underwater version of the porcupine to see how far it had moved. Today I see it has migrated to the far side of its little home. Sometimes I sit and watch the urchins and try to see them move. It's like watching the hour hand on the clock in our bedroom while we lay still in the morning waiting for sunrise so we can start our day. I like to watch the more animated crabs as they scuttle around the rocks in search of anything they can put into their tiny mouths. They are pretty much the creepiest of the creatures I find here, with the exception of the parasitic flukes (I think that is what they are called) that attach themselves to the little leg joints of the crabs and suck out their juices.

It doesn't take long before the bitterly cold water numbs my hands and sends them into unbearable pain. I sit on a boulder and stick my hands deep into my coat and wait for the blood to return to my foolish fingers. I look out over the inlet that leads out to the Atlantic. The bulk of Ukasiksalik Island, where we live, protects the mainland shore from the crashing fury of storm waves that come through. Today, the waters are calm, the sky is clear, and the air is a perfect twenty-two degrees Celsius. I close my eyes to face up to the midday sun and feel its heat. I hear the motor of a distant fishing boat as it heads back out to the deep waters for another run. The sound is mostly covered up by the cries of the seagulls that nest on the nearby rocks and feast on the same creatures we have been looking at, as well as a not-so-nourishing diet of garbage that comes flowing endlessly out of our village. I pull mussels from the nearby rocks and throw them up at the seagulls to watch their aerobatic motions as they swerve mid-air to catch what they have learned to be a free meal. Jacob joins my game of mussel throwing, though his trajectories might go straight up into the air only to come down on his head, or they might altogether fail to attain any altitude and go straight into the water just a couple of meters in front of him.

I find a fairly fresh dead fish in a shallow tide pool, "Watch this Jacob, a flying fish!" I throw it straight up, admiring its slow motion dance as it gracefully twists and spins its way to the apex (that means the highest or most extreme part) of its flight, pauses in space for the shortest of moments, and dives back toward me. The fish picks up speed (9.8 m/second/second, according to Mrs. Sally's science lesson) to end its descent just one arm's reach in front of my head, at which point a black blur rushes by me, grabbing the fish from the air. Startled, I trip backwards and fall on my butt. I turn to watch a large raven fly off with its prize. Jacob laughs at my antics. The raven lands on a nearby rock to join my brother with its own corvid cackle before picking away at the small fish snack.

This is a perfect day. The longest day of the year. The summer solstice. Each year we take this day off to celebrate. This morning we awoke shortly after 4:00 a.m., 4:17 a.m. to be exact, and looked out our window at the water, alive with the first sunlight. We could not actually see the sun rise, since the rock was blocking our view of the northeast. "The Rock." That is what we call Ukasiksalik Island, because it is just that: a big old rock. It is so hard that you cannot even dig a well or bury a sewer pipe in it. We get all our water from a stream that runs off the cliff beyond our house. It has been cold and rainy most of June, but today we are rewarded with blue skies.

This is one of the few days in the year that Father allows us to spend the entire day outside. We sing, we run circles around the weeds and scree that make up our backyard, we throw rocks, and we lay on the ground soaking in the sun's warmth and pretending we are seals taking an afternoon nap while patting our bellies with our flippers. We build rock towers by stacking one rock on top of the next until we dare not tempt gravity anymore. At the end of this game, we will have constructed twenty or more rock sculptures randomly spaced along the water's edge. Jacob gets frustrated at this game, as his towers are no more than four or five rocks high before falling.

We have been outside playing for a couple of hours now, and I am getting hungry. We should head back into the house, where Mrs. Sally will fix us fish sandwiches and potato chips. Maybe not yet. I want to sit for a while longer with my eyes closed and enjoy the sun. Jacob has run off again to look for special rocks, and I daydream as I listen to a fishing boat. Occasionally I hear a man's voice as it carries across the water. I listen intently to try to detect my father's voice amongst the others. My father is a fisherman during this time of year, when the waterways are clear and before the sea fills with ice again. My father said he would have to go out today because *you gotta run 'em while the runnin's good*. But he swore he would be back a little early to celebrate the solstice.

I get up, brush myself off, and I'm about to call Jacob to go inside with me for lunch. Suddenly, I hear him screaming my name from the water's edge just around the bend. He appears before me, running my way with wildness in his eyes, screaming something about a monster. He is as scared as I have ever seen him. "Robert! It's over there. Crawling out of the water. It's the cracker monster! I saw it. I saw it. It's going to eat us!" He runs right past me and toward the house, shouting, "Mrs. Sally! The cracker monster!" He barges through the backdoor and into the kitchen. I can hear a commotion as he cries hysterically to Mrs. Sally about the monster by the water.

I stand looking at the water, seeing nothing. Monsters don't come out in the daytime. Father says they are only to be feared at night. I decide not to follow Jacob into the house. In an act of bravery, I hesitantly step toward the direction Jacob came from. I feel the tingle of fright prickling the back of my neck, but I have to see. I realize this might be the first time I have ever acted like a *man*. I feel like my father, who is afraid of nothing. I stoop down low and hide behind little boulders that pepper the tidal zone. When I get to the edge of our property, I pause. My brother and I are strictly forbidden to go beyond this line. Still, Jacob was there. He saw something. I look around to check if anyone is watching, and I take a step over the line. The thought of getting caught leaving the yard without permission is more frightening than that of seeing a monster. I take another step, and another, and I see something on the ground crawling out of the water. I stand, unable to move. My heart is beating my chest open, trying to run back to the house, even if the rest of my body stays behind.

Frozen in place, I watch as a giant tentacle lies still on the rounded gray stones and pebbles that make up the small beach. One end of the tentacle arm is stretched out pointing toward the unfamiliar land before it, and the fat end of the arm is rolling in the waves generated by a passing fishing vessel. I realize that it might be a monster, but only a small piece of a dead monster. I don't get too close to it, because I am afraid that it might not really be dead. I can see the large suction cups running along one side of the arm. It is as long as two grown-ups lying head to foot, whitish with a tint of pinkish-brown, and it smells strongly of fish. As I get braver, I take a couple more steps toward it and I see green crabs scurrying out from underneath it. They look at me with their beady eyes, scolding me for interrupting their dinner. A crazy thought runs through my head, *Little tiny crabs eating a giant monster. Maybe we should fear the crabs*. Only this isn't really a monster. This is the arm of a giant squid. I have read about how they are rarely, but occasionally, washed up on shore, or caught in a fisherman's net. In my *Deep-Sea Fish* book there is a picture of a line of men holding a stretched-out squid they had just caught. Another picture showed the squid's eyeball alongside an equal-sized soccer ball. Squids and octopi are cephalopods. They have arms or tentacles.

"Quite a find, huh?" The voice came from the bank just above the waterline. "You're the Scotsman's boy, aren't you?"

I look up, startled. A short Innu man in an unzipped white hooded jacket, dark sweater, black pants that taper at the ankles, and a woolen cap that reads *Arctic Cat*, stands looking down at me. He laughs. "I didn't think John ever let you kids out of the house. He afraid you might talk to us?" In one hand, the man carries a plastic bag, occasionally holding it up to his face and breathing in. The other hand is waving back and forth slowly, directing an unseen musical orchestra with no quantifiable rhythm. "Well, your daddy's an asshole, and you can tell him that Billy Cloud said so." The man steps down toward me and holds the plastic bag to my face, "Here, have some. It'll take you off this goddamned rock."

I turn and run back to the house just as Mrs. Sally is opening the backdoor to call me in for our lunch. I get to the door, out of breath and pale as snow. *Never leave the yard. Never leave the yard.* I run past Mrs. Sally and take the stairs two at a time to the second floor, where my bedroom awaits me. I jump into the bed and lie there, buried in blankets. I am scared as can be, but I don't know why. I cannot understand who that man was, and why he said those things. I only know he was the only monster I saw out there. When my father hears that I left the yard and talked to someone, he will be angry with me. "You are still a child," he will tell me. "You are not ready to go out into the world." If all the people out there are like that man, then he is right.

I have not been out of this yard or house often, and of those times, I cannot remember talking to anyone, except my grandmother or Mr. Dave. We saw a lot of people on those occasions, but Father would not let us talk to them. They all seemed to stare at us, like we were different. I know we are a *little* different, especially me. My father once explained it to me. He said that he was from Scotland and came over here *to work the waters and run the fish*. He was a young man at that time, meant for the sea. He met my mother, an Innu girl, she was just sixteen, and they fell in love. He has lived here in this fishing village ever since. Jacob looks like my mother and all the other people here, but I have my father's curly, sandy-colored hair. I am tall and thin, as he was as a young man. *The people here are different*, my father would tell me. He didn't just mean they *look* different. *They don't belong on this rock, in this fishing village. They are from the mainland, from the forests. They are from a people who hunted caribou and wolves. They have their own ways, and they are lost here.* He looked at me fiercely, *Robert, they have their own monsters*.

My thoughts are interrupted by a light tapping at my bedroom door. Mrs. Sally stands in the doorway looking at me in her quiet way. Like my mother, she is an Innu. Short, a little chubby, black hair, round face. Pretty, like my mother. She comes into my room and sits on the bed next to me.

"What's the matter, Robert? Did you see the monster too?" She is not making fun of me; she is completely serious. She looks me straight in the eyes. This makes me a little uncomfortable. I look down at my hands as she continues. "There are monsters everywhere, but they cannot hurt you if you don't allow them to. Robert, you control the monsters. They can control *you* only with fear. Overcome your fear, and the monsters will become nothing but a small tit-dog. Do you understand?"

I wonder if she is talking about the giant squid tenta-

cle, about the man called Billy Cloud, or something far more important. She is like that when she speaks. Sometimes Mrs. Sally knows things that no one else knows. She might be the smartest person in this village. I guess that is why Father hired her to be our sitter and tutor. She comes out here most every day while my father is out on the boat. In the winter, she is here maybe three or four days a week. Father is home more often in the wintertime, and that's when he homeschools us as well. When Father teaches us, he gives us facts and tells us the black-and-white things of the world. When Mrs. Sally teaches us, she fills us with information and makes us come up with our own conclusions and opinions. She offers her viewpoint on how the people in this village think and live, how the Canadian government runs and how they treat indigenous and First Nation people, and how men and women have different ways of seeing the world. Mrs. Sally says that I am one of the smartest kids she knows and that I should go to Memorial University of Newfoundland in St. John's. She says nobody from Davis Inlet ever goes to college. Nobody from here ever goes anywhere. But, she says, that will all change one day. She says that the Innu are a strong and proud people, and once we learn to fight our monsters, we will be a great nation once again. I cannot help but feel proud that she counts me as one of the Innu people.

Mrs. Sally gets up and leads me downstairs to the kitchen where I smell pan-fried fish with garlic and onions. Jacob is just washing down his fish sandwich with a big glass of milk. I sit at the table and look at Jacob. "That wasn't a monster on the beach. It was a giant squid tentacle." I show him a picture from my *Deep-Sea Fish* book that I grabbed before heading down the steps.

Jacob looks at the picture, takes his hand and covers all of the squid except one long squid arm. He smiles and gives me a satisfied look. "No monster," I tell him.

After I eat, we go outside again and sit with Mrs. Sally in our white plastic chairs. Mrs. Sally places a blanket over each chair because they are old and dirty-looking, and also, we can wrap the blankets around us if we get a little chilled. Jacob and I are still a little wary from our monster encounter from earlier, so we are happy to stay near Mrs. Sally for now. We watch out over the waters of the inlet, looking to see if my father's fishing boat is coming in. At the same time, I keep a watch toward the side property line to see if the scary man will appear. Some bushes and boulders are arranged in such a way that they offer privacy to our yard, but if someone wanted to watch us, they could still get a view through the sparse foliage or from the very edge of the water. Mrs. Sally senses our unease, so she begins a story.

"On the mainland, there is a place where the pine trees stop growing and there is only tundra as far as one can see. It was at this spot that a porcupine family lived among the pines at the tundra's edge. They spent much of their time in the tall trees, gnawing on bark and hiding from the wolves that came by from time to time to eat them. Occasionally, the porcupines had to get down from the trees to waddle about on the ground to find pine cones and green plants and lichen to eat. It was at this time they had to be most careful of the wolves. One day, when the porcupines were on the ground, they could hear a great thundering and feel the ground shaking. This frightened the small animals and sent them running back into the treetops. Looking out to the north, where one could see forever if they had sharp eyes, which porcupines do not, they saw a huge creature far off. They saw that this creature was so large that it covered a wide expanse of land. They knew this was the cause of the rumbling and thundering. The porcupines reasoned that if this creature was so large that it could shake the earth, even from such a distance, then if it ever came closer to their pine forest, surely all the trees would be shaken to the ground and the porcupines could no longer hide from the wolves.

When the wolves eventually came around looking for a porcupine to eat for dinner, one of the porcupines looked down at the wolves and said, "Brothers, we have a gift for you." The wolves looked up at the porcupine questioningly. "There is a monster that lives out on the tundra. It is bigger than any living thing you have ever seen. You cannot see it from the ground, but from up here in the trees, we have a good view of forever. The monster is large enough to shake the ground when it moves. We, the porcupines, are very fearful of it, but you, the bravest creatures of the forest and the tundra, would not be afraid at all. In fact, we believe that if you could catch this monster, it would be of such a size that it would feed your entire pack for a very long time.

The wolves discussed the idea of hunting a large creature on the open tundra where there is no hiding place for the creature to go. They all quickly agreed that they should hunt down this monster and see if it were worth eating. The family of wolves set out upon the tundra, while the porcupines watched on, hidden in their pines. It did not take long for the wolves to catch the scent of the creature. They ran for hours before they could catch up with it. When the wolves closed in on the monster, they discovered it was not a monster at all, but a massive herd of caribou. The wolves had never seen caribou before, just as the caribou had never seen wolves, and did not know to fear them. The wolf pack quickly killed a large caribou and devoured it. The taste and the ease of hunting the caribou was so that the wolves never again bothered with the porcupines. And the porcupines, they never again had to fear the wolves."

As Mrs. Sally finishes her story, she sees that Jacob is sound asleep in his chair, and I am close behind. We had been up since 4:00 a.m. after all. She gets up, covers us with the blankets, and goes inside to clean up the kitchen.

2

Solstice Celebration

June 21

I imagine some time has passed since we fell asleep in the sun. It is always difficult to say how long I have been in that state of being where time has no meaning. I see the sun has moved from its previous vantage spot in the sky to a new one. As it scooted over, it dripped some of its heat down onto my face. My mother once told me I was cursed with my father's fair skin, then she laughed. I wipe the afternoon nap from my eyes and stand up from my chair, stretching my legs and arms, ready to begin the second half of the day. Jacob is still asleep in his chair. I hear the roaring of my father's voice coming from within the house. It can hardly be missed or ignored. He does not say much to us, but when he does, we listen. There is something in his voice that frightens me. A deep despair, or hidden anger. At the same time, his gruffness warms me: a reminder of a safe home that protects me from the outside world. My father must have been home for a while, for when he steps out into our backyard he is washed clean of his fishing clothes and dressed up in his flannel and jeans.

He is a giant among the Innu people. He stands just short of two meters and is a massive man. His thick sandy-colored wavy hair, heavy reddish beard, and strong-featured face remind me of pictures I have seen of Vikings in my history book. He walks over to me, wraps his arm around me, and says, "Robert, my son, good solstice to you. I have something for you in the kitchen."

Jacob begins to stir, and Father picks him up like a chubby sack of flour and jostles him around until my brother gives out a little sleepy giggle. He carries Jacob into the house and I follow behind. The three of us sit down at the kitchen table where Mrs. Sally has left us a snack of fresh blueberries and slices of cheese. She had left after Father had got home. I guess she had to go home to celebrate the solstice with her own family. Father told me once that most families do not celebrate this day because they do not think Christians should partake. He said it is thought to be a pagan holiday, but I think it has a completely different meaning for us. Not one of religious beliefs, but rather one of survival. It is cold in the house, and Father keeps his jacket on. He will not stir up the embers in the stove until early evening, just before the temperature plummets.

Jacob looks at Father with wide, black eyes the color of night, and asks, "Do you have presents for us?" He gives our father a wide smile.

Father lets out a deep laugh and reaches into his jacket pocket and produces two boxes. To Jacob, he gives

the larger box, which he pulls open and is ecstatic to find an assortment of beautifully wrapped chocolates. Jacob asks if they are all for him, and my father returns his question with a wink. With that, Jacob runs off with his treasure.

After Jacob disappears, my father turns to me. "You are twelve years old, Robert. You are ready for something besides chocolate." He slides the smaller box across the tabletop to me. At first, I am disappointed. I was hoping for a new book. I had recently finished *Moby Dick* and I was ready to devour more words. Mrs. Sally says that the reason I have such a grown-up vocabulary is because I *actually* devour the words, and they grow inside me. As I look at the box and hold it in my hands, I feel just a little ashamed: I know I should be nothing short of grateful for receiving a gift. I carefully open the package, not knowing what to expect. Staring up at me is an old, tarnished silver lighter. The kind where you have to replace the flint from time to time and fill the little fuel compartment with lighter fluid. Engraved on the lighter is a ship, with the terrifying arms and body of a giant creature emerging from the waters to wrap its enormous writhing tentacles around the hull of the vessel. As I look at the intricately etched drawing, I am reminded of the giant squid tentacle I saw on the beach earlier in the day. This brings me back to the frightening man on the beach. I shiver, but I don't understand why.

"When I was a lad, growing up in the north of Scotland," says my father, "my own father gave me this lighter. He told me this would always keep me safe in the darkness. He told me that it would reliably light the fire in the fireplace that would keep our house warm, for this was one of my responsibilities as it will now be yours.

But also, it would light the candle that burns through the night, to keep away that which prefers darkness." He looks at me with menacing concern and a little fear, which always lies at the edge of his demeanor.

I have not seen this lighter before. Usually, my father uses an old Bic lighter to get the fire going in the wood stove, or to light a candle in the evening. I turn it around in my hands, flip the top open, and spin the steel wheel until I see the spark and flame. My father watches me, and he tells me that each morning I must make sure the wood stove fire is burning, and each evening I must re-light it so we don't freeze during the darkness of these Labrador nights. "And," he says, "I want you to keep one of our small oil lamps on your bedside table for emergencies. You can put the lighter in the table drawer. This is not a toy, Robert. This is a responsibility. You are the keeper of fires." With that, he gets up from the table, places a hand on my shoulder, and leaves it for just one second before walking off to go outside. I have come to recognize this small gesture as a show of his love.

I take my lighter into the living room and sit on the worn sofa that is covered in blankets. I wrap one of the blankets around me, a wool blanket that my father brought over from Scotland and had given to my mother before they got married. I sit, loosely cloaked like a cabbage roll, running my fingers over the smoothness of the lighter case. There must have been an inscription on the bottom edge of one side, but it is far too worn from years of handling and from the buffing of pocket linings. The engraving of the sailor ship must have been a deeper cut, as it is still plainly visible. And the giant marine creature, maybe the one Father often speaks of – the *kraken* – gives me an uneasy feeling. As I sit here, my father returns from outside with an armload of wood.

"Well, son, it is still early, but why don't you get the fire started for the evening? We don't want to give the cold any reason to settle in here with us." He sets the wood down on the rack near the wood stove and goes about his business.

I watch as my father goes upstairs, where he would sit at his desk in his bedroom, writing. Writing letters, preparing our lessons, recording his catch of the day? Sitting by himself, he is a lonely man. He misses Mother. I think he misses Scotland. He often tells us stories of the myths and monsters of the north of Scotland. He says his hometown of Kirkwall is much like Davis Inlet, but the grass is greener, the town is more civilized and beautiful, and the Viking influence richer. But here, he says, the women are just as lovely, the monsters are just as frightening, and the fishing is more plentiful.

Back in the living room, small but big enough for the three of us, I open the wood stove door and carefully begin to stack the kindling as my father has shown me countless times. I hold my lighter in my hand, feeling the cold metallic case, and I am overcome by the feeling of anxiety. The giant tentacle on the beach? It's in the room with me. I sense it. I open the lighter and roll the steel wheel. As soon as a flame appears, the creepy sensation dissipates. I light the tinder in the stove, blow softly on the flames like I have seen my father do a thousand times, and close the stove door; the fire seems to know how to do the rest on its own. The pine will burn quickly, but pines are the only type of trees to be found on this island, or for that matter, on the mainland. Pines, lichen, rock, and tundra. This is our world.

I sit back on the sofa feeling proud and grown up

with my new responsibility. And a little disturbed by the haunting feeling that quickly came and went through me. I look around the familiar living room, taking in the still-life of my home. Nothing strange or unusual. My father's chair sits in the corner under a reading lamp. Some buoys that washed up in our yard hang from nails in the wall. A small coffee table sits between the sofa and the wood stove, mostly for my brother and me to play games on. There is a checkerboard on the table where Father will occasionally play a game of checkers with Jacob or chess with me. Father is a good chess player. He says he learned while he was young and used to play as a young man in the pubs of Kirkwall. He is always going on about Kirkwall. I imagine every house and every pub might look just like our own living room.

The room is dark, with three windows, small to keep the heat inside. The walls are decorated with a few paintings and pictures. There is one large painting of a ship crossing the Atlantic in a horrific storm. I often look up at that scene and imagine what it must be like to be a sailor aboard that ship as it is thrown about in the waves like a toy in the bathtub. *Tossed about in the playground of the kraken*, as my father would say. We have three framed cartography maps as well. One is a detailed map of Scotland. Another, a map of Labrador and all of its waterways. The third map is an odd one. It shows bits of the British Isles, Iceland, Greenland, and northeastern Canada, but it seems to focus on the empty north Atlantic. There are longitude and latitude lines, marked shipping lanes, the active feeding banks, and then there are some strange marks – arrows, crosses, circles with plusses and minuses inside, and some indecipherable symbols that are no doubt spelling out nautical warnings or instructions. This map is old and yellowing, hand-drawn, and blemished with tears and wrinkles from use. Still, nowhere in the room is there a sign of the monster tentacle. It wasn't real.

Partially separating the living room from the kitchen is a stairway to the bedrooms. The stairway is open, giving the illusion of a larger living area. The house was built by my father. Most houses here were built by the government, I think, when they moved all of the Innu people from their original homelands to this rock island in the sixties. The Canadian government forgot that people need water and use the bathroom, and so wells and sewers were never blasted into the solid rock ground. We are lucky. My father built us a bathroom with primitive plumbing – that's what Father calls it – attached to the back of our living room, so we don't have to use a bucket (except at night), emptying it out the backdoor like many other families do. He was able to run a pipe from a creek to our kitchen and on to the bathroom for our running water. The pipe freezes in the winter, along with the creek and the rest of the world. So, winter comes to find us melting snow, buying bottled water, and using the water we managed to bottle ourselves in the early autumn.

Tonight will be our celebratory Solstice Dinner. After sitting on the couch for an hour, reading, I call out for Jacob to come help me make peanut butter cookies. He runs down the stairs screaming with excitement. I have been making these cookies since I was four, when my mother taught me how. Now I have taught Jacob how to make them. I told him he can be in charge today. We will make a mess of the kitchen, and we might even burn some of the cookies, but that is all part of it. While we start getting the ingredients, Father goes into the refrigerator and retrieves the large piece of caribou meat he bought yesterday. There is a man in town who goes off into the tundra for a week at a time, like in the old days, and hunts caribou and sells the meat for a living. Father takes the meat and brushes a marinade on it before taking it out to the grill in the backyard. The smell will probably attract all the dogs in town.

After we have the cookie dough mixed up, we make fun cookie shapes on the greased sheet. First, I make a sun with little rays around it to represent the summer solstice. Next, I make the shape of a fish and a badly shaped caribou. I look at Jacob's cookie. He is rolling out a long snake and attaching it to a side view of a dragon or dinosaur head with its mouth open and sharp teeth showing.

"What's that?" I ask.

"That's the monster I saw on the beach this morning."

"Jacob, that wasn't a monster. That was an arm of a giant squid. And besides, there was no head on the beach." I am not totally convinced of my own words.

"Yes, there was. I saw it. It was at the edge of the water. It was chewing on something big, like a rubber snake." Jacob's wide eyes look directly at me as he tells his story. "You saw it too. You said you did."

"I said I saw a long tentacle. There was no monster."

"But there was. I saw it. It must have swum back into the water. You don't believe me. I saw it!"

My brother always had a big imagination. Sometimes it is hard for me to know when he is telling the truth or making something up. Or, in this case, whether he is making it up or whether he truly *believes* it is real. I decide to let him have his story and his monster. Father once told me that we all have our monsters, and each one of us somewhere deep inside knows they are real. I tell Jacob, "Well, maybe you should draw a picture of it. That way you won't forget how it looked, and I will be able to keep a lookout for it."

Jacob looks up at me, grateful that I believe him now, and he gives me his wide smile smeared with chocolate. I look at his face, and my gaze drifts past him to the portrait of our mother hanging on the kitchen wall – the same wide smile, minus the chocolate. Father hung her picture there so that she could watch over us when we have our meals. I guess she is watching us now as we make our cookies and prepare to put them in the oven. Jacob grabs the cookie tray to put them in. "Careful, the oven's hot. You can put them in, but Father says I have to take them out, so you don't burn yourself on the hot pan and drop the cookies all over the floor." Jacob slides the cookie tray onto the bottom rack, careful not to knock the potatoes that have been baking on the top rack.

My father walks into the kitchen carrying three slabs of grilled caribou steaks. Three menacing looking dogs are trying to follow the aroma of promising dreams into the kitchen. Father turns around, growls at the dogs, and kicks towards the closest one, sending them all off whining. "Robert, throw a salad together. I'll get the potatoes. Jacob, you set the table and pour your brother and yourself some milk." Father pours himself a large glass of water. "Oh, and Robert, would you like to light some candles?" He winks at me and puts a cover on the steaks to keep them warm while we finish up the table. I quickly throw together a salad with a sliced tomato, a sliced cucumber, and some lettuce that we grew in containers with the help of Mrs. Sally. Just before sitting down, I go to the oven to pull out the cookies. I hold the tray just above the stovetop and check the peanut butter goodness. They are all done to perfection with the exception of Jacob's monster cookie. The monster is burned black, and smoking. The entire cookie is twisting around and the tentacle arms wave in tortured arcs as if writhing in pain. From outside in the distance comes a sharp crack, followed by an ominous rumbling sound. Startled, I drop the tray on the stovetop with a bang. I look out the window on the far side of the living room and see the dark gray clouds over the sea. A streak of lightning, followed by another cracking thunder.

"Looks like our celebration has some company. A little thunderstorm for entertainment," says my father.

I look back down at the cookie sheet. The monster cookie now looks just like the others, waiting for the milk dipping. I close my eyes, take a deep breath, and look again. Nothing unusual. I guess my brother isn't the only one here with a vivid imagination.

We sit down at the table, where my father gives a short prayer for the caribou before we begin. He tells us we must respect the life that gives us life. We eat our dinner, mostly in silence, each of us relishing his own caribou meat. At one point during the meal, Father tells us that when we return to Scotland, a promise he often speaks of, we will be treated to the best food – bere bannocks, partan toes – or 'taes', as he pronounces it, – Orkney cheese, and stews made from the North Ronaldsay sheep that are fed exclusively on seaweed.

After we finish eating, we go outside and sit on our yard chairs, wrapping ourselves in blankets as the distant storm keeps to the water. Two more hours of daylight. We stare out at the sea and watch the gulls fly by in hopes of fish or trash meals. Jacob turns to me and asks, "Robert, what was our mother like? I hardly remember her. Everyone says I look like her."

"She was nice. Kind of roundish like Mrs. Sally. She looked short when she stood next to Father, but tall when she stood next to you. Long black hair, and she used to smile a lot, then she stopped smiling so much. Sometimes she would sleep all day." At that, I stop and think for a minute.

"I remember nothing about Mom's family." Jacob's words cut my silence with a note of melancholy. "Do you know any stories about them?"

I searched my memories for a moment. "I remember once, when we were little, she took us on a ferry ride to some village where we have some cousins. I remember going to a fire at night where we sat around and ate marshmallows and drank hot cocoa. There was a man, I think he was our uncle or cousin somehow, who was drunk, and he kept running through the fire. I thought that he would burn up! Then he stood in front of the fire and started howling like a wolf. All the other grown-ups stood up and joined in and they were all howling and looking up at the moon. They started dancing around the fire and moving like birds and wolves and fish. One very old man, all bent over and wrinkle-faced, stood above us, looking down, and he started barking and growling. You were so scared of him; I guess we both were, and we grabbed on to each other and hid our heads under a blanket. Some of the older kids were laughing at us. After that trip, we were kind of afraid of other kids. We thought they were all laughing and making fun of us. I still think they are."

Jacob says, "I'm not afraid of them. I'm not afraid of anything. I know some boys …" he stops there and doesn't say anything more for a while. Then he adds: "Hey Robert? Are you afraid of anything? I mean, like, wolves? Mrs. Sally says wolves are bad spirits. Sometimes, I think dogs are wolves, and I'm not afraid of dogs."

I say, "Sometimes I'm afraid of Father. Like at night when he makes monster noises in his room. I think, what if he is the monster that he is trying to protect us from? Then I think he is turning into a *kraken*, the giant squid. Then I think, if he turns into a squid, and people say that you take after our mother, and I take after our father, then am I going to turn into a giant squid?"

Jacob turns his head toward me and simply says, "You're stupid." I've never heard him say anything like that before. We don't say that in our house. We fall silent again and watch the sky turn colors.

As it gets closer to sunset, Father takes us inside and we all sit in the living room and play checkers. Jacob, seated on the sofa to Father's left, asks about his tattoo for the one hundred millionth time. Jacob loves to hear the story, and our father never seems to tire of telling it. My father's tattoo wraps around his left forearm and crawls up into his sleeve. He tells us it is a *kraken*, the giant octopus-monster that lives in the sea in the North Atlantic and attacks sailor ships. He should know about these things. He was a sailor before he met my mother. Now, he is a fisherman. My father *looks* like a sailor, or maybe a pirate. He has muscular arms and legs, a barrel chest, and leathery skin from the constant exposure to the sun. His eyes are the color of water – a pale blue-gray that is almost empty. He says that the *kraken* sometimes comes out of the sea at night, and ravages small coastal villages. In the water, the *kraken* smells food from miles away, but on the land, the sea monster feels vibrations. Anything that moves on the ground always makes even the softest vibration that only a *kraken*, with its fish-like sensory abilities, can detect.

Jacob asks my father, "Why do we have to live near the monsters?"

My father holds him with his giant arms and looks at him with his watery gaze: "Son, I told your mother we should move inland to get far away from the *kraken*, maybe to Saskatoon, as far from the ocean as possible, but she would not leave this small village that she grew up in. Besides, she knew that I made my living from the sea. And now, we are bound to stay here to surround ourselves with her memory. It may be that when we have saved up enough money, and you boys are old enough for the journey, we can return to Scotland. You'll see: the Orkney Islands make the beauty of Labrador look like a vacant lot in comparison."

"Sing one of your sailor songs!" demands Jacob. We both love to hear father's deep singing voice. When he is not around, Jacob and I try our best to imitate him, then we fall down laughing at how bad we sound. My father agrees to one song before bed. He encircles us both with his monstrous arms and sings one of our favorite songs, which we have heard many times before:

My ship, she is called the Bonnie Marie
The Scots, they built her sound
The North Atlantic she does sail
To Labrador she is bound

Sail quickly on, my first mate says
Stay with the midnight sun
If darkness comes to the open sea
Each of our lives be done

We sailed up north as far as we dare
Past Iceland we did steer
Past Greenland to the Davis Straits
Whose stormy currents we fear

The gales did come, the seas did roll
So far from course we're thrown
The Bonnie Marie, she took on the sea
Our sails in need of sewin'

And it's oh ma Bonnie, ma Bonnie Marie
Frae brave Scotland came she
And it's oh ma Bonnie, ma Bonnie Marie
Was once the queen of the sea

The currents took us far down south
By midnight the sun was set
An hour had passed, the darkness came
The sea a menacing threat

From down in the depths, the kraken did come
We knew the attack to stave
For a' the sailors feared it would take
Oor Bonnie Marie tae her grave

So brave oor men, kept her afloat
as we fought through the night
One broken mast made a harpoon

And slayed the beast by light

And from the Labradorean coast
She listed her way into Nain
At the dock, tied in the port
The Bonnie Marie'll remain

And it's oh ma Bonnie, ma Bonnie Marie
Frae brave Scotland came she
And it's oh ma Bonnie, ma Bonnie Marie
Was once the queen of the sea

This is the Father we love. These times together make me feel we are a crew, on our own ship. These are the moments we wish would never end. We sit on the sofa and watch the fire as it crackles away. Father pours himself a rare pint of ale and continues to sing softly, more to himself than to us. He used to sing all his songs to our mother, back when she joined us for these warm moments. There is a deep sorrow in his eyes these days. He is like a character from his old songs. Jacob is barely aware of the wounds that lurk below the surface of Father's ways. But I feel them with a frightening strength. And I fear that whatever it is that grips my father will soon have a hold on me too.

Each night, as sunset nears, our father becomes a different man. It is during those times that we try to stay out of his way. With my eye on the clock, always, I do my best to get Jacob up to bed before the sun sinks. It is now half past nine and time we get upstairs before our father turns. The sunset is scheduled for nine fifty-three, and we all know the rules. In this house, we go to bed at sunset, and we get up at sunrise. This has been as it always was. It is my job to protect Jacob and make sure he never, ever leaves the bed at night. We share a double bed, which is good because I do not think I could be brave at night sleeping alone. While we are huddled together under our quilts, the house trembles with the sounds that come from my father's room. He yells out like an angry animal in pain. He *is* in pain. *Anguish* – that is a synonym for pain – I read it in one of my books and I think it more appropriately defines how my father feels.

He shouts to people who are not there. I think he is mourning our mother and talking to her spirit. Father tells us that our mother knew there were spirits in everything, even in the caribou we ate for dinner. Jacob thinks Father actually turns into a monster at night and eats the things that walk on the floor. Jacob says that when we are angry, we all act like hungry animals, eating everything in our sight. Sometimes Jacob scares me when he talks like that. Some nights, the sounds are so terrible that we cry, hiding deep under the covers so my father doesn't hear us.

When we wait too long to get in our bed, Father looms above us and his voice bellows out his unchallengeable demand that we get upstairs before darkness begins to creep in. My little brother and I fear our nighttime Father and his rules. "Remember," he tells us, "if you step one foot on the floor during the night, you *will* be eaten alive!" We shudder at his words. We cower in his shadow. *You will be eaten alive.* This we know as a fact. "Remember your mother?" This is not a question, but a threat by example. We do remember our mother, but that memory is slowly fading to a dimmed image of a distant figure. A portrait on the wall. She died when we were much younger – Jacob was two, and I was eight.

She was eaten. It is a possibility. She broke the rules. She touched the floor, we were told.

Never.

Touch.

The floor.

At night.

We know this rule because we were told this every night of our lives. We dare not speak of it outside of the house, to our distant family, to anyone, with the exception of Mrs. Sally. We are alone with this terrible secret.

Our father has other rules besides the bed rule. Like, we have to keep the kitchen spotless, we have to put a bowl of cat food outside the back door every evening after we eat, we have to do our studies before dinner. But the bed rule is the most important one. Mrs. Sally is mostly the only other person we ever talk to. We rarely talk about the bed rule with her though. We assume she knows about it too. For that matter, we assume the whole world knows not to touch the floor after sunset.

I look out our window by the bed. The view is that of our backyard and the sea. I watch as the sky slowly turns to purple, ending our longest day. Now, it is the night's turn to grow in length. I can see just beyond our property line to the beach where the squid arm rested. Now the arm, the beach, and many of the large rocks all lay beneath the soft waves as the tide creeps in to devour the land. And on one large rock that stands like an island a few meters from the land's edge, there is the dark silhouette of a man. It seems to be the same man I saw earlier in the day – the man who called himself Billy Cloud. His right hand waving back and forth in slow motion, like a drunken maestro leading a sleepy orchestra. I watch as he teeters on the rock, drinking from a bottle and peeing into the water at the same time. I giggle a little at the sight, my hand covering my mouth so as not to wake my brother. Suddenly the man turns toward the house and appears to be staring straight into my window. He could not possibly see inside our darkened room, yet he starts laughing and puts his hand over his own mouth as if he were mocking me. His dark form then starts to flail its arms in a slow writhing motion and sends images into my head of Jacob's blackened monster cookie that I pulled from the oven. The wind carries his laugh to our window and I hear him yell out, "Did you tell him? Did you tell your Celtic-Viking Daddy that he's an asshole?" The man begins to laugh wildly. He pulls a plastic bag from his jacket and says in sing-song, "I have something for you. Come on down and get it."

I bury my face into my pillow. I want to scream. I look over at Jacob's sleeping face and find myself wishing I too were asleep. I can't help but to look back at the man once more.

But he's gone.

3

Nain

July 12

The time is 4:30 a.m. and I am awakened by my father as he shakes me and tells me it is time to get up. "Wake up your brother, too. Dress up warm; it'll be cold and windy on the water. I'll have breakfast ready for you in ten minutes." And, as if he had never been there, the room is empty of his presence. I know better than to waste time. I wake up Jacob from his quiet slumber and tell him we have to get dressed and ready like right now. I pull on my long underwear, wool socks, wool pants, and long sleeve shirt with a sweater over that. I find my old down coat and carry it with me downstairs. Jacob is right behind me, complaining that it will be a nice day and why would he have to dress so warmly.

"Because," I tell him, "remember the last time we spent the day on the water? The wind was so cold that you cried the whole time. Father threw the two of us in a big quilt and made us lie on the floor of the cabin to keep warm. I thought he was going to throw us both overboard for fish bait."

Down in the kitchen, our father is moving about and getting things together for our trip. He is not in the best of moods. He did not want to have to take us with him, but Mrs. Sally would not be available today. He doesn't want us to be left at home alone all day. He tells us there are some bad people that might try to take advantage of the situation. I do not understand what he means by that, but I do know that he is not happy. "Hurry up and eat," he barks at us. He is an angry sled dog daring the rest of the pack to try his patience. "We're wasting daylight." We sit down to our bowls of oatmeal and some pan-fried bait fish that we often eat after father comes back from seining the back bay. I don't know what a bait fish is and I don't know what the back bay is, but that is how my mother used to describe things. We are quiet. We eat quickly. We await Father's instructions. When it's time to leave, our father squats down in front of us – he does this when he is serious and needs us to pay attention – and he tells us, "Stay by me. Do not talk to anyone. When we get aboard the boat, Mr. Dave will be waiting for us. He will make the trip with us. You can be polite, say hello, but do not get in his way. You know he likes you boys and enjoys a bit of banter, but mind you, lads, he'll be busy with the boat, steering through some tricky waters. So be on your best and stay out of his way. Do you understand?" We each nod in agreement and follow Father out the door. Walking through the town with Father does not happen much. And the times I have been allowed to walk through town on my own, that was like finding red seaglass on the beach – far more of a rarity. But it does happen when Father needs something done and I am his last resort.

It is a cold morning with an unwelcome crispness in the air. Every morning is cold here. I ask my Father, if there were tropical places with palm trees and warm beaches all yeár long, then why don't we live there? He tells me, "It doesn't matter where you go, there are always monsters awaiting you. Besides, we do not belong down there. Your mother's people are here, and my people, well," he hesitates, "we may return to them one day." I consider this for a moment. I wonder what Scotland is like. Does everyone look like me and Father? Do they speak English? My father tells me that they have running water – hot water – in all the houses. He says that everyone has a car and that all the Scottish lasses would lay eyes on me and they would eat me up with my Canadian/Innu accent. I am not sure if I want anyone to eat me up, but he says it as if it would be a good thing.

"Are you …" I start, and then decide to put the question away for another day.

"Are you what?" asks my father.

I wish I hadn't said anything. Then I continue, "Are you allowed to touch the floor at night in Scotland?"

"Nay, lad." His voice gets quiet. "Not in Kirkwall you're not."

Mrs. Sally once told me that people touch the floor at night all the time. "Maybe," she confides to me, "Your father has this rule to keep you in the house and away from the bad people of the village. Or as he calls them, the monsters. Your father is the most protective man I have ever known when it comes to his children." This she told me in confidence. That means like a secret. I gathered that from one of my books.

We continue in silence making our way down the road without seeing anyone. The town is dead. It is a different place from the nighttime, when I can hear people yelling, screaming, and laughing wildly from outside my window. My father says that even though the people laugh, they are sad and desperate, and they must fight against their own monsters. I wonder to myself: how many different monsters are there? Mrs. Sally once told us a story of the Witiko, that wandered through the forests of the north and devoured lonely hunters. She said that some of the more superstitious people think it followed us to Davis Inlet when our people were moved here thirty years ago. She told me she didn't think the Witiko could get across the water and onto the island.

It is dead quiet this morning. We can hear the water tasting the shoreline as we arrive at the docks. It is a quick ten-minute walk in a village that is only fifteen minutes long. We walk down the dock to the *Bonnie Marie*, my father's boat. He named it after our mother when they just got married. "That way," he would say, "I can be with my bonnie wife even when I am out to sea." I heard father remark that when he bought the boat, it was holier than St. Magnus Cathedral. He patched the holes, refurbished the entire boat, and then he painted over the old name, *Rat's Arse*, and renamed it *Bonnie Marie*. I don't know if it was really called Rat's Arse, but I do know it is bad luck to rename a vessel. My father said that one day we would get aboard this boat and we would leave the dock and not come back. He said he thought it would be possible to make our way to Scotland if the weather and the water were in our favor. Stopping over in every small town in northern Canada, Greenland, and Iceland that we could manage for refueling. I asked about the sea monsters of Davis Strait, and he told me we were a strong crew and we could see our way through such dangers. The thought of such a voyage both excited and scared me.

As we step aboard the *Bonnie Marie*, even Jacob's small body is enough to rock it in its mooring. The dock creaks and groans as the ropes that hold the boat tight to its anchors are stressed with the commotion of our boarding. Father's friend, Mr. Dave, is moving about the deck preparing everything for the trip. We have to navigate around the fishing supplies carefully stowed around the back deck of the boat. Jacob and I take a seat on a large rolled up net that smells of fish, and we duck low beneath the gunwales so that the wind can't get to us. We see Mr. Dave and I look down shyly. "Get comfortable, boys. It'll be a long ride out." He gives us a quick, friendly smile and a roughing of the hair. He and my father say little to each other except to look over the map, the tide chart, and the weather forecast. We are in a hurry to take off. It will be a five- or six- hour ride each way to Nain and back. The motor kicks to life with a low, guttural sound. It always makes me think of what a polar bear must sound like in the morning as it wakes up – deep chested and menacing. The waft of the exhaust drifts briefly to our noses before being lifted away by the ocean breeze. We inch away from the pier, slowly gaining momentum as we venture out into the inlet. We track through the islands where we can in order to avoid the full brunt of the sea.

Father said Mr. Dave is the best navigator he knows. Mr. Dave grew up south of here in the village of Hopedale. Like my father, he came here for the love of a woman. Father says that one day I will understand that.

Mr. Dave has been running the coastline from Red Bay up to Nain for most his life. He goes out with Father almost every day to fish the banks. Once in a while, Mr. Dave stops by our house for dinner, "Just to keep John in line and, since I've no kids of my own, I may just steal you away from him."

The trip goes well for the first couple of hours. Jacob is mesmerized by the scenery as it glides past us. We see a couple other boats, but we do not pass near them, so it is hard to tell what they are doing out here. There is a lot of gray: gray skies, gray water, gray rocks on the passing landscapes. The wind is cold, making me glad that we brought the blankets. Father has some extra blankets as well, stashed away on the boat. After a couple of hours, the drone of the motor eventually gets to me, and I fall asleep in our fishnet and blanket bed on the deck.

Time passes, and Jacob and I are awakened by a change in the tone of the engine. I look about and see the town of Nain coming into view. It is so seldom that we get to leave the house, let alone our village, that I feel butterflies in my stomach fluttering in circles with excitement. The village is surrounded by steep cliffs running down to the sea, and pine forests, and scrubby tundra. I think Labrador is the most beautiful place in all the world. I haven't been anywhere else, but I can't imagine anything more striking than the starkness of our winters and the calling of our summers. As we slow down and move in toward the docks of the port, I am aware of the number of people walking the road. There is a small cruise ship just off the shore that Mr. Dave says brings in the tourists for the day but leaves before sundown. Must be to keep them from touching the floor at the wrong time. Just up a short road that leads to the water, I see a pretty church building. Father tells us it is the Moravian Church that was built two hundred years ago. I have a hard time imagining a building that has been around for so long. Our own house is less than twenty years old, and already there are parts of it falling off.

Mr. Dave eases the *Bonnie Marie* sideways to the dock as Father jumps off the boat with ropes in hand to tie it to the big iron horns. He grabs his backpack, lifts Jacob onto the dock, and allows me to get out of the boat on my own. We wait for Mr. Dave to finish up with the boat, and the four of us make our way up the gray, stony dirt road filled with shallow puddles of murky water. Each puddle carries its own reflection of a piece of the cloudy sky. We head toward the church where a group of tourists are taking pictures of it, and taking pictures of the waterside, and taking pictures of the locals walking down the street. Father says the tourists don't see the real world; they only see little squares of reality through their cameras. He says that each of those cameras they have cost as much money as he makes in one month. The tourists are easy to spot. They are all white people, and they walk in circles, so they can see everything, with no destination in mind. The local people (who look white to me, but Mrs. Sally told us that they do not consider themselves "white people") walk with purpose. One tourist man dressed in bright colors and carrying a particularly large camera aims his camera at us as we approach him, and Father yells at him and tells him to "Bugger off!" The tourist man takes our picture anyway before quickly buggering off.

Most of the local people who are walking or biking through the streets are Inuit. Mr. Dave is an Inuit as well. Father once told me that the Inuit and Innu are all about the same, "But," he added with a wink, "don't tell that to your mother. She will remind you that the Innu live among the trees rather than trying to scrape a living from the tundra, eating lichen and snow. She will tell you that the Innu are the greatest storytellers, hunters, and craftsmen in all of the Americas. And then, if that weren't enough, she would lull you to sleep with her Innu stories of mysticism. Calling an Innu an Inuit would be like referring to a Scotsman as an Englishman." Mr. Dave and Jacob look like everyone else here. I wonder if the locals would mistake Father or me for tourists. Mr. Dave knows a few of the local men we pass by, and he stops to talk grown-up stuff with them. I look at the kids we pass and stare at their dark eyes, but I am careful not to speak to them, as that would make Father mad at me. It is nearly noon and the day is warming up a bit. Father pulls up his sleeves, revealing the *kraken* crawling up his arm. A couple of the passing kids see it and make remarks of awe, and Jacob and I both walk a little taller with pride.

Our first stop is a small brown house that backs up to the water. There is a lot of junk and boat stuff littering the yard, so I guess the man who lives here is a boat mechanic or something. Jacob and I are told to stay outside on the street while Father and Mr. Dave go in to talk to the man. As we stand outside waiting, I get a little chill, like scared goosebumps. We are in a place we don't belong and everyone passing by seems to know it. They don't look at us as if we were tourists, but like we are in a cage, on display. Three girls walk by, looking sideways at us, whispering to each other and giggling. I don't know why, but I am embarrassed. Do they see my Scottish face and hair and think I look strange? They must think that Jacob is one of them, an Inuit, because he looks like them. Most people seem to ignore us as they go about their daily business, but I know they are secretly thinking things. Jacob picks up some stones and throws them into a nearby puddle. I join in and we make a game of it. We have to watch for cars that come down the road. I don't know why people drive cars in such small villages. I guess they could use them, especially the pickup trucks, to haul stuff around.

A large sled dog comes up to us with a hesitant gait and a tilted gaze. Its white body and black head give it the appearance of having stuck its face into a bucket of midnight sky. Jacob is immediately wary of it and takes a step back. The dog slowly edges toward me and lies submissively on its belly at my feet. I slowly stoop down and stick my hand out for the dog to sniff. The dog licks my fingers, which I take as an invitation to pet it. I fall to the ground and rough up the dog's thick fur. The dog, with its fierce look, gently play-wrestles with me, making sure not to knock me over or hurt me. I am happily surprised, as I have always heard, mostly from Mrs. Sally, that many of these dogs were meant only as work dogs and were often treated harshly, so that they ended up not liking people so well. Maybe this was just a house pet, but in our village no one has dogs as house pets. Wanting to play with the dog too, Jacob walks towards us. Suddenly the dog stops its game with me and takes two menacing steps toward Jacob. It bares its teeth and lets loose a deep, rumbling growl. Jacob takes slow steps backwards away from the dog, and it swiftly turns back to sit by my side, amicable (friendly, my books tell me) once again.

Jacob says, "I don't think he likes me. You should

leave the dog alone. It's mean."

The dog continues to stare at Jacob, raising one side of its lips in an Elvis-like snarl, hairs bristling up on his back. I look around, unsure of what to do. I consider getting my father, but I am afraid he would be mad at me. Jacob picks up a stone and throws it at the dog, hitting it square in the head on his first try. The dog runs off with a yelp and Jacob chases after it with more stones, running around the side of a nearby house. I go after him. Father said we are supposed to stay put and I don't want to get into trouble. When I round the corner of the house, I see Jacob on the far side of the backyard, the dog gone. Instead, a strange man, mostly concealed by brush, is squatting down and talking to Jacob. The man looks around, and he whispers something to Jacob. He hands Jacob something, which Jacob slides into his pants pocket, and the man, seeing me, stands up tall and walks off into the brush. Jacob turns and walks over to me with a smile. "I scared the mean dog away."

"Who was that man?" I ask.

"What man?"

"The man who was talking to you," I say.

"There was no man."

I give Jacob a confused look. "But I saw him give you something you put in your pocket."

"There was no man." Jacob was looking a little irritated with me.

Did I even see a man? I begin to question myself. "Come on. We better get back to the brown house or Father will be mad at us."

We walk back to the front of the house just as Mr. Dave is coming out, followed by our father and another man. They are carrying some fishing utensils and boat stuff that Mr. Dave and the other man will take back to the *Bonnie Marie*, while Father takes Jacob and me on other errands. First, we go to the Everyday Store to pick up supplies for our house: kerosene for the lanterns, soap, new bath towels, some hinges and screws, and a whole list of stuff. Father said we might as well load up while we are here. It takes forever in the store. I feel like everyone is staring at us, and talking about us while we walk down the aisles. Our father does not seem bothered by it, and Jacob does not seem to notice anything different. I am relieved when, finally, we check out and leave the store, each of us carrying a couple of bags.

Our last stop before leaving is the Nunatsiavut Government Administrative Building. That's what it says on the front. It is the biggest, fanciest building I have ever seen. Father told us that this building was nothing; just wait till we see the amazing buildings in Kirkwall! Every one of them made of beautiful ancient rocks and blocks. The churches are each magnificent in their own way. St. Magnus, the Church of Scotland, people come from around the globe to see it. History is written in the streets. Father suddenly stops to close his eyes and recites a stanza from a poem by his favorite poet, George Mackay Brown:

> As I came home from Kirkwall
> The ships were on the tide:
> I saw the kirk of Magnus
> Down by the water side:
> The blesséd brave Saint Magnus
> Who bowed his head and died.
> His shining life was shorn away,
> His kirk endureth to this day.

As I came home from Kirkwall
The ships were on the tide.

"It's called 'The Road Home', bairns; best kens when we'll tread it too. Mackay Brown was from my ain Orkney, and he aye makes this Orcadian heart sing." Whenever he speaks of Kirkwall, his eyes brighten up and his Scottish accent seeps through more strongly. His accent always comes out when his emotions are heightened. When I see him like this, I get a giddy feeling – those swooping butterflies – inside me. He told us we were coming here to see about getting us a passport so we could one day leave this place and go to Scotland. I am not sure I want to leave my home, but the thought of a new adventure sends my mind dreaming. Jacob and I sit in a row of chairs as Father goes to the counter to talk to a lady who works here. I overhear them talking about papers to fill out and identifications and proof of residency and other boring grown-up stuff.

We have to sit for a while and wait while Father fills out the paperwork, grumbling about this and that. He hands it back to the lady and she tells us to wait until we are called back. My father and I sit in the chairs, and Jacob sits on the floor playing eight-year-old games, pretending he is a dog. My father continuously checks his watch. I can see he is worried we will not be back before sunset, even though we have a lot of time still. When the lady calls us back to the rooms beyond the waiting room, we follow her through the carpeted hall, past a bunch of offices (some with people in them, some without), and into a room with a white screen that we are meant to stand in front of to get our pictures taken. This room has carpeting. I have never seen or walked on a carpeted floor. It is like walking on moss. I wish we could have carpet in our bedroom. It would be so quiet to walk on, and maybe we would not have to stay off the floor at night.

The lady starts with me. She tells me to stand in the little square marked out on the floor and look straight ahead without moving or smiling. A bright flash leaves me blind for a second, and I see a dark spot in the front of my vision. It takes a couple of tries to get my brother's picture because he keeps moving or not looking in the right place. After three tries he must have a lot of dark spots in front of his eyes, because he keeps reaching out like maybe he could catch them.

The lady looks at us as we are about to leave, "Well, it's always good to see that the camera still works. We don't get many people in here wanting passports. People kind of like to stay put in this part of the country. Now, I hear they have to do this a dozen times or more a day over in Ottawa, but I guess you would expect that in a big city." She gives us a look of someone who is starving for conversation. "It might take two months to get these processed and sent out to you all the way down in Davis Inlet. Are you planning on doing some international travel? Down to the States, maybe?" My father gives her a grunt and we follow him out the door and back into the street.

It is going on two o'clock and we are hurried along with remarks that we need to get on the boat and get moving. When we get to the dock, I see Mr. Dave and the boat mechanic guy sitting on our boat with a bottle of something the color of weak tea being passed between the two. They are just staring out to sea, and their lips curl over their teeth at every swig. They see us coming and Mr. Dave goes into the cabin and wakes up the boat, enticing it to purr out its deep-chested song. The other man walks up to my father, shakes his hand, and slurs something to him that I cannot understand. We get back aboard the boat and prepare to leave. Jacob and I lie down on the fishing nets, snuggled under the blankets. Our father and Mr. Dave are in the cabin discussing things and waving their hands around emphatically. Father looks irritated, and Mr. Dave looks apathetic. As we start to move, Jacob and I take one last look at the town. The tourists are still out there, but they are dispersing to sit in the rocky tundra just above town, or looking for a sad, lonely, rocky shore to cheer up. The locals go about their business just like they do in Davis Inlet, up and down the street, dodging into houses and sheds and back out again.

And there, standing on the edge of a pier, is the black-headed dog. It is staring at me, its mouth open, tongue out, head tilted. I smile and wave hesitantly at the dog. *He's saying goodbye.* Then the dog moves its gaze the slightest bit and looks directly at Jacob. The dog lowers its head just a little and bares its teeth. It starts barking ferociously, dancing at the edge of the pier as if it were to leap the thirty meters across the water and onto our boat to tear Jacob apart. Standing a couple meters away from the dog is a man who looks a lot like Billy Cloud, with a crooked, drunken smile. The man I saw Jacob talking to after he chased the dog. He points at the dog with his fingers as if he were holding a gun and drops his thumb as if to shoot. He stares back in our direction and holds up his middle finger, throws his head back, and lets out a most hideous laugh. I duck back down into the blanket, and Jacob joins me. But while I am shaken by the man,

Jacob has a little smile on his face as he reaches secretly into his pocket.

The day seems to have turned a more dismal shade of gray as the hours pass. The sun cannot penetrate this world. The clouds are falling to the sea and we cannot see much as we motor out into the water. I feel the dampness of the air crawl into my clothes. My father looks out to the sea and says, "It's mighty dreich in this northern coast. Mind, Dave, swing clear of those rocky outcrops out there. They'll take us down quicker than a rogue wave." At least the wind has died down and the sea is calm. In fact, the sea is still as glass. The sounds of Nain fade away as we head into oblivion. My brother and I crawl deeper into the blanket with our heads underneath to escape the thick grayness that infiltrates everything. Soon, we are left alone with the drone of the motor. No one speaks. Each of us is lost in his own thoughts. Jacob is asleep in five minutes. He has the gift of falling asleep at any given time or place. It is an instant escape for him, though I do not know what he is escaping from. I envy him that skill, for the anxieties of our small world keep me awake.

I pull my head out of the tedium of the blanket-covered nest and stare out at the water. The grayness is so complete now that the fog has cut our line of sight to just a few meters. The entire boat is in a blanket-covered nest of its own. There are no waves. There is no wind. I watch my father as he runs his fingers through his red and golden beard, as if doing so would conjure up a wind to blow away the fog. Mr. Dave keeps an eye on the compass and his hands on the wheel. The two men speak in low voices, as if whispering secrets they dare not let the ocean hear. "We need to head out to sea in order to avoid the hidden surprises through here. This damned rock-strewn mess of islands will surely destroy my *Bonnie Marie.*" We head farther out, I guess, but who can tell?

Two or three endless hours pass. The only thing that has changed is a light clunking sound from within the engine. My father looks at Mr. Dave, "How much farther do you figure?"

Mr. Dave looks deep into the fog, as if the answer lies just ahead. "Truth is, John, I can't know how far we've gone. All we have is this needle to follow. With no landmarks, for all we know, we've gone all the way down to Hopedale." He smiles, "Of course, we haven't been gone *that* long."

"That engine doesn't sound good. I'd hate to be stranded out here in this soup," my father says. The engine lurches once, as if on cue. "We'd better cut her off and see what's making that racket, before she blows something."

Mr. Dave nods his head and shuts off the engine. Suddenly all is silent. The fog is so thick that nothing, save for a dim semblance of daylight, could penetrate this little piece of world. All of our sounds are dead. Cotton blocks my ears, and my eyes are filled with the gray lint from a clothes dryer. Even the water that surrounds us lies dead. The unexpected lack of sound wakes up Jacob from his slumber. He sits up next to me, rubs his eyes, and asks "Are we home?" As he looks around, he becomes noticeably uncomfortable with the stillness. Realizing we are in the middle of nowhere, he leans into me, "I'm scared, Robert. What if it's out there, the *monster*?"

"There's nothing out there, Jacob. We just stopped so Father can mess with the engine."

We sit, saying nothing for a while. We listen to the silence, broken only by my father's occasional cussing and the empty clanging sound of metal tools being set on the boat's deck. I hear Jacob's rapid breathing. And now a large splashing noise comes from somewhere beyond the fog wall. My blood freezes. Jacob grabs my hand and squeezes hard. He lets out a soft scream or gasp that is turned to mush before it gets out of his throat. Mr. Dave looks out over the water, which is now swelling with oversized ripples, "A humpback, I'd bet. Didn't think we'd be so far out. What do you reckon, John? A whale, huh?"

Father turns his face to him while his head is still half inside the engine. "Aye, that or a feckin' *kraken*."

Mr. Dave rolls his eyes and looks out toward the origin of the ripples. Again, we hear the sounds of something large rolling around in the water just out of sight. The boat starts to rock with the new waves. I wasn't worried before, but now Father's suggestion of the *kraken* starts to tease me. My eyes sweep the water's surface. Another thick kerplunk of water, this time followed by a fluttering sound like heavy rain on the water's surface. Out of the fog comes the flash of thousands of silver fish, each one about the size of my hand. Jacob says feverishly, "They're running from something, Robert. Something is trying to eat them."

My mouth gapes to find words, but I can say nothing. We hear another walloping sound of water movement and displacement. The *Bonnie Marie* rocks abruptly, knocking Mr. Dave off balance. Father curses and yells out, "Start her up, Dave!" The engine comes to life and dies immediately. Father reaches back in with a screwdriver as the whole ocean seems to tilt. We slide hard against the hull. We hear a bump on the bottom of the boat. Jacob shrieks and reaches deep into his pocket and brings something out that he holds tightly in his hand. He closes his eyes and hunkers down deep into the pile of fishing net we are lying on. I bury myself down with him. "Try her again, Dave," we hear Father say from the entrails of the boat.

This time the engine kicks in and continues to grumble in its throaty voice. The engine hatch slams shut and finally the boat starts moving forward. I hear Jacob whispering to himself through clenched teeth, "It's under the boat. It's following us." I look at him and he is holding whatever was in his pocket and staring at it, as if he were talking to it.

I see a flash of white in his little hand. A bone? "What is that?" I ask him.

He answers with a guilty look.

"Is that what the man gave you?"

"I found it. It's my secret." With that, he puts it back into his pocket as if afraid I would try to take it from him. He gives me a suspicious look and curls into a ball, facing away from me.

I sit back up and watch the fog go by as the boat kicks its speed up a notch. My father yells out over the roar of the engine, "Take her full speed for about an hour. Then we best bring her in toward the islands, slowly, so we can figure out where we are." He looks at his watch, and I in turn look at my own watch. Father says, "It's nearly seven. We have just two and a half hours to get home. We sat in that water longer than I expected." He looks toward Jacob and me. I know he is thinking that he is responsible for getting us in our beds before sunset. For some reason, I think it would be partly my fault if we don't get home in time. I know my father expects me to take care of Jacob and protect him, and if I don't make sure he gets in bed by sunset …

Another hour passes and Mr. Dave cuts the speed. We must be heading in toward the coast. The boat slows to a crawl. Father, Mr. Dave, and myself are looking intently at the fog, willing it with our eyes to part and reveal our whereabouts. The tide should be turning around soon, bringing us in and hiding the ship-wrecking rocks. Again, I hear something in the water. I cannot tell which direction it is coming from. Something slaps the outside hull of the *Bonnie Marie*. A soft, wet, floppy sound, as if a large fish were being slammed on the side of the boat to knock it unconscious. Father is looking over the edge with a fresh coating of concern on his face. I see in his left hand he is holding the machete he uses for cutting up fish as he tries to see under the water's surface and through the fog's robe. Again, we hear the thudding noise hitting the hull.

"We must be hitting a shallow bank. I'll see if we can slow her down and navigate through this invisible maze," Mr. Dave says.

"Aye, could be. All the same, I want you to speed it up some. I have a bad feeling about this, I do."

Mr. Dave usually knows better than to disagree with Father, but this time he replies, "*Aye*," in a mocking manner, "perhaps your bad feeling is that we're going to rip a hole in the bottom of the boat."

Father turns toward Mr. Dave and gives him a look like he might knock him right out of the boat. He lets a moment pass as he takes a few deep breaths. "Now mind you, mate, you're a damn good navigator, I'll give you that, otherwise I wouldn't have you on my boat. But there are a few things in this world you don't know. I'm not disagreeing with you that there may be some rocks under this water, but I'll bet my house those aren't rocks that are reaching up and slapping the sides of this boat."

Mr. Dave is about to reply, foolishly if you ask me, but his expression changes. He points starboard and we all look. The fog lifts just enough to make out land. "Sioralik Island. I'd know those rocks anywhere. They nearly devoured a postal boat I was once crewing on." This seems to dissolve the tension that was quickly building up. We soon lay eyes on our own rock of Ukasiksalik, and I know we will make it home safely and in time for bedtime.

Soon, we are tying the *Bonnie Marie* to the dock, and Father tells me to get Jacob to the house and the two of us need to get to bed. As we make our way down the road, I feel good to be back in a familiar place. I never want to leave here again. We have been gone just for the day, but it feels like forever. I look around the street and notice how the familiar strangers in this town look like the same people we saw in Nain. The kids all stare at us like we are zoo animals. A funny thought comes over me – what if they *are* the same kids as we saw in Nain? What if we just went around in circles on the water for five hours and landed right back here in a part of town that we have never been to? I will have to tell Mrs. Sally this idea. She will think it funny and probably have me write a story about it. We studied "irony" last month. I wonder if this would be a kind of irony.

Back in the house, Jacob and I go upstairs and get ready for bed. It is nine thirty-five and the sun sets at nine forty-four, according to our chart. Without time to waste, we quickly brush our teeth, throw our clothes on the floor, pull on our pajamas, and jump into bed. The sun sticks to its promise and sets precisely at nine forty-four, leaving us with a slowly fading daylight to see us to sleep. I lie on my back, thinking about the day. I think about the whale, *kraken*, monster, or whatever was in the water. I think about Father getting cross with Mr. Dave.

"Hey, Robert?"

"What?"

"Why didn't he like me?"

"Mr. Dave? He likes you alright. I think he just doesn't talk to us much because we're only kids and he's a grown-up."

"No, not Mr. Dave. I'm talking about the dog. He didn't like me at all."

Thinking about that dog as it growled at Jacob gives me an uncomfortable feeling. "I don't know. Dogs are temperamental like that."

"Do you think the dog was afraid of me? Like maybe he thought I was a polar bear?"

"That's silly Jacob. Go to sleep."

As I say this, I feel something new come between us. We see the world with different eyes. Jacob sees scary dogs; I see scary men. I know that Jacob is different from me, but I now worry it's in a bad way. But I also worry that it might be *me* who is different in a bad way. My eyes float across the room and down to the floor where our clothes from the day are thrown. I see Jacobs' pants wadded up and my mind wanders into the pockets to find what his secret object is that the man gave him back in Nain. The pants are just out of reach. Fifteen minutes pass. I look over at Jacob, asleep already. I look at the pants. I reach out with my right foot to try to hook the pants with my toes. I can just about touch them, but not enough to get them any closer. I lightly touch down on the front pocket with my toes and feel an object about the size of a finger. Moving slowly, so as not to disturb Jacob, I reposition myself for a better reaching angle. My big toe just gets under the waist of the pants. I can get them. Just a little further. I lose my balance at the edge of the bed and my foot slams onto the floor to catch me. *No. I didn't mean to!* Fear pours over me and I choke a scream of terror before it escapes my lungs. I squirm my way back into bed and under the covers, eyes wide open. Ears alert. *I touched the floor.*

The front door of the house slams open. I hear a loud roaring noise mixed with a flash of lightening, followed by thunder.

My blood freezes, my heart pounds too loudly.

A storm.

A monster.

A polar bear.

A *kraken.*

I hear and feel the pounding of footsteps up the stairway. My father's voice roars out, "You boys best be in bed!" His weight plunders back down the stairs and I hear him banging around the kitchen and out the back door. Still his voice carries with indiscernible shouts, cursing, and I clearly hear him yell out, "*Bonnie Marie.*" I don't know if he is referring to the boat or our mother. The rain pummels the world with a sharp suddenness as distant rumbles are heard and strobe lights decorate our room in nightmare flashes.

4

June Bear

July 27

This evening we are sitting at the table for a late dinner. Mrs. Sally joins us for the meal. Father has had a long day on the boat, as he does most days in the summertime, and he is tired and quiet. More so than usual. Jacob and I sit at the table across from each other looking from Father to Mrs. Sally. We don't turn our heads, but exaggerate our eye movements so that it looks as if we are watching a ping-pong match. We both start laughing at the funny spectacle we create. Mrs. Sally looks at us, gives us a short smile, and tells us to eat our dinner. The mood of the grown-ups is dark. Jacob and I soon dampen our own spirits as a heavy conversation seems about to loom over the meatloaf.

In short time, Mrs. Sally looks at Father and says, "Did you hear about June Bear?"

I hear her say *June Bear* with the emphasis on the

second word. And I ask, "What is June Bear?" Only, I put the emphasis on *June*, because it sounds like a cartoon character – *April-Bear, May-Bear, June-Bear* ... Mrs. Sally gives me a look that says I need to shush.

Father says, "Aye, 'tis a pity." All goes quiet for a moment while Father puts some food into his mouth, savors it, and says, "Good meatloaf." With that, Father commences (that means *to start*, or *to begin* – I looked it up in the dictionary this morning), the tale of June Bear.

"Not what. Who. When I first moved here some fifteen years ago, June was a right bonnie lass, she was. About the prettiest girl in town, aside from your mother, of course. At that time, she had not yet started up with her future husband, Tom Bear. I can't say why, but she took an instant interest in me. Maybe because I was new blood in town. Well, she tried hard to get and keep my attention, but I just wasn't interested in her. She had a way with the boys here in Davis Inlet, and I was told she went through men like a nor'easter rips through the Canadian coastline. Maybe that's okay for the women in Montreal or Quebec City, but here, just like back home in Kirkwall, that kind of behavior can only poison a community. I stayed away from her. Besides, my Marie had cast her magic spell upon me, and I was soon to be hers.

Now June, she was a heavy drinker. I guess when she met Tom, she about met her match. They found themselves in trouble more than they were out of trouble. Everyone was surprised to see June finally settle down with one man, but no one was surprised to see that it was Tom. They each had the temperament of a full-on hurricane. She was the fierce wind, and he was the devastating flood waters. From the moment they got married and settled into their house, they went at each other with cussing and screaming fights that could be heard clear across the island. I can't say which of them got the worse end of the abuse.

Just a couple years back, June called the police and said she had killed Tom. I guess it was his night to get too rough with her, and she went and stabbed him. When all was said and done, Tom's body was cut up pretty bad, but that is not what killed him. According to the coroner, Tom Bear had enough drugs running through his veins to get this entire village high. His death was ruled an overdose. No one ever doubted that June had sliced Tom up out of fear for her own life. June was a lot of bad things, but a cold killer was not on that list. Since then, June just sort of disappeared. She stayed home, lost in depression and unable to step outside for fear she would be the victim of a revenge killing by Tom's brothers, who were just as mean as Tom himself. I've seen her slinking around the grocery store a couple of times, and she was not looking like the beauty she once was. Life was unkind to her."

Mrs. Sally spoke up, "This morning she was found on the mainland, just across the water. A hunter came upon her. They say she followed Tom out the door – filled with OxyContin and with gasoline traces on her face and clothes. Only, *she* was half eaten. They say she must have died and then was lunch for some wolves or an errant polar bear. But the guy who found her, he said it looked to him like she was eaten *alive*. He said it looked like she was crawling out from the water's edge and up the rocky beach, as if to escape her tormentor. I don't know. I feel she took a boat over there to be alone and end it all. She had near forty years of a hard life, she deserved a better end than that."

I think about this story and I get a little shiver. The thought of being eaten by a pack of wolves or, worse, a bear (worse, because I get the impression it might take longer) frightens me. But if she was crawling up from the beach, what if it was something else? I picture writhing arms reaching out from the water, trying to pull her in to get better bites out of her. Monster beach.

5

Other Kids

August 25

I sometimes see the kids living down the street riding their bikes past our house. I never much thought about it before, but now I am beginning to question why they can go out into town when we are told we must stay in. I know it's dangerous out there, but why aren't those other kids afraid?

Today, our tutor Mrs. Sally let us outside in the front yard for a short playtime and I see one of the kids, a girl about my age, walk down past our driveway. She stares at me for a long time, as if I were an exotic animal. Her friend comes to join her and together they watch me and wait for me to say something.

"Hello," I say to them. I don't know what else to say. I am never in a situation where I need to talk to a stranger. So, I just stand and stare.

The two girls look at each other and start to laugh.

The taller one whispers something in the other's ear, and they giggle some more. I am confused, and maybe a little angry, at the way they stand and stare at me. The tall girl is wearing a teal blue hooded sweatshirt with a picture of a wolf on it. Her hands are shoved in the front pocket and she stands in a relaxed fashion that makes her appear as if she were the one that belongs here and I am the intruder in my own front yard. Her friend stares at me from inside a hooded coat that might belong to her mother, and she never loses the mocking smile she has glued to her face. The tall one asks me why I don't go to school. I tell her she's being silly. I go to school every day with my tutor or my father. She tries to explain that she means *real* school, like walk to school at seven in the morning and get home after three in the afternoon. The school building where classes are held Monday through Friday. She says that there are at least thirty kids in her school and they have different teachers and they have lunch and something called *recess* and all her friends go there. She says her mother told her that the reason we couldn't leave the house was because of what happened to our mother, and that my father is a murderer and a *paranoiac*. I look at her and yell, "You're a liar. My father is not a murderer and a paranoiac. And you don't go to a *real* school. You can't touch the floor that early every day!" I put my hand over my mouth and run inside the house and curl up on the sofa and cry into the sofa blanket. Mrs. Sally, in her soft way, comes to sit on the edge of the sofa, and puts her arm around me. She says she saw me with the girls outside, and that I should not worry about what a couple of mean kids say, and we won't have to tell my father what happened. Mrs. Sally knew she wasn't supposed to let us play in the front yard anyway. Another rule.

****

This evening my father returned home, we finished dinner, and we were spending some family time on the living room sofa playing games. I ask my Father what a *paranoiac* is, and he tells me that it is a person who knows that monsters are real.

6

On the Floor at Night

September 15

It is the middle of the night and I am in the kitchen getting a glass of water. What am I thinking? I don't even remember getting here. Was I sleep walking? The water tastes funny, that is, it has no taste at all. Our water is piped in from a small trickle of a creek that comes off the cliff across the road and is supposed to taste like rocks. I look at the jar I am drinking from and I can clearly see the rocks that lie on the bottom of the water. I shiver. I think I hear a voice from somewhere. It is outside the kitchen window. There is a silhouette of a man looking into the window with his hand on his forehead to offer a better view into the house. Our eyes meet and he laughs, "Your daddy's an asshole, and you can tell him that for me. Now come out of the house and I'll show you how to float right off this goddamned rock."

And now I hear Father thumping and roaring down

the steps to see who is up. The man at the window is gone. I look at my feet and am surprised to see that I am standing barefoot on the floor. *How could this be?* I think, *I was only just in bed.* It is too late to do anything about it. Father's footsteps are getting closer. His bellowing roars getting more frightening, I try to hide under the kitchen table. Maybe, I think, he won't notice me. On the far wall of the room, where a photograph of my forgotten mother hangs, I can make out my father's shadow as he approaches. But it is not my father. He has turned into something worse. I hear a voice announcing, "Ladies and Gentlemen, come delight yourselves! Watch the shadow dancer appearing nightly on your local kitchen wall!" The shadow is that of an octopus' arms flailing about, and a profile of a dragon head with gnashing teeth and floating tendrils all around it. My father yells out in his horrible voice, saliva spraying from his mouth. A long rough octopus arm, covered in scabs and scales, snakes along the kitchen floor toward me. I hear wet gurgly sniffing sounds as the father-monster smells me out. The tentacle finds me and touches my leg. I scream, but make no sound. I get out from under the table and stand up, cornered against the pantry. I yell at the monster that begins to fill the doorway, "I didn't mean to break the rule!" Then I begin to float off the floor just a couple of centimeters, and my father disappears.

I wake up, still screaming. Still in my bed. Tears wetting my pillow. With the familiar sounds of roaring in the next room, my brother at my side shushing me to get back to sleep, and the moon shining through the window, throwing unfamiliar shadows around the room, I crawl under the quilts and fall asleep waiting for sunrise.

***

This morning, after Father leaves for the day, I go downstairs and sit on the couch staring at the cooling wood stove. I have brought down my silver lighter. I light up the stove, comforted by my father's words, *this will always keep me safe in the darkness*. Once the fire is blazing and the room begins to take in the heat, Mrs. Sally comes to join me on the couch. I tell Mrs. Sally about my dream. She tells me it was only a dream and I should not worry about it. But as she says this, I see her shiver just a little bit, even though we are sitting in front of the wood stove. Mrs. Sally says that the monsters are just in our heads, and that my father is a very nice man. I like Mrs. Sally. She is kind to us and always makes sure to give us a hug whenever she sees us. But she is not like us. She is not a *paranoiac*.

7

Swimmer

September 30

It is snowing outside. The first snow of the year. It won't stick, but it is our first celebration of winter. I step out this afternoon, into the sitting area in the back, and I look around and marvel at the falling flakes. The sun is out, but still the snow finds its way. It will probably continue to fall for the next eight months, by which time I will hate it. But for now, it is exhilarating. Jacob is in the house with Mrs. Sally doing his lessons. I finished early and have some free time without Jacob hanging over me. Still, I will have to get him out here soon so we can chase the snowflakes together, and I will tell him they are being dropped from the sky by the snow fairies.

From here, in our backyard, I can see I am not alone in celebrating the first snow. I have a partial view of monster beach, as we have come to call it after the "monster" Jacob claimed he found there in the summer, and I can see three older kids sitting on the rocks. Maybe they're kids; they are at that strange age where some days they are older kids, but other days they are young grown-ups. There are two girls and a boy, and they are laughing loudly and saying things that I can't quite make out. They are acting funny like people do when they are drinking alcohol. A *celebration of inebriation*. That is called a *lazy rhyme*. I came up with it during my poetry sessions with Mrs. Sally. We do not have alcohol in our house, except for a couple bottles of beer, so I don't really know much about it. Father says alcohol kills people and it will very soon destroy our village. He says we will need to leave this place one day before everybody's monsters come to life and eat this whole town. I don't actually understand what he means when he talks this way.

I stand near our back door watching the three loud kids as they throw stones into the water and laugh. They have a large radio blaring out some pop music. I don't know much about music because we have had no radio or tv in our home since my mother died. One of the girls stands up with a big grin on her face and starts to spin slowly in circles and dance to the music. I can see her clearly, even with the view partially blocked by boulders at our property line. She holds up a plastic bag and brings it to her face. When she lowers it, she is laughing even more. She looks directly at me and I fear I am in trouble for watching them in their secret fun time. The girl's gaze leaves me and seems to blur away as if she is barely aware of anything around her. She scares me because she is beyond my experience of how people act. The girl steps closer to the water's edge and removes her coat, throwing it toward her friends on the rocks. She must be freezing; the winds are so cold coming off the water. She takes off her boots and socks, and dances barefoot on the cold strewn beach pebbles, snowflakes pirouetting around her. The girl brings her plastic bag back up to her face and breathes into it again. Now she drops the bag and peels off her pants, followed by her underwear which she drops at her feet, uncaring. Her friends start yelling and laughing wildly as the girl continues her dance, stripping off her shirt and bra. I stand unable to look away. I have never seen a naked girl before. I feel I am dreaming it all. The snow falls and I can actually see the snowflakes melting on the girl's bare shoulders. I don't know how she can stand the cold, nor can I understand how she can stand naked in front of other people.

Again, the girl directs her gaze toward me. This time she stops her twirling dance and locks eyes with me. She is just about thirty meters from me. She grabs her breasts and shakes them at me, moves one hand up to her mouth, blows me a kiss, and continues her twirling dance. The sunlight reflects off a silver bracelet that hangs on her wrist. Blood rushes to my face. I want to run inside the house, but I can't move. I can only stare, transfixed. I can't tell if I am breathing. Now the girl walks slowly into the water. She screams and laughs as she gets deeper. I watch her legs sink, and the water creeps up over the girl-hair covering her crotch. Her tummy goes under, her breasts seem to float for just a second, her head goes down, and then she disappears beneath the surface. Her friends get up, grab the radio, and run off laughing. The music fades as they disappear. I wait. The girl must have swum out of view before getting out of the water, because I do not see her again.

Jacob busts out of the back door, filled with energy,

ready to play. I stand staring at the water where the girl disappeared, a ghost of a ripple to show someone has just dipped in. I barely register Jacob's presence. "Come on," Jacob yells, "let's throw rocks into the water."

I hesitate. What if the girl shows up while we are on the shore? Jacob runs past me and throws his head up toward the falling flakes. His tongue sticks out to catch one and he laughs at his own spectacle. He spins around with his arms out and falls down dizzy, still laughing. This goes on for about ten minutes before my little brother skips to the water's edge and picks up a handful of rocks and throws them at a large black raven. A member of the corvid family – I learned this when reading Edgar Allen Poe with Mrs. Sally. Edgar Allen Poe was a famous writer from the eighteen-hundreds. We read a story called "The Tell-Tale Heart," which scared me afterwards every time I could feel my own heartbeat. Then she read me a long poem, more like a story, about a raven who said "Nevermore." She told me it was Edgar Allen Poe's most famous work. It was a creepy poem that made me a little wary of ravens, but also a little curious, hence why I went and looked them up some more.

Jacob's aim is off, but not so far off that it doesn't alarm the bird. It takes flight over the water and circles around to dive toward Jacob's head, missing him by just a meter. "Stupid bird!" he yells. Forgetting his short-lived wonder of the snow, Jacob runs after the bird, throwing the remaining rocks in his hand. I could see frustration, and maybe anger, drawing across his face.

Hoping to relieve Jacob's mounting anger and escape the possibility of the reappearance of the naked girl, I yell out, "It's cold out here. Let's go upstairs and play pirates."

Jacob's smile returns and he runs past me yelling, "AARGH!!!" He races into the house and up the stairs. By the time I get up there, he already has his stick-sword in hand and black bandanna on his head. "Come oan, ye scallywaggin' salty dug! Why, I'll run ye through wi' ma sword like a rat on the cuttin' board!" He yells out in his best imitation of our father's Scottish accent.

I take a sword in the belly as I break past him into the room. I grab a towel and, pretending it is a net, throw it over him, "I've got you now, you land-lubber nix-nox! Now 'tis time to walk the plank." I see the two pairs of binoculars on the dresser top. "Wait, Matey, is that the British Royal Navy I see on the horizon?"

We grab the binoculars and scan the waters. Jacob looking for the navy, and I looking for the girl. Small gentle waves come in with never-ending stories, but *the sea does not give up her secrets*, as my father often says. I see the girl's body floating, face up, in the distance, but upon a closer look it turns out to be nothing more than a mass of seaweed, bleached white by the sun. I swing my gaze over to the monster beach rocks in hopes of finding the other two kids. All I see is the pile of discarded clothing that the girl left near the receding tideline, awaiting either the return of the girl or the following high tide to take them up, like a pile of shoreline seaweed.

8

Evening Discussions

October 7

We sit at the dinner table, Jacob, Father, Mrs. Sally, and me. I have finished my dinner of baked fish, potatoes, and broccoli, and I am waiting for everyone else to finish so I can be excused. I run my fingers along the edge of the wooden table, feeling all the scratches and marks that have landed on the surface since my father made it twelve years back, about the time I was born. The table is heavy, sturdy, and built to last forever. Somewhere back in a foggy memory, I hear my mother saying, "It is a simple design, but it is more beautiful than any furniture you could ever buy." It was because she loved this table and saw it as such a special thing, that I too loved it. Now, I mostly take the table for granted. It has always been a part of our house, as Mother was also a part of the house. Mother is gone, and the table remains. For some reason, I think of the table as my mother's gravestone. Mrs. Sally says she goes out to visit her dead husband's gravestone every week, and she talks to him. I guess I visit the table many times a day, and I often talk to my mother inside my head when I'm sitting there. Father goes to the sea to talk to my mother; I go to the dinner table.

I watch as Jacob takes a never-ending amount of time to eat. He pushes his potatoes around the plate like they are little boats in the harbor. His fish becomes the rock island, and broccoli make for the sparse pines that litter the landscape. From time to time, my father eyes Jacob and gives him a look that says he should be getting finished with his dinner.

"Boys," Father addresses us, "I've asked Mrs. Sally here to stay with you for the next couple of days, maybe even three or four days. I hate to leave you two for so long, but there is talk of a cod run out on the banks. An old-timer fisherman in the inlet, Albert Skanes, is getting together a small crew to make a go at them. The cod fisheries have been shut down for some time by the government, so we'll be making a small jump on the fish while no one is watching." Our father gives us a little wink. "I'll be gone first thing in the morning. Robert, you take care of Jacob and the fire. Jacob, you take care of Mrs. Sally. And remember," my brother and I join in with his chorus as he says, "*don't touch the floor after sunset!*" Jacob and I both laugh, but only because it covers up our deepest fears.

* * *

The sun is now long gone. Jacob and I sit up in bed, neither of us tired. Jacob plays imaginary games with his small, brightly-colored plastic dinosaurs. He makes little growling sounds as he reenacts the classic Triceratops versus T-Rex fight to the death. He creates mountains and valleys out of our blankets and forms the Jurassic setting of the dinosaur world.

"Robert, do you think there are still dinosaurs? I mean hiding from people in the Northwoods where no one lives?"

"I don't know. Maybe little, tiny ones that can hide in the rocks and not be seen. Definitely not big ones like there used to be. We would have seen them."

"Do you think a polar bear would win a fight with a small dinosaur?"

"I don't know, Jacob"

"Do you think a polar bear would win a fight with a big dog? Like the one we saw in Nain?"

Without waiting for an answer, Jacob says, "Robert, I don't like it when Father leaves. Do you think Mrs. Sally will let us play outside?" Jacob looks at me with sad, hopeful eyes as he puts up his dinosaurs.

"I don't know. Sometimes I think she would like to see us off running with the other kids for a while. I heard her talking to Father once, telling him that."

Jacob rolls over and stares out the window at the water. "Robert …"

I say nothing as I close my eyes for the night.

"Robert." I can hear the annoyance in Jacob's voice as he waits for my acknowledgment. "Robert." A little whine in his voice.

"What?"

"What if Father doesn't come back? What if he is eaten like Mother was? Would we have to live with Mrs. Sally then?"

I let a silence hang in the room for a moment before answering. "Nothing is going to eat him. Nothing eats people except maybe sharks and polar bears. Sharks only eat people when they are swimming, and polar bears don't live on the water. And besides, Mother wasn't eaten. She just died, that's all. Now go to sleep."

"But there's a monster …"

"Go to sleep, Jacob."

9

My Mother's Death

October 9

I awaken with the sun far above the horizon. Jacob has already gotten up, leaving a turned down blanket for the cold air to slip into my own sleep sanctuary. I sit up and feel the chill of the morning air as it brings my body to life. Throwing on a sweater and warm pants, I make my way down the steps to find Mrs. Sally preparing breakfast. I smell pancakes and my stomach speaks to me. I notice only one setting on the table and look questioningly to Mrs. Sally.

"Your brother has been up for quite a while. He ate his breakfast and ran out the back door. He's becoming a squirrelly one, he is." She fills my plate with a pile of pancakes and hands me the bottle of syrup.

I guess that Jacob wanted to be the first one out to see what the tide brought in during the night. Usually, we find nothing more than plastic bottles, and remnants of old fishing nets. Sometimes we get a buoy from a lobster or crab trap that floats in, and we add it to our collection of sea treasures. I will have to go out after I finish breakfast and see what Jacob has found.

Mrs. Sally sits down at the table with me and says, "Robert, I need to take care of some things at my own house today. Keep an eye on Jacob and stay out of trouble." She winks at me, knowing that I never get into trouble. With that, she finishes up the dishes, puts down her apron, and gets her things together.

I run upstairs to get my jacket and sneakers on so I can go out and see what Jacob is up to. From my room I hear the front door close as Mrs. Sally leaves for her errands. I look out the window to watch Jacob, but he is not visible from this vantage point. So, I go downstairs and out the back door. Our backyard is not big. It is mostly rocks and weeds, and an ever-fluctuating tidal line. But one thing it does not seem to have is Jacob. I call out his name. Nothing. I wander over to the monster beach to look among the boulders. Nothing. In the back of my mind, I hear the drunken, wavering voice of Billy Cloud: *Looking for something, Scotsman's boy? Scot-tot. Maybe some woman's clothing? Well, I found them first. I took them home. Finders keepers. Maybe you can come to my place and I'll let you touch them, or sniff them. What do you say, Robert? I'd tell you to bring your brother with you, but he doesn't seem to be here, does he?* I yell out, "You're not real!"

I run around to the front yard and out onto the street to escape the haunting voice of Billy Cloud as much as to look in desperation for Jacob. I feel like I am disappointing Father just by the act of stepping onto the street without him nearby. I look down the road, and in the distance, I see three boys walking away from our house. I can't tell from this far away, but the boys look to be about Jacob's age. And the boy on the left *could* be Jacob. I call him, but not too loudly so as to remain inconspicuous. I don't like attracting attention. Seeing as the boy doesn't acknowledge my calling him, I go back into the house and see if he is in there somewhere. Walking through the kitchen and living room, I call out for Jacob. I go upstairs and look in our room, and then I hesitantly open the door to Father's room. I softly call out, "Jacob." No sign. Where else could he be? I am now quite sure that it was in fact Jacob that I saw walking down the street. Where could he be going with those boys? Who *were* those boys, and how does he know them in the first place? Maybe he went to the boat.

I will be in such trouble if something happens to Jacob. I step back out onto the street, frightened of the big world, and stare down the road, now empty. I see a couple of grown-ups going on about their grown-up lives, and a small pack of dogs dominating their territory. I stand motionless, talking myself into walking down the road alone. I make up my mind and head straight toward the docks where our boat lay snug in its home. There is no other place that Jacob knows of to go. He surely must be hiding out in the *Bonnie Marie*. As I walk, I look around in fear that I might run into Mrs. Sally or some other person who might know who I am. I remember Father once telling me, *Everyone knows who we are because we stick out like a sore thumb – a couple of handsome sandy-haired Scotsmen thrown into a bowl of dark-haired Innu people*. Then he would look at my predominantly Innu brother and add, *Not that the Innu aren't the most beautiful people on this planet, but face it Lad, your mother and you could hide in plain sight among the locals.* Then Father grabbed

Jacob and wrestled him to the floor and allowed young Jacob to get on top and pin him down while they laughed and squealed. That was a rare day of happiness. Father doesn't laugh much anymore.

As I get to the docks, I see a few old fishermen, some women with toddlers, and that's about it. I get on the pier that houses the *Bonnie Marie* and walk tentatively to the side of the boat. I step over the gunwale and hop down to the deck. A bunch of fishing supplies are laid out as if the *Bonnie Marie* were always in wait for a willing passenger to ride her out to the banks. With no sign of Jacob among the ropes, nets, buckets, and other paraphernalia, I venture to the cabin. I step inside and am first hit with the strong smell of tobacco. I am startled into a sort of muffled scream as Mr. Dave sits up from his chair. He has somehow blended into the clutter of the cabin as if he himself were a part of the *Bonnie Marie*.

"Well, if it isn't young Robert Kidd. Come to escape the island, have you?"

My initial startled surprise soon turns to embarrassment at my own reaction. I look down at the floor feeling as if I had been caught in the most heinous of crimes. I feel my face burning and I stutter as I say, "N-n-no, I was looking for Jacob. He r-ran off."

"Have yourself a seat, Robert. No worries, I can use the company." Mr. Dave takes a drink from a glass at his cabin table. "I hear ol' John went out on a big fishing excursion."

I want to run. If Mr. Dave tells my father I was out here on my own, he'll be so cross with me. But I know that I cannot leave while talking to a grown-up until I am excused. "Yes sir," I answer while studying the glass in his hands. "I'm looking for my little brother. He ran off with some boys, but I need to get him home."

Mr. Dave looks at me, saying nothing for a while. He takes a long drag on his cigarette and slowly blows the smoke out his nose. "I saw your brother. He was running with some other kids down the road. He was happy. Laughing. The kid needs to get out more. He fits right in with the others, you know. You, on the other hand, Robert, you look just like your father: a Scot who does not belong here. I don't mean that in a bad way. I'm just saying, you're different people. Listen Robert, let your brother run off and have a little adventure for a change. A boy needs it. And God knows your father won't give it to you." He looks at me long and hard. "Now sit yourself down and let me tell you something about John." He opens up a small cooler that Father keeps on board and he gets out a root beer – the closest thing to alcohol that my father ever drinks when on the sea. I used to think it was a kind of beer, and I guess it kind of is, but I soon learned it was just sugar water with some flavor to it. Maybe it tastes like real beer, but never having had either one of them, I wouldn't know. My father mostly keeps root beer, Vienna sausages, and sardines to snack on while he is out on the water. Mr. Dave pops off the cap and hands me the dark brown bottle of root beer, which I take. All I could think was that if Father found out about this, I would be in huge trouble. He would never trust me again. Mr. Dave must have read my mind, because he says, "Now don't you tell John that we were in here drinking up his root beer and talking about him, because if he knew that, he would surely beat the shit out of you, and throw me overboard." Mr. Dave laughs and takes a sip from his glass.

He looks at me with his stern face, which does not

really seem to fit his personality. He closes his eyes for a moment, then says, "Let me tell you what no one else will tell you about your father. I don't want you to get the wrong idea, I love your father. He is a good man, but he is broken. I think you know that. Ever since your mother died …" Mr. Dave pauses as if to consider if this was a wise thing to be telling me. "That day your mother's body sunk into the sea, your father's heart fell from his chest and followed her down to the depths of the ocean. Sometimes I think that John would be better off packing you boys up and heading back to Scotland. That's where he truly belongs, and maybe where he desperately needs to bury his sorrows. It sure as hell isn't here on this rock," he pauses and sighs. "Well shit, none of us belong here. Most of the people here in the inlet are haunted by depression as it raises its ugly head and casts its shadow over us. Like your father, we have all been displaced. Look around you, boy. Alcohol has ravaged us all, yours truly included." With that, Mr. Dave takes another sip. "It is our last salvation. And those who get bored with the drink, they turn to the cheaper alternative, a bag of gasoline or spray paint, as their next best friend. Drink one, sniff the other, it all turns out the same. It all adds up to darkness. In the end, Robert, there's only one way off this rock. Your father knows this. That is why he has been planning your escape aboard this surprisingly seaworthy boat. In the meantime, he has turned into an over-protective guardian. You know what I'm talking about." Mr. Dave pauses, maybe to let the alcohol steer his words to a place he knows they shouldn't go. He does his best impression of my father and says, convincingly, "Never touch the floor after the sun sets, lad. The *kraken* will get you!" A shiver runs through me. "I'll tell you, Robert, there is no *kraken*. This is your father's plan to keep you from sneaking off into the night and getting involved in the atrocities that have overtaken this village. And it seems to do the job, at least with you. Your brother, now he has a different mindset altogether. You are right to keep mind of Jacob and keep a good eye on him."

We sit silently for a while. Me sipping on my root beer, Mr. Dave sipping on his demons. I look out the cabin window and watch as the gulls take to the wind from their resting place to survey the shallows before returning to their piling that they have claimed and guarded from their rivals. I watch as a lone raven flies uncaringly through the seagull community and lands on the rail of the *Bonnie Marie*. The raven seems to be looking through the window right back at me before taking flight again.

In time, Mr. Dave carries on. Clearly, he has much to say to me, and limited opportunities to do so. "What exactly happened to your mother? You certainly must wonder. Well, I can only tell you what I know. As I said, depression is everywhere. No one escapes it, not really. Your mother and I, we are cousins or second cousins, something like that. I guess everybody in this community is related in some way. From time to time your mother and I sat on this boat and passed the bottle back and forth. She alternately laughed and cried about life. You should know, Robert: you boys and your father were everything to her. But the sickness of depression is not always healed by the closeness of loved ones. The healing only comes from deep within. Sometimes your mother would tell me how she would prefer to be far away from this place, whatever it would take to get there. She mused over the number of suicides in this village. She thought of those people who killed themselves as strong and brave souls who can face death and the afterlife. She insisted that though she had thought about it, she was not strong enough to end it all. Were I a wiser and smarter man, I might have talked her into leaving this rock, but mostly I gave her my ear and my shoulder. Marie stayed close to the bottle and began to befriend the gasoline bag as well. You were young, and maybe you didn't know or understand it, but your mother spent her last couple of years drunk or high. Your father, he knew of the addictions and the sadness that lived within Marie. He tried to convince her to go to Scotland with him and take you and your brother as well, but she did not want to leave her family. She did not want to leave her community and her home, as much as she detested living in it. Your father was beside himself to see her in such pain. Finally, he made a decision. He would leave you two boys with your grandmother and take your mother out to sea on the *Bonnie Marie*. He told me his plan was to stay out there until she sobered up. Until he could fix her. *The Great Purification Voyage*, he called it. He did not care how long it would take."

Mr. Dave took a moment. His face contorted as if the memory hurt him. I suppose it did. "The morning that Marie stepped onto the boat was the last that I saw of her. It was the last that anybody saw of her. Marie did not want to go. She kicked up a fuss. She smelled of gasoline and liquor, but she did not want to leave your side." Mr. Dave makes a dramatic pause to emphasize his point. "Robert, it could not have been later than nine in the morning. Your father must have dragged a week's worth of food and water on board. As the onlookers watched them put her out to sea, there was much head-shaking and muttering. Your father was not a popular man. He was an outsider, and his ways were strange. Most people in the village, with the exception of other fishermen who knew him better, did not trust him. Perhaps it was because he was different, perhaps it was because he married one of theirs, or perhaps because he kept to himself and did not get involved with the rest of the community. Five days passed since anyone had seen any sign of the *Bonnie Marie*. That is when the storm came. It was the remnants of a hurricane that came up the coast to say hello in a very angry voice. Thunder and lightning clashed. The waves pummeled the shore and ripped out a couple of the docks. Only a fool would be out on the water in those conditions. Again, people shook their heads, murmuring about this crazy Scotsman who took his wife to meet their ends. It was yet another five days before I saw the *Bonnie Marie* limping into this inlet. She was listing to one side and there was visible damage on the hull. John, your father, staggered off the boat and came walking down the pier. I waited for Marie to come out, but there was no sign of her. I walked onto the boat to assess the damage and to look for Marie, who I assumed was sleeping in the cabin, but she was not there.

10

Jacob With the Street Kids

October 9

As I leave Mr. Dave and the boat, my head is swimming. So many thoughts are going through me. Monster. Murder. Suicide. Stormy seas. Depression. Grief. And maybe the one word that was not spoken – Madness. So much conjecture. So many truths. Perhaps a hopelessly tangled fishing net that is thrown to the sea of frustration – no known solution to finding the truth that lies within the story. Does Mrs. Sally have her own version? Does Father ever talk about it? Does the entire world, other than myself or Jacob, know the truth?

My feet take me unknowingly to a boulder that overlooks the water. I sit and slowly digest Mr. Dave's story. It slowly becomes clear why my father does not want Jacob or me talking to Mr. Dave while he is not there. It only takes one drunken morning for the story to crawl out of him. I stare at the water, but it has no answers to

offer. Today my life has changed. I have lost my innocence. I can feel my mind and the world open up before me, and it is terrifying. As I look down the shore toward the docks, I feel tears seeping from me. I close my eyes and try to shut out the world. I sit for quite a while and suddenly realize I have been gone from home for far too long. I look up and there is a girl watching me. A look of sadness shadows her face. I realize she is sad for me, for the image I must portray as I sit in my grayness, exposed to the empty sea. We look at each other for an awkward moment, holding our gaze a little too long. There is something feral in her lack of inhibition. She is a fox, a deer … no, she's more of a bird, and the image of a raven flies through my head. She gives me a little smile and a short wave of empathy, and she is again a girl. I get up from my boulder, scamper across the rocks to the high tide line, walk within ten meters of her, return her smile, and step up to the old, rutted road.

Up the street toward the center of town I see Jacob. He is walking now with a group of boys, five or six, of varying ages, and heading my way. I stand in the street and wait for them to come closer.

"Come on, Jacob, we have to go home."

Jacob and the boys stop where they are. Jacob says something to the others, and they turn to me, laughing. Every one of them, Jacob included, wears a strange, almost frightening smile. One boy wearing a red hoodie stands a little taller than Jacob, and yells out loud enough for me to hear, "Hey Jay, is that your brother Scott?"

Jacob says nothing but laughs aloud with the other kids.

"My name isn't Scott, it's Robert." I say in a breaking voice. I don't know why I am suddenly so nervous. My arms are tingling.

"Hey Scott," yells out the oldest of them, maybe my age or older, "why don't you go home and get your kilt?" They all burst out in laughter, Jacob joining them and looking at me with dark, unfocused eyes that I do not recognize.

The boys are made of liquid metal and rat poison. They hang on to each other like sled dog puppies of the same litter when they sleep, piled up on the other puppy bodies. Even Jacob, who seems to have been assimilated into the group, leans on a fat kid next to him as if to prop himself up to keep from melting.

Jacob says, "Go on Robert, I'll meet you at home."

"Yeah, go on Bobby-Lad," yells the red hoodie kid.

They give me the creeps, these unknown kids. I think of the mean kids in *Lord of the Flies*, and I suddenly feel like Piggy. I turn around and run home with the sound of laughter fading behind me.

I arrive home and run through the front door to find, with some relief, that Mrs. Sally hasn't returned yet. I go into the kitchen and make some hot chocolate and a peanut butter and jelly sandwich. I grab an apple and go into the living room, curl up on the sofa with my lunch and some blankets, and stare absently at the cold wood stove while my head swims. I dig into my pocket to find my lighter. I rub my thumb over the engraving and think, *this is the worst day I can remember, except when my mother died*. Really, it's like a continuation of that day – many years later. As the winter air creeps into my body to echo the thoughts in my head, I get up, step quickly outside to gather some wood, and bring it back into the house. I carefully stack the small pieces and in turn, the larger ones. I grab some paper from the trash, roll the wheel of my faithful lighter, and produce a flame. Lighting the paper, I put it in place under the kindling, and revive the memories of the buried embers from early this morning.

I recall some of the events of the day my mother died like they were yesterday. Other parts of that day, well, it's like people say: time makes a mockery of our memories. I recall that we were staying at Grandmother Alice's house. She likes us to call her Alice. We were excited about the sleepover. We did not have many chances to get away from our own home, but Mother liked us to stay with her mother sometimes. She would say that it is how a family stays together. I don't remember how long we stayed, but it seemed like forever. I was getting homesick for my own room and for my parents. It was the late afternoon of a strange day filled with crying women and quiet men that I looked out the window into the street. And then I saw Father. I was so surprised to see him. I shouted out to him and ran toward the front door, nearly tripping over my feet. At the door, Alice stopped me and said, "You need to leave your father be for right now. He's sick." Again, I called to him, but Alice swept me into the house and set me down on a kitchen chair. She sat next to me and put her arm around me. I could see her crying. She pulled me closer to her and told me that Mother would not be coming home. She said that the storm took her. I remember being confused by this, unsure of what she meant. How could a storm take her? I broke away from my grandmother and ran outside. Father was gone.

I yelled for him and, not waiting for an answer, I ran down the street to the water's edge, all the time calling out "Mother! Father!" I stood at the seaside, crying and yelling out until my uncle came down and picked me up in his large arms and carried me back to the house. Jacob and I stayed at Alice's house for a few more days, seeing Father a couple of times, but he was quiet and not really our old Father anymore. It felt like a long time before he remembered how to laugh again. When we returned to our own house, the rooms were always silent. We were afraid to say anything because Father would either yell at us or he would act like we did not exist. I felt like a ghost, even though Grandmother Alice told me that it was Father who was a ghost.

And now, with drunken Mr. Dave's revealed secrets, I find myself back in this confused world. I get up from my sofa seat and head upstairs to my room. Mr. Dave's words come back to me.

What happened to your mother, you might ask? Well, there are three versions of what took place during those ten days. The first version, which is the popularly held belief, was that John killed Marie. He had seen that she would never change, which led to deep sorrow and horrible fights, and he threw her overboard. Naturally, Marie's family wanted revenge. For some reason, John kept you boys in your house out at the edge of town rather than leave the island. People approached John and told him in no uncertain terms that he was no longer welcome in our community. John easily stands one foot taller than any other man here, and he would not be intimidated easily.

The second version of what may have happened, and I believe this to be the truth, is that your mother took her own life. I understand the anguish and turmoil that lurks inside an addict or an alcoholic. I've been there and, as you can see, I am still there. Your mother's depression, guilt, lack of self-worth – these are things that are endemic to our people. It is not our fault, rather it is the hand of fate. It was far too heavy a load for your mother to carry any longer. I feel she took her life far from shore to spare you boys.

Then, there is a third version, the one that is held firmly by your father and perhaps by some others here in the Davis Inlet. Your father has gone over this many times with me. He told me that while the hurricane was ravaging and tossing their boat, he was fighting for their lives to keep the boat from smashing against the rocky islands that had been their harbor for the past five days. Finally, he had gone further out to sea where the waves were bigger but broader and less likely to smash their boat. Marie was not doing well, sick from withdrawal symptoms. She continually walked out of the cabin onto the deck where she was torn by waves and rain and wind. Darkness set in and the seas still did not calm down. The boat was at the mercy of the storm. While John was busy trying to keep the boat upright, keep the water out, and make some makeshift repairs where the hull was damaged, he heard an unearthly scream behind him. His first thought was that a seagull had landed and taken refuge on the boat and was shrieking. He turned and watched in horror the events to follow.

It was as dark as ink, and the rain was coming down in heavy sheets. The angry flashes of lightning gave instant images of progressing still-lives. And what John saw was the thick arm of a kraken come up from the sea, grabbing Marie, and taking her down underwater with it. John said he could smell the beast and hear the loud roaring noises that came from its bellowing body. John himself let out a thundering anguished cry into the air.

And she was gone.

It was as if she had never been on board. Was it a wave that reached up and tore Marie from the boat? Was it the outraged passion of the storm that seized the opportunity to carry out Marie's destined fate? Or was there in fact a sea monster that reached up and grabbed her? Perhaps the question is irrelevant. Perhaps the sea monster came into your father's head to protect him from the truth. Only God knows.

You and Jacob are all that your father has left. He is a hard man to understand, but he has his reasons. All he wants to do is shelter you and your brother from harm. Your father has not drunk alcohol, save for an occasional pint for special get-togethers, since that day of the tragedy. A hard thing for a Scotsman, I should think. And I can tell you one thing Robert: if you or your brother ever mess with gasoline or alcohol, you will break that man.

I sit on the bed, and again, I pull out the lighter that Father gave me. I look closely at the *kraken* that is engraved on the metal body of the lighter. A chill runs through me as the realization sets in that, yes, monsters *are* real. I stopped believing in Santa Claus a couple of years ago when my father would always make sure the wood stove was burning hot on Christmas eve to keep the monsters out of the chimney. The house was always shut up tight in the frigid winter months when the nights were insufferably long. How, I wondered, would Santa get down the chimney if Father was making sure that nothing could get in? And yet, there were presents awaiting us in the morning. While Father succeeded in keeping the flames of the stove burning, he inadvertently snuffed the flames of my Santa beliefs. When I confronted Mrs. Sally with my reasoning, she looked at me, with some pride, and said that I was a very clever boy, but I should keep the Santa story a secret from Jacob. I have continued to let Jacob believe in Santa, but I always told him that monsters were not real. Now, I am no longer convinced that there are no monsters. My father could never kill another person. My mother was always happy and laughing with Jacob and me, so I don't believe she was depressed. And the storm, maybe it was the storm that carried my mother away. But if my father actually saw the *kraken* come up from the stormy seas, then I believe it was a combination of storm and monster that took my mother.

I flick the lighter and watch the flame come alive. I quickly extinguish it, frightened by its light. I slide the lighter into my pocket, and I hear the front door open. It must be Mrs. Sally. What if she asks about Jacob? What if she knows I have been talking to Mr. Dave? No matter, I feel scared and I need a friendly face. I run downstairs to see her, but it is not her. Jacob wanders in the doorway and walks by me and up the stairway to our room without a word. As he passes me by, I smell the lighter fluid from my Zippo. It must be leaking in my pocket. I am confused about what to do with Jacob. I should go upstairs and talk to him. I can't. Instead, I go out the back door and walk to the water's edge to let my mind wander. I throw rocks into the water. I look over at monster beach. I think about the giant squid arm we found there. Mr. Daves's story keeps playing in my mind.

Could it have been a giant squid that Father saw come out of the sea on that stormy night? No, he would know the difference. I once asked him how they differed. I had read in *Twenty Thousand Leagues Under the Sea* how Captain Nemo and his crew were attacked by a squid and it sounded a lot like a *kraken* to me. Father told me there is a difference between fiction and reality, between a gentler creature of the deep and a monstrous devil creature that sinks ships.

I look up at our bedroom window and I see Jacob looking out and watching me. As soon as our eyes lock, he ducks out of sight. And just like that, my mind is made up. I will not ask him about today. And I will not tell him of my talk with Mr. Dave. We now each have our secrets.

11

Father's Return

October 10

It has been three days since Father's departure, and now he returns. Mrs. Sally told us he and his crew had come into the docks and had apparently brought with them a huge haul of fish. Probably enough to see us through the winter with meat and money. Such was the talk as they pulled in. But there is something else; something Mrs. Sally is leaving out. I can see a shadow of deep trouble across her already dark eyes. Adults do not like to tell complete stories, and those who are able to read faces can see where those stories veer off or end abruptly. I guess I am a face reader. While Jacob jumps around in excitement, I feel a shadow approaching, as if the barometer had fallen and a massive nor'easter is coming down. I look into the eyes of Mrs. Sally, searching for the unspoken story, but she quickly looks away and begins the business of preparing a large feast of a dinner for my father when he comes home.

It will take most of the day for Father to take care of his catch and help clean up the boat, so I don't expect to see him until early evening. I wander outside to the shore, where the tide is quickly receding, to look through the tide pools for treasures – living and otherwise. I don't invite Jacob to join me, as things are still strange between us. I don't know who will get in more trouble when, or if, Father finds out our secrets. Mrs. Sally once said, *There are no secrets in this village. Except, this whole village is a secret from the rest of the country. The Canadian government relocated us here with promises of a better life, and then they abandoned us. No running water. No sewer. No fertile soil. No livelihood. No road in or out. No sense of pride. We have been tucked away out of sight from the world. It is no wonder that that so many people take their own lives.*

I poke through a familiar pool on the upper end of the tidal zone. A couple of sea urchins, dressed in their formidable jackets of spines and needles, are tucked away in crevices. I pick up a loose rock to see a muddy green crab, the size of a loony, scuttle to another hiding spot. There is a small fish, no longer than my pinkie, swimming back and forth, trapped until the next incoming tide can release it from its prison. Petite shrimp-like crustaceans, scuds, dart here and there. Limpets, living in their half-shell houses, cling tight and become a part of the rock. I am a limpet. I cling to this house on this rock, seemingly immovable by any force. Or, I am the small fish, trapped in my own tidal pool, pacing about, awaiting my release. Sometimes I am the crab, hiding under rocks, afraid to be seen. Mostly, I think I am the sea urchin. A fragile creature with mushy insides, and my father playing the part of the formidable green jacket of spines and needles. I am stuck in my low-tide world, fearing what the high tide may bring.

The water is cold on my hands, so I leave the pools and wander toward the left side of the shore to look at monster beach. I look over at the house to make sure no one is watching, and I climb the boulders that separate our shore from the monster's shore. I walk onto the beach of small gray rocks and pebbles, and look around to find what the sea might have brought me. Nothing, really. A couple of plastic bottles – one of laundry detergent, and another of bottled water. Bottled water, a necessity for our survival on this rock. I laugh to myself to think that it is now empty of water and has transformed into bottled air. I wonder if the whales in the ocean find the bottled air and take it down deep to the sea bottom to insert into their blowhole for an extra second or two of submersible time. I see what I used to think was a tiny plastic bottle, but when I brought one into the house, Mrs. Sally had to explain what a tampon applicator was, and she told me to throw it away. Mrs. Sally also explained what menstruation was. It is a word and a concept I was not familiar with. I tried to use menstruation in a sentence the next couple of days – there is a *menstruosity* of litter discharged by our community that washes up on our shore at high tide. Mrs. Sally told me that that form of the word is not a word (but it is – I looked it up. It is now obsolete and forgotten) and I should not use the word anyway.

I sit down on the rocks that have been warmed by the sun, and stare out at the sea. I am drawn to the water as if I belonged in it. A sea creature stranded in the drying tidal pool. I remove my shoes and walk barefoot over the smooth stones. I know the water will be cold, but I somehow need to feel the sensation on my skin. My feet go in, and after the initial flash of stinging there is instant numbness. The gentle waves that lap the shore caress my ankles, my calves, and tease my knees. I close my eyes to lose myself in the moment. I belong here, in the water. I recall the girl dancing naked in the water a month back, and I think I know why she did it. She, too, must have felt the calling. As I take one more tiny step toward the horizon, I hear a peal of laughter behind me. Startled, I quickly turn around, lose my footing, splash around, and soak my rolled-up pants halfway up the thigh. I look up into the grimacing face of Billy Cloud.

"Look at you, boy. You're a fool, just like Marie. If I were you, I'd stay far away from that water. According to your asshole father, there are monsters – or did he say demons? – in that ocean." The drunk man wipes the drool from the corner of his mouth, stumbles for a moment of uncertain balance, and continues. "I told Skanes not to take fucking John-the-Fucking-Scotsman out with him. Now it seems another 'monster' took one of the crew out to lunch while they were heading back."

I am no longer aware of the knee-deep water I am standing in. I am mesmerized by the swaying motion of this man, and I can't help but wonder how he is still standing.

The man continues, "Your family is a curse upon our people. I should drown your sorry little Scottish ass right here and now and bring an end to your lineage." The man stumbles closer to the water's edge, brings out his plastic bag from his coat pocket, opens it, and places it over his mouth and nose. He inhales deeply. I watch his eyes lose their focus for a moment.

And I run.

I leave my shoes on the beach and feel nothing of the

barnacles on the boulders under my numb feet. I get up to my back door and bolt inside, shivering in fear. Mrs. Sally eyes me as I round the corner to go upstairs, and says, "Robert Jonathan Kidd, look at you! Wet and shivering. Are you trying to get sick? You get up there and change those clothes and then come down and help me out in the kitchen. What are you thinking, playing in the water this late in the year? And I thought you were the one with common sense."

I go up to my room and Jacob is at his desk painting funny faces on rocks – a new hobby of his. He has twenty or thirty of them littered around the room and the house. They're pretty good, actually.

He looks over at me. "What happened to you?"

"Tide pool accident," I lie.

"I saw you out the window talking to that man."

I look at him as if I were in trouble, but then I say, "I saw you with those boys on the street."

Neither of us say anything for a minute. We just stare at each other. Then Jacob slowly puts his finger to his mouth and makes a long exaggerated "Shhhh" sound. He goes back to his painting, and I change into some dry warm clothes. This is how our awkwardness ends.

I go back downstairs into the kitchen to help Mrs. Sally. She gives me a knife and six potatoes and tells me to cut them up into wedges and throw them in the bottom of the big roasting pan. I do as I am asked, and I cut some carrots and onions as well. Mrs. Sally gets out a large piece of caribou meat that has been defrosting in the refrigerator for the past day, and places it on top of the potato-carrot-onion medley. She rubs salt on the roast, sprinkles it with a healthy dose of thyme, rosemary, and pepper, and places it in the oven. In another hour, this house will smell so good that the wolves will come down from the hills in hope of devouring the feast.

We clean up the kitchen as the day grows longer. I hear a thumping at the door, and in walks Father, laden with fishing gear and smelly clothes. He gives us a quick smile, says, "Good to be home," and rubs the top of my head as he passes by to clean up. "Let me go wash and be human again." I wonder what he is if he is not a human.

Or what he is...when he is not a human? I almost hear my mind whisper. I shake the thought out of my head.

It is nearly five o'clock. Sunset will be six twenty-one tonight. The smell of dinner has filled the house and we sit at the table to eat this special meal to celebrate Father's return. Mrs. Sally joins us for dinner tonight, which is not unheard of, but unusual. Jacob is digging into his roast caribou like he hasn't eaten in a week. Father slowly starts with his potatoes and carrots, "because they're no good when they're cold," as he always says. He looks at us and he says in a deep, quiet voice, "There was an accident on the boat last night." He pauses dramatically. He has our complete attention.

He slowly cut up his meat and looks at us with serious eyes. "There was a full moon, or close to it. Just about three in the morning we found a large looming shape on our radar, just below our boat. The captain knew it had to be a school of cod. He figured there was enough light with the moon that we could lower the nets and get one last haul. Don't be a fool, I told him, there are things that lurk in these dark waters that we have no business messing with. The other men scoffed at my words. Skane was in the cabin keeping the boat steady, while Stephen Cloud and George Ankron laid the nets. I had no choice but to help out. We trawled the waters, dragging the nets in the area we knew the cod were running, and after an hour we could feel the heavy load bogging us down. Ankron started working the winch and pulling the lines in. Cloud and I made sure the nets came up properly. We could see what looked to be a net filled with cod illuminated by the moonlight and the spotlights on the boat. As the net came up even with the gunwale, the fish started wiggling and jumping in the oddest way. Cloud got right in there to see what was going on. Something wasn't right. That was about the time we figured out that there were not as many cod filling that net as we had thought. The net was filled with the massive body of a single creature from the depths. An arm snaked out of that net, tossing full grown cod aside like they were nothing. It wrapped around Stephen Cloud's waist and began pulling him into the net. Cloud was yelling something about his leg. The boom was bouncing about with the weight of the catch and the commotion raised by the creature. The boat was becoming unstable. I could hear Albert Skanes yell out 'It's a giant squid. Stand clear!'

Only it wasn't a squid. I could see it clearly. It was the *kraken*: a beast filled with hate and anger. It has the strength of a whale, and the wrath of a protective she-bear. The *kraken* can eat small ships and all its inhabitants; this is how you know it's not the smaller, more passive giant squid, who is content with eating fish. 'Cut her loose, I tell you!' I yelled out, 'It'll destroy the boat, and us with it.' But Ankron kept pulling it up, yelling something about it only being a squid and we didn't want to lose all those cod in the net with it. Cloud was cursing the arm that had entangled him. 'My God,' I yelled, 'it's a *kraken*! I swear, as soon as that net lands on the

deck, we'll all be dead.' I had to move fast. I jumped on Ankron and yanked his hands from the winch. I heard the winch handle whirring like a cyclone as the net and all its contents fell back into the sea to empty out. And gone forever were the *kraken*, the cod, and Cloud. The devil creature, still wrapped tightly around Cloud, had pulled him down with it. After all that commotion, we were suddenly engulfed in the heavy silence of the night. The moon looked down on us in all its innocence. We three who were left aboard the boat were lost. Ankron looked at me with violence in his eyes. Skane said a quiet prayer, looked at Ankron, and said, 'If John Kidd saw a *kraken*, then so be it. There are mysteries in these dark seas that no man could know; and John has seen far more of this darkness than any man should.'"

The three of us stare at Father in disbelief. Cold shivers run through me as the truth of the story from Mr. Dave runs through my mind.

"'Tis truth," my father says. "The stories will spread through the village and, no doubt, people will choose the truth that suits them best. But I am telling you, if I had not let the net drop, the search crews would be scouting the water for all four of us and the boat in the coming days, and they would find naught, save for a plastic bottle or two."

Father looks at Mrs. Sally and says, "I'm sorry to bring the news of the passing of Stephen Cloud. He was a good man. He was from down in Cartwright. Did you know him?"

Mrs. Sally shakes her head no.

Father tells Mrs. Sally that this might be the best caribou he has ever tasted. He looks at us and says, "Boys, you help Mrs. Sally clean up so she can get home. It's getting late. Sun sets at six twenty-one."

12

Lone Wolf

October 20

I dreamed I was a beast, a wolf or a wild dog, walking through the village, nose to the air, filling my senses and my brain with sensations I could not imagine in a waking life. Colors were vivid and terrifying. Apprehension coursed through me. Rage filled my head. I felt I might explode at any moment. The wind was blowing through me to remind me that I was little more than a spirit.

Then I heard the song. A beautiful melody, floating down the street. It was a woman's voice singing out a soulful song of sadness. I followed the song up the road, past all the houses and to the end of the village. I could see the string of music floating down from the bare hill beyond town, carrying with it the scent of pines, bare earth, and the ever-present sea air. And another, more unfamiliar scent – an acrid animal smell that was unfamiliar, yet I knew instinctively what it was. The scent of a woman. I had never known that one could smell a woman – not in this way. I continued up the hill and into a small copse of pines, where I saw her. She sat still, on the pine needle-covered rock floor. She stared at me, uncaring, unafraid. Edging cautiously closer to her, I saw the blood. It was covering her. There was blood running from her arms, and a blood stain in the crotch of her pants. The stream of blood ran down the rocks, carrying with it the woman's life.

That is all I can remember. Even those vivid details are quickly dissolving from my memory. When I awoke, I found that I had ejaculated in my pajamas. I had been told about how boys started having wet dreams. This was my first one. I am troubled by it as it is connected to a gruesome dream. It is still dark outside. So, I try to go back to sleep, feeling uneasy and sticky.

***

Morning comes with the sun on the far east side of my window view, and a small piece of the moon straight up. I wash, change my clothes, and go down to breakfast. I feel like everyone knows that I had a wet dream last night, but no one says a thing. In fact, it seems to be quite an unremarkable day. Father goes off to his boat, Mrs. Sally goes on with breakfast cleanup, and Jacob is getting his schoolbooks together. And soon, I find I too am carrying on as if it were any other day, which it is. I start on my math assignment while I eat my pancakes. Mrs. Sally fusses over the syrup I am dripping on my school paper. Jacob is running up and down the stairs, pretending to be a mountain climber racer. I tell him there is no such thing. He tells me I am just mad because I can't go as fast as him.

Yep, just another day.

Mrs. Sally spends most of the morning on the phone. She is talking very seriously, saying a lot of grown-up things that I'm not really interested in. Jacob and I finish our lessons just around lunchtime. Today, Father comes home for lunch. I guess there wasn't much to do on the boats. He said the fishing wasn't good and that it would be a waste of time. Besides, there was a storm approaching in the afternoon, which will likely kill the remainder of the day for any outside work. I know father does not like missing a day of work, so it must truly be a bad day.

As we sit down to lunch, Mrs. Sally fidgets about and acts as if something is weighing on her mind. Finally, she looks at Father and says, "Something horrible happened today. My neighbor, Len, told me his wife, Jan, went out late last night and did not return. That is not like something she would ever do. So, this morning, he spent a lot of time calling up her friends and family to see if they had seen her. Nothing. He gathered some of the men together and they went searching the village. After coming up empty, they got together some of the dogs and tried to find a scent. Well, the dogs found a scent, but they were acting all funny and scared, like they didn't want to follow the trail." At this point, Mrs. Sally pauses, sits down at the table, and gathers her thoughts. "Well, they found Jan up in the woods. It was carnage. The poor woman had slit her wrists, and I guess the blood attracted wolves. Or maybe only one wolf, because the body was ripped open at the abdomen and only the organs were eaten."

Father says, "Aye, likely a lone wolf, otherwise there'd

be little left intact. Why do you reckon she killed herself?"

"Well, she recently lost a son. He died in a snowmobile accident late last winter. He had been drinking pretty heavily. Only twenty. A tragedy. I don't suppose she ever got over it." Mrs. Sally thinks for a moment, "You know, there is a waning quarter moon in the sky. A time for release. A time for letting go. A time to fly. Perhaps that is what happened. She needed release."

Shreds of the dream come back to me, but I cannot make sense of them. A few images and short snippets. I ask to be excused. As soon as I get up, my head starts swimming. My vision is graying out. I make it to the sofa, and plop quickly into its soft embrace. The full dream pours back into me.

13

Drowning

October 24

"Robert Kidd. We meet again." Billy Cloud sits on a snowmobile in the middle of the road. His now familiar parka loosely draped over him, as if the frigid temperatures meant nothing to him, and his arctic cat wool cap glued to his head. I feel fear creeping through me. An ominous cloud sliding across the sunny sky. I would take time to appreciate the accidental pun if I weren't so scared. "Hey, you give a proper respectful greeting to an adult when he speaks to you." The man waits for me to speak.

My voice shakes as I reply, "Hello, sir." I look down at the ground. I should not be talking to him.

My father sent me to take a package to the post office this morning. He told me there was a small rock from our property in the box, and there was a letter. It was addressed to his brother, my Uncle William. The rock is significant, he told me, because it meant we were returning to Scotland. When Father came to Canada for the first time, he brought with him a small rock from the shore of Kirkwall. That rock sits on the windowsill above our kitchen sink. It is rare that Father lets me go out on my own, but he said it was with honor that I help deliver this package to our future home. He gave me thirty dollars and said that he thought that should cover the postage. He also told me not to talk to anyone and no one should know what was in the package, not even the postal woman.

And so, here I stand, holding a package bound for Scotland, in the middle of the road, on an overcast morning that hovers well below zero Celsius, confronted by a man who frightens me. I glance around and see that there are few others outside this morning. The man wants something, but I am not sure what. His right hand wavers in the air in front of him, maybe not a maestro, as I had thought before, but a man controlling the strings of a marionette. And I am the puppet.

"Well Robert, young Scotsman, I've something to show you. It is down here," he points to the docks, "down by your father's boat." The man gets off his snowmobile, leaving it in the road, and he starts down the short drive to the fishing boats. He turns and looks at me as if to say,

Of course you will follow me down here. We walk down the pier where Father's boat is tied down. As we pass the *Bonnie Marie*, the man simply says, "A fine boat, she is." I walk behind the man and stare at his old well-worn brown jacket with fur around the hood that lay back off his head of bushy black hair. I take in his short stance and slightly fat body shape. He points out at the sea and says, "Your father is a fisherman and a skilled captain. I prefer to be in the forests hunting the caribou. But I envy your father's ability to go out and be free on the water. In a man's own boat, out on the sea, he is the ruler of his own world. He can catch what he wants, eat what he wants, fuck what he wants, and he can kill who he wants, too."

He stares through me with no real focus in his eyes, then lunges out and grabs my coat. He pulls me toward him, knocking my package onto the pier and into the sea, breathing his alcohol-laced breath into my face. "If John Kidd wants to throw his wife into the sea, that's his business. But when he kills my cousin and good friend, Stephen Cloud, when he throws him into the sea and leaves him behind to be eaten by the fish, he needs to be held responsible. He needs to atone for his murderous ways. Maybe when he finds his own Scottish-fuck son drowned in the sea, then he will know what retribution is."

All the while he is saying this, he is shaking me with an inescapable grip. I try to push off his chest. One of his hands releases me and pulls back, only to come back around to hit me hard in the head. I see a flash of light and feel my body jerk sideways. I am falling. I fall farther than I should fall. I expect to hit the dock, but instead, plunge down into the water. Dazed by the punch, I am unable to swim. The sea is ice cold as it overtakes my winter attire and devours me. The current rips me out from the pier and sucks me deeper down and out. I flail my arms. Movement is difficult in my thick waterlogged clothes, and I feel myself sinking. My eyes open wide as I search for the surface. The grayness of the sky seems forever away as it wavers in the undulating surface of the water. My chest heaves in an attempt to get more oxygen. My restricting clothes mock my starving lungs. The grayness of the sky above turns darker. I give in to my need to breathe and take in a deep breath of seawater.

All sensations within me change profoundly. No longer am I aware of the iciness of the sea. My clothing slides off my body. I breathe in, but it is not as I am accustomed to. The saltiness of the water is life-giving. My body constricts and relaxes in an odd way. My vision is all-encompassing, and all colors change to shades of blue-gray. I look up and I see the moon, a black hole in the sky, sucking all the colors from the world. It's a new moon, it should be invisible. How could I possibly detect it?

I sense my body changing.

I am becoming my worst nightmare.

Has this happened before? It feels both strange and familiar at the same time. My spirit is filling with rage. I come to the surface and let out a thunderous sound. My arms spasm and reach out for something, anything, to spill my wrath upon. The current and tide of the new moon have delivered me far from shore. I am barely aware of my life as Robert. All thoughts quickly drain from my brain, as a new sensation enters to fill the spot. I am a raw beast.

And now, my rage drifts away as I sink deeper into the depths of the sea. Weightless in my world. The light fades, but I am still able to make out the slightest distinctions of grays. I am carried deeper yet, and I am entering a space that is home. Away from danger.

And now, I feel a constriction in my chest. Pain racks my rib cage. I feel a hard surface below me, and I am rolled onto my side as water gurgles up from my lungs.

I cough and spatter out sprays of salty liquid. A pounding on my back. I try to fight but my arms no longer move. There are hands all over me. My lungs scream out and sweet oxygen enters me. My body is shaking uncontrollably. I hear voices. My father. Other strange men. A woman. Blankets are thrown around me and I am picked up into strong, thick arms. I hear my father talking quietly in my ear and then I hear him barking out at others around us. Then nothing.

And now I am waking up on our sofa. I don't know how long I have been sleeping, but it is dark, so somewhere into the night. An over-stuffed wood stove is blaring out its heat. Blankets are wrapped tight all about me. Still, I shiver. It is dark outside. Father sits in the chair next to me. He sees me waking up and he sits me into an upright position, leaning against the arm of the couch with my legs outstretched along the cushions. I am offered hot tea and told I must drink it.

My father looks at me with tear-filled eyes. "I thought I'd lost you, son. We were lucky to find you so quickly."

I take a sip of the tea and nearly burn my lips. I look at my father, a man I barely recognize in his state. "Father," I say hesitantly, "I am a *kraken*."

"What are you talking about, lad?"

"I … I don't really know. I was in the water. I was afraid, and then I was filled with hate and anger. And I became a *kraken*."

My father looks at me with eyes that half believed my story. "Aye, son. That would explain how you survived in the icy waters for so long. Though I'm more willing to believe that it was your tough Scottish blood that saved you. Actually, it was Mr. Dave who saw you go in. Cloud ran off while Dave jumped into the *Bonnie Marie* and acted quickly to find your submerged body. You were under for nigh ten minutes before he found you, with the strong currents sucking you out to sea, and he pulled you out with our nets. The doctor said we were lucky you're such a small lad and the water was cold enough to send you into some kind of a state of hibernation. Or, maybe, like you said, you're a *kraken* at heart."

"Father, I didn't get a chance to take your package to the post office."

"And it was a good thing. It went into the water with you and floated back to the surface, allowing Mr. Dave to track where the currents might have taken your body. And now," my father continues, "I'll heat up some soup for you, get you a fresh pot of tea, and I want you to stay sleeping here on the sofa. Here's a can to piss in. I don't want you to leave this spot till sunrise. I'm going out for a short time. I've business to tend to. I'll be back in an hour. Mrs. Sally is in the kitchen if you need anything."

Father brings me soup and tea, and I am asleep before he leaves the house.

14

The Beating

October 25

"Dammit, John. You can't just go beating a man as if you mean to kill him."

"You'd do the same, Dave, if that were your kid. What kind of father would I be if I just let him walk away? The man is lucky I stopped when I did."

"He's only lucky that he *was* able to walk away from such a pummeling. If I hadn't pulled you off him, you'd be facing a lifetime in prison. What kind of father would you be then? You're turning into the monster from your own stories."

I'm still wrapped up in blankets on the sofa. The sun has just come up from its place of sleep and I can hear the popping of fresh wood in the stove. Mr. Dave and Father have been arguing in the kitchen for some time.

I hear Mr. Dave, his voice lowered now with some real concern in it, "So, how is he?"

"He'll be alright, considering he was already dead."

What? Who is he talking about?

My father goes on, "It was a wonder you found him in time. Almost as if someone placed him in your nets as you went by. The boy was filled with stories of his drowning, but I could barely listen, as my heart had turned black with murderous vengeance, as well, I was right disappointed in myself for allowing him to go out on his own." Father pauses, "You know that was Stephen Cloud's cousin. I guess I should thank you for pulling me off him. To be truthful, the man is a waste of human life. His blood spilled out thinner than water – diluted with alcohol, and his piss was pure gasoline."

"I swear to God, John, this whole godforsaken village is headed that way. The government brought us out here onto this rock and left us to rot. And if you ask me, we're doing a damn good job of it." I think of my mother and her addictions and wonder if Father will get angry with Mr. Dave. But they just murmur some soft words, and Mr. Dave grabs his coat and heads out the front door.

Father yells for Jacob as he passes the stairway, and he comes into the living room to check on me. He leads me into the kitchen for eggs and thinly sliced pieces of caribou. Jacob joins us for breakfast, and we sit in silence for a short while. Jacob looks at me solemnly and says, "They said you were dead and came back to life. What was it like? Did you see a white light?"

Father gives Jacob a look that makes him silent. I wait a moment, and I say, "I didn't die. I *changed.* If I'd died, I would be dead." I feel myself becoming irritated. "Do I look dead?" Jacob and Father are staring at me as if I said something wrong. "What? I didn't die!" Anger creeps into me. My blood runs cold as I relive the sensation of turning into the *kraken*. I notice the colors of the room are draining and everything is turning to shades of gray. I try to get up from the table and my legs fail me, as if there were no bones inside. I fall to the floor.

My eyes flutter open to see my father splashing water on my face. "Son, you were under the sea for ten minutes with your lungs full of saltwater. You're weak, as anyone would be. I want you resting today." With that, he carries me up the stairs and lays me in my bed.

"One day, Robert, we'll go to live in Kirkwall, where the worst that will happen to you will be to break a couple of ribs in a good game of Kirkwall Ba'. I've played many a game where we might have two hundred or more men in a scrum, pushing, punching, and trying our best not to be trampled. That's a lot of bodies and a lot of weight to move the ba' through the streets. I played against the Uppies, for I was a Doonie, as will you if you decide to play. Of course, you'd be playing in the boys' ba' game until you're sixteen. I'd tell you how to play, but that would be difficult, for there aren't a lot of rules. We Doonies simply had to get the ba' doon the streets and into the harbor to win the game."

Father sometimes gets lost in his walks down the road to sentimental memories. If you can call getting destroyed in the largest game of barbarism ever *sentimental*. His longing for Scotland is always evident to me.

15

Raven Girl

October 25

Here I lie, curled up in my blankets for the day to think about what has transpired. I don't want to go outside anymore. I'll stay in my room and live here forever. The night, as well as the day, holds only danger for me. I told Mrs. Sally I would not be going downstairs. Father tells her and Jacob to let me have my space, "He's been through a lot." Jacob looks at me like I'm a freak. And me, I am lost in a dream. I mostly spend the day looking out the window at the sea. The sea – the place where I died. The place where I lived. The tide goes out. The tide comes in. It never ends, in its vastness or in its movement. It is forever fluid. It changes those who enter it. It changes its colors to suit its moods. It is angry. It is calming. It is seductive. Seductive. I try that description on. I only recently learned that word. It is a grown-up word with many sides to it. Like the sea.

I don't know if I should fear the sea or if I should embrace it. Part of that sea is still in me. I can feel it in my chest when I breathe. I try to cough it up, but I think it has become a part of me forever. I lie in bed and feel like I'm floating – like I'm swimming.

I died yesterday. I died. But death was not empty. It was not a void. Nor was it a golden gate surrounded by a chorus of angels in the clouds. No: the space was filled with the *kraken*. Father said we all have a monster inside of us. I thought he meant that figura … figuratic … figuratig … figuratively, that we could all be mean people when we wanted, but what if he meant we had an actual monster living inside our bodies? What if I turn into a *kraken* in the middle of the night and eat Jacob? What if I become a Frankenstein and all the town's people come to our house with torches? My skin feels cold and rubbery.

My thoughts are interrupted when I see, flying past my window, a pair of ravens. And more come by. It is rare to see a large group, a *conspiracy* of ravens. They prefer a group of two. So close they come that, were the window open, I could reach out and grab one. They call out to the world in a voice that would not be defined as a beautiful song, but a bold statement. I have found that most of the birds along the shore have ridiculous voices. The ravens continue to call out in a frantic storm. Something is going on. I close in on the window and look around the landscape below. The birds swarm around a moving figure at the water's edge, on the boulders, just beyond monster beach. It is hard for me to make out the figure. It appears almost as if it is wearing a coat of black feathers, or as if the person is in fact a large raven.

I find myself unable to stare for too long – the sun is

shining from a spot in the sky just above the ravens, and straight into my eyes. The birds all take to the sky, make a path for the sea, and circle around again. I get a better look at the person on the rocks. A girl wearing a black coat, throwing slices of bread into the air to feed the ravens. I cannot make out her face, but her hair is long, black, and flowing in the breeze. The ravens, a conspiracy of fifteen or twenty, again pass by my window and return to the girl, who is now retreating down the rocky beach. This time, the birds flap their wings all about the girl, creating the illusion of a single black undulating mass. Surely she must be suffocating in the onslaught of feathers. After half a minute, the ravens dissipate into the air like smoke in the wind. As the cloud of ravens clears, they leave no trace of the girl.

I continue to stare out of the window at a now empty scene that contains nothing more than rocks, sky, and water. I wonder if what I saw really played out, or if it was a figment of my imagination, much like the burnt cookie episode. Below me, I watch Jacob exit the back door and walk out into the scrubby backyard. He is wrapped in three or four coats and a wool cap. A seagull lands on a large rock by the water, not far from him. He reaches down, grabs a small rock that fits his palm, and throws it at the gull. The rock flies wide of its target, scaring off the bird who releases a shrill laugh at its eight-year-old attacker. Jacob looks around and walks quickly off to the side yard, vanishing from my line of sight. He returns and starts making little rock towers which he then uses as target practice for his slingshot. I haven't seen that slingshot in quite a while. He got it last year, but never used it much. He is a terrible shot.

He stoops down and gets a big pocketful of small,

rounded stones. After a few completely errant shots, Jacob turns to shooting the larger targets like tide pools and boulders. He steps within three meters of one rounded boulder and hits it squarely with his weapon. Unfortunately, the rock ricochets the small projectile back, hitting Jacob on the forehead. He calls out once, in pain or frustration, I cannot tell which, and then he does what appears to be a little monkey dance. I can't help but laugh at his antics. At this point, Jacob turns, looks up at our window, sees me looking out, and a strange grimace comes across his face. He reaches into his pocket for another stone, loads up his slingshot, and lets loose a shot directly at the window. The rock hits the wooden frame that separates the top half of the window from the bottom.

I cannot believe he just did that. What has gotten into him? I don't know if he was trying hit me, break the window, or if he was just playing around. He looks mad. He sticks his slingshot into his coat pocket and stomps off to the side yard out of view again. He is sneaking down the street. One day he will get caught, but he can't resist hanging out with his new friends. I haven't said anything to him, or anyone. For some reason he scares me when he is with those other boys and when he returns home, acting weird and looking at me in a way that I cannot explain. Like I am an animal in a cage. Like the kids in Nain looked at me. That is what I am – an animal stuck in a cage. But I don't mind it; I like staying here at home. Jacob, on the other hand, is not complacent with his captivity. I fear that one day he will not come back from his adventures with his friends.

I pace around my room, needing to put my mind somewhere else. I glance down at Jacob's desk and notice a strange object mixed in with a pile of five plastic dinosaurs. I pick it up – a large tooth. A bear tooth? I put it down quickly, feeling guilty for touching his stuff and wondering where he got it from. Was that the secret object that strange man gave him that day we went on the boat with Father to get our passports done? I return to the window. Soon, hunger drives me out of my room and downstairs into the kitchen, where Mrs. Sally sits drinking coffee and reading a book. When she sees me, she gets up and gives me a warm hug. "I thought you'd be coming down here soon. I have a sandwich and some soup for you. You shouldn't let your belly go empty." I sit down to the sandwich, peanut butter and jelly, while she reheats the soup. "Now," she says, "what's on your mind?"

"Well, I keep seeing," I pause, thinking how best to phrase this, "seeing or dreaming of people and animals. Like, they are turning into animals, or the animals are reading the person's thoughts." My mind runs through images of the dog in Nain, the raven girl, the *kraken*.

Mrs. Sally looks at me for a short while before answering. "You get that from your mother. She had a way with animals. She thought of them as spirit people, and she believed in all the Innu myths and stories handed down through the generations. Most people now think they are just stories. But there are some, like your mother, who *felt* the power of them. Oh, Robert, don't be worried or frightened of this. It is a gift you have been given."

The soup is heated through, and Mrs. Sally sets the warm broth in front of me. I feel it warming me from the inside. New life.

16

A New Dog

November 1

Today, Father invites me to the boat to help clean it up and work on the engine. He is always working on the engine. He says that a boat is like a woman: treat her with love and respect, and she will stay true. When we work on the engine, it actually means *he* works on the engine while I hand him tools or hold a light. I am not good with mechanical stuff. Maybe I just haven't got the confidence. Even the tools confuse me. I don't know a ratchet wrench from a monkey wrench. I get nervous when Father asks for something because I am quite sure I will hand him the wrong tool and he will think less of me. He tells me that I may not be a mechanic meant for working on engines, but I am smart enough that one day I will attend college, and then I can design new, better engines. I smile inside and hand him an awl when he asks for a Philips. Today he has me washing down every surface of the *Bonnie Marie* with bleach water to avoid any algae growth or any bacteria that contaminate the day's catch. As I look overboard into the water, I feel a sudden flush of anger and a desire to slide into the shallow waves and disappear. I don't understand this feeling and I fight it off.

After a couple of hours of me cleaning and scrubbing and him banging and cursing, we take a snack break. Father gets out some canned sardines, a large loaf of bread, some cheese, apples, and a two-liter bottle of Coke. We sit back on a couple of large fish coolers and allow the sun to warm our faces. I feel pretty special out here with Father. Just the two of us. Jacob is at home getting extra lessons from Mrs. Sally to keep him caught up to grade level. Sometimes other fishermen pass by and yell out, "Hey John, I see you got young Robert out here learning the trade." Or they might not know my name and they say, "I see you got your kid out here cleaning up your *Bonnie Marie*." I am both proud and embarrassed when they call me out. Then the conversation moves on to grown-up talk. I wonder how grown-ups learn to talk like that – boring conversations about matters that they think are important. When I grow up, Jacob and I will still talk about the really fun things, like the tide pools, dinosaurs, and the best hiding spots in the house.

A troubling thought goes through me. What if Jacob grows up and moves away? He likes to sneak out and go down the street for new adventures with the other kids. What if he one day wants to go live in Ottawa, or Quebec, or St. John's?

As if reading my mind, Father takes a long, hard look at me. He watches as I finish the last of my sardines, and says, "You haven't really got any friends. I noticed that you and Jacob don't play together like you used to. Also, there are some very dangerous people in this village. I am not saying they are bad people, but there is something about this place that brings a heavy darkness down on us all, which leads to sickness in the minds of many people."

I stare at Father, not really understanding where he is heading. I am feeling a little lost, like maybe I am missing something. And just at this moment, as if orchestrated by my father, Mr. Dave comes walking down the pier towards the boat. At his side walks a large sled dog. Mr. Dave gives us a wave and comes up alongside the boat.

"Here she is. Like I told you, she's a handful. Lois was a little afraid of this dog and couldn't control her. She is useless as a proper sled dog because she doesn't play well with others. She'll make a good watch dog because she tolerates very few people. I'm surprised she let me lead her here without so much as a snarl, but she seems to like me somehow. She knows me pretty well." Mr. Dave stood there, not sure if he should bring the dog on board or not. "Maybe this isn't a good idea," he says, having second thoughts about the dog's disposition.

Father looks at me, "What do you think, Robert? Every boy needs a best friend, and there is no better friend than a loyal dog."

I look at the dog. She is mostly white and has a few random splotches of black on her with no symmetry or planned design. Her fur is thick and not too short. Her eyes are as blue as the sky. We stare at each other, the dog and I, and she tucks her tail down between her legs, lowers her head, and lets out a soft whine. I expected her to take an aggressive stance and growl at me, but she seems afraid, even. Dave leads the hesitant dog onto the boat. I stay seated where I am and wait for the dog to come to me. The dog creeps forward with head down and eyes looking up. I hold my hand out for her to smell me. I look up at Father, who is looking over at Mr. Dave. He gives Mr. Dave a small nod.

Mr. Dave hands me the leash and says, "Old Lois will be happy to see someone give this dog what she needs. She calls her Fleur." The dog lies down next to me, giving me a sideways look of suspicion.

My father says, "Thanks Dave. Bright and early tomorrow morning, then."

As Mr. Dave turns and walks away, Father says to me, "You take care of that dog, and she will be yours for a long time. She's not a pup anymore, but she's not old either. Now you keep her in the cabin with you while you finish up, then we'll take her back to her new home. Your brother should be about sick of Mrs. Sally by now. That boy does hate his studies."

I finish up my cleaning while Fleur curls up in the corner, leaving as much distance as possible between us. People say that animals are more afraid of us than we are of them, but I do not believe this. I am nervous and untrusting of this dog. I have very little experience with dogs. Father says my unfamiliar Scottish blood makes dogs see me differently. So now, I keep one eye on the dog, and she keeps one eye on me. And we spend the next hour sizing each other up.

Father grabs his tool bag and cooler and, hesitantly, I grab the dog's leash. We walk down the road toward home. Fleur, my French-Canadian dog, walks next to me, but she keeps a meter away, as far as the leash allows. I get some odd looks from people on the street because dogs are either chained up in the yard or left to wander on their own. It is not often that someone leads a dog around on a leash. As we arrive home, I stop at the door. I am not sure if the dog is supposed to stay outside or come into the house. I look at Father for guidance, and he motions to bring the dog in with me. I enter the house and the dog looks around, uncertain. I take off the leash and she paces the living room and kitchen, sniffing around for a while before finally settling down in the far corner behind the sofa. Father had already bought a large bag of dog food and stashed it in the cabinet under the kitchen sink.

"Son, you had better make a food and water station for the dog, so she knows this is her new home. Grab a couple of large bowls and set them on a folded towel on the floor."

I spend the next half hour sitting near or next to the dog, talking to her, scratching her neck, running my hands through her thick fur, and watching as her tail lazily thumps on the floor. Jacob comes in from outside and looks at the dog, tilts his head and asks why there is a dog in the house.

I look at Jacob, "Father asked Mr. Dave to get me a dog."

"Is that because that man killed you?"

I flash him a frustrated glance and say, "That man didn't kill me. He pushed me into the water. And I didn't die. You might have noticed that I am right in front of you, alive."

Jacob watches me as I sit on the floor petting Fleur, and he takes a step toward us to get a closer look at the dog. Fleur immediately sits up and growls softly at him. Her hair bristles up on the back of her neck and her gaze focuses on Jacob. With that, Jacob quickly backs up and slips out the back door again. The dog whines gently and returns to resting her head down onto her front paw.

Father has been sitting in his chair reading the latest *National Geographic*, with a lead article about the collapsing fishing industries, half watching me and Jacob interact. After Jacob leaves out the back door, Father says, "It looks to me like that dog already knows who she belongs to." I look down smiling. "When you take her out make sure she has her leash on. At least for now, until she learns that this is her home. I would hate to have to go retrieve her from Lois's place."

17

The Body

November 8

A winter storm is coming through. Jacob and I are hiding in our room listening to the screaming north Atlantic winds as they fly down from the Davis Straits. Fleur is tucked under the bed, innocently unaware of the oncoming blizzard and of the floor rule. I wonder why it doesn't apply to her. What makes dogs immune from the *never-touch-the-floor-at-night* rule?

Those winds are so strong you can smell the warming dinners from the kitchens of the Greenlandic Inuits a thousand miles away. That is what Father says. Pellets of frozen sleet hit the windows like sand. As the temperatures slide down the scale, the sleet gives in to snowflakes oblivious to the existence of gravity as they shoot around in all directions. It is black beyond the glow of our house lights. We can hear the angry waves of the inlet as they smash with uncharacteristic violence against the boulders of our backyard.

There is a thrill of excitement in the air for Jacob and me. But not all the excitement is good. After a couple of hours of the monstrous howling of the wind, I hear frightening voices filled with pain and sorrow riding along on the ripping forces of this nor'easter. It is all the souls lost at sea crying out their final thoughts before dying. That is something our father once mentioned when telling Jacob and I his terrifying stories of the sea. I think of my mother. Is her voice among this chorus of spirits? No, these voices are not human. I cannot shut the sounds out of my head. Fleur lets out a long mournful howl in answer to the winds. Goosebumps run over my body. The house shakes, the windows rattle, and, impossibly, Jacob sleeps. I hide beneath the blankets with my pillow over my ears. There *are* monsters. I count backwards in my head to take my mind somewhere else. One hundred, ninety-nine, ninety-eight, ninety-seven …

***

I open my eyes to the slanted sunlight sliding into our room. The room is freezing. It feels as if the window had been left open. I see something odd on my bed. I reach for the hand-sized object and immediately recoil from its slimy feel. I shriek in surprise. There, in the middle of our bed, lies the body of a squid. Jacob wakes up from my scream and sits up wide awake, like he does.

"You're bleeding," he says, pointing at the bed sheets just above the blankets' top edge.

"What?" I look down to see blood on the sheets, on my pillow, on the blanket, and on my left arm and hand. I jump out of bed and watch as a shard of glass, the size of my palm, flies off the blanket I just threw back. I look at my hand and notice a long, deep gash in the fleshy part below my little finger.

Just as I am starting to freak out about my bloody hand, Jacob notices the squid on the bed and simply says, "Why is there a squid on the bed?" This is followed by, "Why is the window broken?" And with more excitement than for his other discoveries, "It snowed! The yard is all white!"

I look at the window and seem to have a vague recollection of a crashing sound, followed by raucous laughter and cursing that had entered my early morning dreams. Maybe not a dream. I shiver at the thought of Billy Cloud throwing squids at my window from below. I remove the squid from the bed and we run downstairs to the breakfast table to find Father sitting with a cup of coffee in his hand and a pot of hot oatmeal on the stove top. I smell the fire in the wood-burning stove as it rids the house of last night's winter storm. "I'll tell you young Robert, there was such a rage last night, I had to keep the fire burning full on to keep us from freezing on the inside. I know it's your job and your honor to wield your lighter to stave off the winter, but I felt it could not wait."

I sit at the table and tell Father of the squid and the broken window. He looks at my hand, "We'd best wrap that gash up so you don't lose *all* your blood."

"Why would someone throw a squid through our window?" I ask with a shaky voice, picturing a drunken Billy Cloud in our backyard. "And how can a squid smash a window, for that matter?" Father gives me a look of confusion and concern as he bandages my wound.

We go up the stairs and into my room to look over the damage. My father runs his finger along the edge of the broken windowpane, making me cringe at the thought that he would surely cut his skin open. He peers out the window and then turns to the squid that is now set on a piece of paper on my desk. He picks up the squid, turns it around in his hands, and looks closely as if examining it for something in particular. "I'm not sure that any person threw it through the window. Who would have been out in that storm last night but a fool? Not that there isn't a shortage of fools around this village; all the same, I believe 'twas the sea that tossed this squid to you. If not the sea itself, then something that may reside in the sea."

Father looks at me, as if the squid were meant for me. As if maybe it was my fault. And then he says, "Go get some duct tape and the roll of plastic from the storage shed. We'll see if we can get this sealed up until I get a chance to replace that window."

I put on my shoes and coat and open the back door. Fleur follows me out. I am immediately blinded by the brightness of the day. Brilliant white snow covers everything where the wind hasn't taken its turn to uncover it. The frigid air freezes the inside of my nose, and a trail of steam pours from my mouth. There was only an inch of snow on the ground, but I knew there would be more snow farther inland, where the ocean wind could not carry it away as soon as it landed. There is a ten-meter swath of bare rock that the tide waters had cleared before retreating. I can see a fair amount of driftwood and plastic that was washed in by the storm. After helping Father, I plan on going out to see if there are any other squids or treasures that were brought in.

I open the small storage shed filled with building utensils, tools, fishing supplies, and boat engine parts.

When I was younger, I used to come in and play with the old wooden captain's wheel that will forever hang low on the side wall. There is a long wooden box, polished and finely made, with a lid and a latch that holds all of Father's nautical maps and an old brass sextant with a working telescope on it. The box has an engraving on the lid: a ship on a tumultuous ocean, frightening clouds up above, reaching their wispy arms down to encircle the ship. This box used to be kept in the house, almost as artwork, but Father said Mother never really liked it, so he moved it out here. Fleur sniffs around and gets herself acquainted with this new, unfamiliar shed, but seems comforted by the scents of mustiness about the junk. I grab the roll of clear, translucent plastic and go back to the house with brittle fingers and a face that feels as if it had been slapped by the winter gods of the north.

I walk into the living room from the back door to find Jacob curled up on the couch, covered in blankets, while Father is sticking another small log into the stove. Father looks at me, "Robert, see what you can do with the window. As soon as Mrs. Sally gets in, I'm going to see what kind of damage the *Bonnie Marie* might have suffered from the storm."

Armed with duct tape, scissors, and a roll of plastic, I look at the window with its jagged hole the shape of an angry mouth, surrounded by shards of glass that hang like feral teeth, inviting me to stick my hand closer so it could finish the slicing it had started in my bed. I begin to shiver from the suggestion of teeth, as much as from the arctic air coming through the window. I roughly measure a piece of plastic to cover the entire window and use a couple of layers of duct tape to let it adhere tightly over the hole. As I finish, the plastic billows inward from the slight breeze that attempts to come in. I open the adjacent window, lean out into the cold morning air, and do my best to reach over and tape a square of plastic to the outside of the window frame. I shut the window and stand back admiring my work. It seems to effectively stop the wind from entering the room, and it should hold until Father gets a new pane of glass.

From downstairs, I hear Mrs. Sally arriving and Father leaving. I go down to warm up on the couch next to Jacob. Mrs. Sally is busy starting a fresh pot of coffee. She looks into the living room and says, "Boys, I will start your lessons in about one hour. Do what you need to do while I clean up around here."

I turn to Jacob, "Want to go out and see what washed up on the shore last night?"

From the kitchen, "If you boys are going out, be sure to dress warmly; it's wicked cold out there." Mrs. Sally spent a couple of summers, years ago, in downeast Maine, working summer camps, where she picked up the habit of saying "wicked this" and "wicked that." I like it. I keep getting the ring of Ray Bradbury's *Something Wicked This Way Comes* in my head when she says it.

We bundle up in our winter coats, scarves, hats, and gloves and run out into the snow. I keep Fleur on a short leash. She still does not trust Jacob, her normally soft top lip quivering in threat every time he's around, so I need to keep her away from him. He seems hurt by her diffidence, but I trust they'll get to know each other eventually.

We try to make snowballs, but it's too powdery. Below the high tide line, I sift through the debris of potential treasures. Lots of seaweed with those little air bladders in their leaves. Pieces of shells and broken crab carapaces litter the ground. I find one half-rotten seagull with a few feathers holding on to help it float. Yellow and green bits of fishing nets weave through the pile of rocks in the tide pool area. Jacob finds three jellyfish lying in the sun – dollops of shiny clear rubber. Empty quarts of oil lie quietly longing for the days of their youth when they sat proudly on the shelves of garages. Tired plastic bags paint the rocks with wrinkled coats of whites and yellows.

And there are squids. The frozen bodies of squids on the upper regions of the tidal zone and, strangely, beyond the tide's reach and into our yard, half buried in snow. There are about a dozen squid bodies tangled on themselves. I have read that these smaller squids travel in schools. The storm must have thrown an entire classroom onto the shore. Most of them are slowly being devoured by the crabs that are brave enough to venture out from their comparatively warm watery homes. My father's words spin around my head – *I believe 'twas the sea that tossed this squid to you. If not the sea itself, then something that may reside in the sea.* Why me? Why would the sea throw a squid at *me*? Is the *kraken* calling me back? That's ridiculous. The ocean can't throw a fish to a second story window. *Or something that may reside in the sea.* I continue walking among the small rocks and I come across something black on the ground. At first, I think it is a bird, then as I get closer, I realize it is a wool cap. I pick it up, and on the front, and wrapped around the side, it reads "Arctic Cat" in white letters. For a moment, I am confused about where it came from, and it strikes me, Billy Cloud. He must have been here during the storm last night, or early this morning. He must have thrown the squid through the window. I look around, frightened that he might be right near. Watching us.

Jacob yells out, "Hey Robert, let's go look at monster beach." He crouches down low and crab-like to avoid slipping on the slick rocks.

A chill comes over me. There ld be more squid. Or even a giant squid, waiting f us. Or something worse. A monster called Billy Cl . I call Fleur over to my side. She seems to feel my t sion and stands in an alert pose. "We should go bac n," I tell him. But Jacob has already gone. Reluctan I follow him over the boulders.

Nothing. Nothing but more tras and seaweed. Jacob kicks around at some lobster buoys the water line, slips on the ice-covered rocks, and his b t fills with water.

"Augh, that's cold. I'm going n before my foot freezes." And Jacob disappears ove the rocks and into the house.

I stick around and stand on the pebble beach a little longer. Fleur sniffs the rocks and the beach litter, and looks up at me as if to ask *What are we doing out here?* I am not sure why I feel so on edge. My skin is crawling, my mouth is dry, my legs are not meant for standing. I close my eyes and breathe the cold sea breeze, deeply, fully, letting the briny air into every cell of my body. I hear no sounds save the gentle lapping of the waves. I count down from one hundred slowly, with each breath.

Just as I feel at ease, I hear my name from behind me.

"Robert," a low guttural voice. Almost an accidental sound. "Robert." I slowly turn. "Robert." There is nobody behind me, just a lone raven hopping here and there. My eyes run towards the boulders, the nearby trees, half expecting Billy Cloud to emerge in his half-open parka, one arm holding his bag of gasoline and his other hand waving back and forth with a squid dangling from a string or maybe a slingshot, but I see nobody.

And yet I hear the same low voice. This time it is more like a groan.

I notice the raven looking directly at me, hopping up in the air and back down slowly, gracefully, almost as if it were dancing on the moon. It lands on a rock, stoops its back, holds its head down, and lets out a raucous screech. Fleur growls deep in her chest. The raven continues to hop around the rocks until it finally lands down on the ground and pecks into a large pile of seaweed. It looks at me, calls some more, and flies off to a nearby roost.

I walk hesitantly over to the pile of seaweed and I see the mangled remains of a half-eaten animal. Fleur whines and will not approach it. She turns in circles, upset at something. I grab a stick and move the seaweed aside. My heart freezes. It is the blueish, bloated remains of a woman. Nearly unrecognizable as a human.

I stare, unable to look away. She is naked except for a glimmering band of silver on her wrist. The raven cackles a laughing sound. There are crabs crawling out from the cavity of her decomposing torso. The remains of one masticated breast stares at me mockingly with one eye. The arms and legs are twisted at unnatural angles. A mat of black hair clings to the scalp of an eyeless face. Her mouth is stuck in a terrible grin, the lips gone, and what is left of the gums is black.

A gull flies overhead, screaming; in my mind it sounds like a wretched laugh coming from the woman's mouth. Like rats scuttling out of a sinking ship, my breakfast rushes out of my stomach. I feel drained of blood and as white as the corpse before me. Fleur stays close by my side, looking worried for me. We run shakily back over the rocks, across the yard, and into the house.

"Mrs. Sally!" My voice sounds weak as my stomach ripples with spasms. "Mrs. Sally!" My eyes are watering as I walk into the kitchen. Mrs. Sally sees me. I must look wretched, because she rushes to me and sets me into a chair and holds me close.

"What is it, Robert?"

I cry and shake uncontrollably.

"Oh, Robert," she says, tightening her grip on me. She looks at me without understanding.

"There's a body," I force out the words, "on the beach." That is all I trust myself to say.

Mrs. Sally stares at me for a long time. Her eyebrows raise up in the middle. "Are you sure?"

I nod my head.

Another silence. "Take me to see it."

Now it is my turn to stare in silence. Finally, I get up and walk toward the back door. Mrs. Sally grabs her coat and follows me. I take her to the side yard and over the rocks, which give her a difficult time with their ice covering. We slowly walk to the pile of seaweed and the body, which is guarded now by a pair of ravens and a lone seagull. They fly off at our approach, cawing and screaming, annoyed that we are interrupting their dinner. I stand back and point. I cannot bear to walk closer and see that image again. Mrs. Sally walks cautiously up to the corpse. She studies it for a long time. She tilts her head slightly, turns to look at me, and she walks back to me with a worried look.

"Robert, you are sure you saw a dead person there?"

"Yes. It was a woman. She was naked and half eaten by crabs and fish and, I guess, birds."

"Robert, this is no woman. It is a harbor seal, decomposed and picked at. It must have been at sea for the past month, and the storm brought it in. Come see for yourself."

I don't move. "But what about the bracelet?"

"What bracelet?"

"She was wearing one, silver and shiny. Look, it's on her wrist."

"No, there is nothing like that. It must have been the sun in your eyes."

I'm confused. Does she not know the difference between a woman and a seal? I step up beside her, preparing to once again be confronted with the corpse. I stop when I get to Mrs. Sally's side. I find myself staring at the old remains of a harbor seal. "No, it was a woman. I saw her!" I swing wildly around to look at the beach. There is nothing else but plastic trash, rocks, and a lot of driftwood. My legs are weak, and I have to sit down. Mrs. Sally doesn't believe me. She looks at me like my imagination has gotten away from me. "But there wasn't a seal. It was a lady. Someone must have moved her."

"Who could have moved her? You were only in the house for a couple of minutes before we came back out. There aren't even any footprints in the snow around here." She reaches down, grabs my hands, and she pulls me up. "Let's get back into the warm house. I have some hot cider going on the stove top."

Back in the kitchen, Jacob and I sip hot apple cider with cinnamon, and we open up our schoolbooks. Mrs. Sally is going over Jacob's math lesson while I am working on my own algebra assignment. I am having a hard time concentrating. The image of the woman keeps coming into my mind.

***

It is late afternoon and my father walks in the front door after a day of working on the boat. He removes his coat, hat, and boots and he sits on the sofa with us all in front of the fire. His face and hands are red and raw from a day in the winter air. Mrs. Sally brings him some hot tea and she has herself a seat on the armchair next to the wood stove.

Mrs. Sally says, "How was the *Bonnie Marie*, John? Any damage from the storm?"

"Aye, but not bad. Mostly the winds threw around the fishing nets and there was a bit of water in the cabin brought on by the pounding waves, I reckon. And how did you all fair on this coldest of days with high waters brought on by a full moon tide and the wrath of the Norse gods?"

Jacob chimes in, "We found more squids in the yard, and a huge jellyfish!"

"I'd be surprised if there weren't a lot more things brought up from that storm," our father says.

I look at Mrs. Sally, expecting her to bring up the harbor seal, but she is silent. She simply smiles at Father as if she is a child listening to his stories of the sea. As if … It is at this point a thought blinks into my mind. Mrs. Sally likes my father. As in, she *likes* my father. I never thought about it before. But I can see it now, the way she watches him. She is *enamorous.* Is that a word? Maybe, she is *enamored* with Father. The way she spends far more time here than she needs to. I don't know if he feels that way about her, though. I think he misses Mother too much. She won't mention that I wandered off and found a seal, because she doesn't want him to think that she did wrong by not watching us closely. It is like the time I was out front on the road and the girl told me my father was a paranoiac. I am now able to relax a little: my father won't know I was out of the yard.

Father looks at Mrs. Sally all serious-like and says, "You remember that girl who went missing about a month ago?"

Mrs. Sally looks at him, "You mean Rita and Ed's daughter?"

"That's right. She was seventeen or eighteen years old."

"Yes. There were all kind of stories of what happened to her. She was a wild one. I heard she was pregnant and ran off to Ottawa or something."

"Well," says Father, "that was one story. Her body was found today. She was washed up on the shore on the back side of the inlet. A boy out fishing this morning found her. She was mostly unrecognizable. The boy who found her thought he was looking at a seal, but then, he said, it was like he blinked the cold out of his eyes and saw that it was a young woman. Naked, and badly decomposed. Took a while to identify her, but someone recognized the silver bracelet on her wrist. Another treasure brought in by the storm."

I feel the blood drain from my face, from my extremities. I would collapse to the ground if I weren't already sitting down. Mrs. Sally looks at me with her mouth dropped open. This is impossible. It is a dream. I could not have seen a dead girl who was not there. Yet, the image remains in my mind. The mangled twisted body. The laughing mouth. The dark staring nipple. The repulsive reaction that it gave me.

And the silver bracelet. I suddenly remember the

bracelet. The naked girl dancing in the sea with her arms out and the sun glinting off the metal band with each turn. The laughing girl, still laughing. I don't say a word.

18

Jacob Caught

November 11

It is not yet three in the afternoon, and already the sun sits low on the horizon. We finished our studies by noon, but I have a paper to write. Mrs. Sally is always assigning me papers. I think it gives her something to read in the evenings. She says she gives me a lot of extra work because I have a gift. While she used to tell me that one day I will get into university in St. John's, she now says I am smarter than anyone she has ever seen. She says that I should attend McGill in Montreal. I guess next month she'll be telling me I am going to Harvard in the US. At any rate, I am forever writing papers. We are also just starting French lessons. Mrs. Sally says that to be a proper scholar in Canada, one must speak French as well as English. And so here I sit at my desk, writing about the culture of the far north of Canada, slipping in a little French vocabulary along with some Innu words for good measure.

I look out my window and catch a glimpse of Jacob over on monster beach. He is playing rock-throwing games with two other boys. They throw rocks at each other and double over laughing. One boy has blood trickling down his forehead but doesn't seem to notice. They run in circles around each other, tripping on their own feet. Now they stoop down behind a rock and are looking at something. I watch curiously. I see the biggest boy as he stands up quickly with a plastic bag in his hands and he puts it to his face and looks in. He twirls around twice and falls down. The next boy does the same. He gets up, laughing uncontrollably from the first boy's antics, and puts the bag to his face. I was mistaken: they are not looking in the bag, they are inhaling its contents. I am not always as smart as Mrs. Sally thinks, because these kinds of things take me a while to comprehend. Like my confusion over the twirling naked girl who drowned herself. How could her friends let her do that? Why didn't they try to stop her? Should I have stepped in? But never in my wildest imagination would I have suspected she was drowning herself, not with her friends all witnessing and then walking away. Could I have saved her, but failed her? The thought sinks deep and leaves a profound sadness in me and disappointment in my own naivete. How little I understand this big world.

After the second boy goes reeling off like a whirling dervish, falling closer to the water's edge, I watch Jacob get up to take his turn. I watch him put the bag of gasoline up to his face and breathe in the fumes. I can hear his brain cells screaming in their death throws. I can hardly recognize my brother when he is with these strange boys.

It is as if Jacob doesn't belong to this family. The boys leave the beach and disappear from sight.

The front door opens and shuts. It is 3:44 p.m.: Jacob is cutting it close. Sunset at four o-six. No, it is not Jacob. I hear my father's heavy footsteps ascending the stairway. At the top landing, he looks into my room, "Afternoon, Robert. Studying hard, are you? You're a good lad. Where has your brother gotten off to? It's getting late."

I keep my eyes on my writing to avoid Father's glare. "He's not in here. I guess he's outside."

Father stands in the doorway for a moment longer, "Hmph. I best go out and grab that boy." He clomps back down the stairs. Just as Father gets to the bottom of the stairway, the front door opens and in walks Jacob. I run to the top of the stairs to see what might transpire. I am sure Jacob is in trouble.

"What are you doing out in the front?" Father quietly asks, thunder grumbling low in his voice.

Jacob looks at Father and giggles. He says, "You can't keep us locked up in the house forever. I'm not afraid of you. I'm a polar bear! The man told me."

"And what man told you such a thing?"

"The man in Nain." Jacob looks as if he were about to say more, but thinks better of it.

He tries to squeeze past Father but is unsuccessful. I stop breathing.

Father puts one giant hand on Jacob's shoulder and sits down on the second step so that he is at Jacob's eye level. I am sure Father is going to explode. Jacob has never looked smaller than he does in this moment. Father says nothing. He just sits and stares into Jacob's crazed eyes.

Jacob yells out, "Let go of me! You're not even my real father! The other boys told me. They said I don't look anything like you."

Father does not flinch, but I do. Father says in a low and steady voice, "Jacob, you reek of gasoline. You've been sniffing gas again."

Again? How does Father know what is going on, even when he is not here? Father says to Jacob, "Now, I am going to count tae five. If you are not in your bed, you are going to sincerely wish that I was not your ain father. One."

Jacob tries to move his feet but falls over.

"Two."

Jacob gets up and squishes his tiny body past our father on the stairs.

"Three."

Jacob does his best to run up the stairs, bumps into me on top. Falls to the floor for the second time.

"Four."

We both jump into the room. Me to my desk chair, and Jacob into the bed. He is shaking. I never hear Father say *Five*. I don't hear anything for a while. Three fifty-nine, I need to get into bed. I grab my activity stuff, crawl in next to Jacob who is hugging the wall and who, in fact, does smell of gasoline. Just as the sun sets, I hear Father get up, go to the back door, and yell out in his most terrifying roar. I dare not look out the window. I fear I may see Father transforming into the *kraken*, which at this moment, I am fairly certain to be a possibility.

19

Goodbye Mrs. Sally

November 12

Sometimes, as I sit in the corner of the living room on the floor, petting Fleur, reading my books, I am invisible. The furniture is arranged so that there is a blind spot to all passing through the house. And if I don't move, it is not immediately apparent that I am here. This phenomenon (I have been waiting to use the word *phenomenon*, as it is my new vocabulary word, though I am not sure if I am using it correctly) of creating an illusion, has caused Jacob to go searching for me outside because he looked right over me, Mrs. Sally to jump out of her shoes because it scares her when I suddenly say something from a room she thought was empty, and it has given me a chance to overhear many conversations that might otherwise have been private. Such is the case right now. I am leaning against the wall with Fleur curled up with her head on my lap. I am absentmindedly running my fingers through her thick coat, while I look through an old *National Geographic* of which we have decades-worth sitting around the house, when a conversation pierces through my lost thoughts.

My father says, "I know the boys love having you here, but it's getting time to stop fishing for the winter. The ice will be forming soon, and my old body is tired of the cold. I need a break to hibernate. So, I really won't be needing you here all the time. I'll take over with the boys' lessons."

There is a pause, and Mrs. Sally replies, "If you're certain. I don't mind coming around here, you know. In fact, I've grown quite used to it." I can hear a strain in her voice as she continues, almost pleading, "I would be happy to stop in and fix dinners, maybe sit around for a short time and give us both some opportunity for adult conversation." As she says this, she paces within my line of sight, and I can see by her expression that she fears she has crossed a line. She gathers up her belongings and, with bowed head, makes for the door. As she is leaving, she adds, "Well, you know my number. If you need me for anything, please call." With that, she slips out the front door to be enveloped by the winter air.

I am starting to understand how grown-ups talk to each other. The way they say things by not saying things. I don't really get it, though. Why didn't Mrs. Sally just say that she wanted to see more of Father? And Father, why didn't he say that he needs to be left alone? Why didn't he say that he thought it was Mrs. Sally's responsibility to keep Jacob from going out with the other boys? Why didn't he just tell her how angry he was last night? The words that come out are just the hard shells that surround the tasty mussel meat. They are like our winter clothes that we present to each other, but the real us is the naked body inside. Father and Mrs. Sally both talk to me and Jacob like that. But Mr. Dave, he talks to me and tells me exactly what he is thinking. Maybe because he is always drunk. Father says *in vino veritas*: when people are drinking alcohol, they say things, true things, that they maybe shouldn't. That's why there are no secrets in this village, because everyone drinks too much. I will never drink, and I will never talk without saying what I most want to say.

Fleur is asleep. I go upstairs and sit on the bed in my room. Jacob is drawing pictures at his desk. I watch him for a while. As I stare at his back, something about him bothers me – a feeling that has been rising within me since the day I saw him on the street with those other kids. He has changed, and not in a good way. He no longer talks to me or Mrs. Sally. He just hangs out by himself, or he seems to disappear. Once, I saw him coming out of the shed all sneaky-like. The door was closed so no one would know he was playing in there. He sneaks off down the street as well, but he is not a clever sneaker. At times I catch him staring at me like he is judging me. Then the jeering words of Jacob's friend haunt me, *Hey Scott, why don't you go home and get your kilt?* Why would Jacob ever hang out with that mean boy?

From my spot on the bed I say, "Jacob?"

"Huh?"

"Mrs. Sally is gone for the winter." I wait for a reply, "Father said he'll be staying here during the day now because the weather is turning too cold."

Jacob says, "Will he be here all the time?"

"I guess. I mean, he'll probably go out to the store and stuff, and maybe to sit in his boat sometimes."

"Hey Robert? Do you like Mrs. Sally?"

"Well, yeah, I think she's nice. I think she likes Father. I wonder if she'll come visit over the winter. I guess she'll mostly just stay home and be lonely." I think about this for a little while. "I think *we* might get lonely. We never see anyone or go anywhere in the winter. It will just be me and you and Father. And Fleur." As soon as I said that, Jacob turns around and looks at me.

Jacob looks funny and says, "Fleur is kind of scary. What if she turns into a monster wolf and attacks us? I heard wolves do that. Do you remember when Mrs. Sally told us about the *Witiko* that runs through the tundra and eats people?"

I roll my eyes, "Fleur is not a monster *Witiko* wolf. She's a good dog." With that, Jacob turns back to his drawing, talking softly to himself. I didn't use to believe in monsters. Not really. But now, I am not so sure.

I think about Fleur. She is not a monster, and I am not a monster.

But I was a monster when I drowned. Or was that all a dream?

And what happened to Mother? Father says monsters are real.

And the giant squid on the beach – what if it wasn't a squid?

And the drunk man on the rocks? Father says there are monsters in us all.

And the dog in Nain, was he a monster, or did he think Jacob was a monster?

And the dead girl who turned into a seal?

My head is spinning.

I stand up from the bed, "I don't care if you don't like Fleur. You don't even like Mrs. Sally, I'll bet! Well, *my dog* is not a monster and *I* am not a monster. The only monster around here is you!" My voice is raised. I never raise my voice. I can't stop my anger from suddenly spewing out. I am not sure where it is coming from. I hear Fleur running up the stairs. She comes into the room and stands by my side. She looks up at me with worried eyes. I place my hand on the side of her head and pull her in against my hip. I stare at the back of Jacob's neck as he leans over his drawing pad. For the first time I can remember, I feel hate for another person. I realize I have been changing since the day I "died." Easy to anger. Very intense feelings. Jacob stands up suddenly, screeching his chair on the floor. Fleur flinches and growls from deep inside. Jacob's eyes get big and he quickly leaves the room. I think to myself, *this winter just got lonelier*.

20

The Laundromat

November 18

It does not take long after Mrs. Sally leaves that Father needs me and Jacob to take over some of her duties. Besides keeping the fire burning throughout the day – lighting the sacred lighter – I find that I am also taking over food preparation (I am becoming a pretty good chef, according to Father), bathroom cleaning, and, along with Jacob, laundry duty. Jacob has to sweep all the floors daily, and when I make dinner, he has to do the dishes. He is also supposed to pick up sticks for firewood and keep the beach clean by collecting the trash that comes in with each tide. Jacob loves his outside duties. Sometimes, still, he sneaks off down the street as soon as he cleans up the shoreline. He doesn't learn.

Laundry day is the worst. I hate walking down to the laundromat and staying there till all the clothes are done. I usually bring a book to read while the clothes spin round. Jacob hangs out with the other kids there, and sometimes goes outside in the small parking lot to play with them. I try to keep to myself and leave my hood up to hide. Sometimes people stare at me. I don't know if it is because I look different or because everyone knows I died. Everyone knows I am a monster. I am no longer afraid of these people; rather, I am angry with them. Today one girl, a couple of years older than me, walks right up to me and says, "You don't look dead. What is it like?"

"What is what like?" I repeat.

"You know, being dead."

I am not sure what to say. "I'm not dead." I get a little flustered with this.

"Yeah, but you did die, right?" The girl sits down in the hard plastic chair across from me. Why does the laundromat owner think that hard plastic chairs are good to sit in when one might spend a couple of hours there? My butt gets sore after a while. I guess they're cheap and easy to clean. I don't actually think they do clean them. Years of food crumbs, summer sweat, oil stains from dirty hands, and general marks of passing time have accumulated on the once bright orange and aqua blue chairs. I once dared Jacob to lick a chair. He was six. He licked it. Of course he did.

"Right? They say you died."

I look up from my book that I am only half reading, and I say, "No. I didn't die. I … I *changed*."

Now the girl is truly intrigued. "I had a dog who died once, only he wasn't *all the way* dead. He changed. He was meaner, a little more nervous, and he bit people a lot. We had to kill him a second time. Only that time, we killed him all the way." The girl gets up to get her clothes from the machine. She gives me a smile and says, "Just make sure you don't bite anyone." Then she adds, "I'm Beck, by the way. And I have to help my mom get the clothes out."

Beck walks off, turns back around once to give me a secret look and mouths, *No biting*.

Our clothes dryer buzzes as it comes to the end of its cycle. I grab Jacob and we fold up the clothes, put them in the two laundry baskets, and head out into the wintry morning. As we walk down the road, Jacob is feeling talkative and goes on about all the different people we saw at the laundromat. "The short round lady with eyes sunk into her face – she works in the post office, which is only open a couple of hours a day. The tallish man who couldn't stop smoking – he has the yellowest teeth, some of the kids call him *piss mouth*. The two younger kids who smelled like they never bathed – they are super poor and have no bathroom or running water of any kind in their house."

"How do you know all this stuff?" I ask him.

"I don't know. I just do."

But I know. It's because he sneaks out all the time, and plays with the other kids. "What do you know about that girl who was talking to me?" I ask, trying not to sound too obvious. She is the first girl that I have really noticed, as in *like*. Maybe it was the way she looked at me when she said *No biting*. She was tall and thin, wore her black hair long and in a braid, and her smile was wide and warm.

Jacob says, matter-of-factly, "I don't know. What girl? I didn't really notice her." Then, Jacob says, "When we get home, let's stick our heads into the middle of the clothes baskets. I bet they're still warm."

* * *

Lunch is finished and I sit on the sofa while Father sits in his recliner. We each have our reading material, and we are completely relaxed in the quiet, warm, cozy room. The fire lets out a loud *pop*, and we both look up. Father speaks out, "Must be a spirit in that wood trying to get out. That's what your mother would have said." He smiles, looks around, and says, "Where's your brother? That boy is invisible when he's not being a clown."

I don't know where he is, but I venture a guess, the obvious guess. "He is probably in our room, drawing." I hope I am right and he is not down the street. Father would be mad if he found out Jacob had snuck out.

"That boy and his imagination. I guess he might make a fine artist one day. What do you think?" I quietly smile and nod. "Well, let him be. I have a job for you. I have some letters that need to get into the mail, and while you're at it, you can ask if we have any mail waiting for us. Take your dog with you. You can leave her outside the door when you go into the post office. I'm sure she won't leave as long as you're in there." He reaches into his pocket and hands me five loonies. "That should cover it. You can keep whatever is left."

Always eager to please my father, I jump up and get my winter gear on. Fleur is at my side as soon as I grab my coat. I felt bad that I couldn't take her to the laundromat this morning. I could hear her howling eerily halfway down the street. Father says that she has some *abandonment* issues. I feel the same for her and miss her when I can't take her with me. Not a howling kind of miss her, though. Father hands me three letters, telling me they are very important, and I should mind not to lose them. I see one is addressed to my Uncle William, my father's brother in Scotland, and the other two to Ottawa. I remember what happened last time I tried to send a parcel to Uncle William in Scotland, and get a shiver down my spine, but I try to remove the thought from my mind. I've never met my uncle. I have heard stories about him and my father growing up, and I've seen pictures, and once, I even talked to him on the phone. But I have not met the man.

I put the three envelopes into my secret pocket inside my parka, and Fleur and I make our way down the crunchy snow-encrusted road. It seems that no matter how cold it is outside, there are always people walking about the streets. Most of them look the same to me because of how over-bundled they are in their winter wraps. The post office is but five hundred meters down the road and then a right turn up to the building. This village is so small, Father says a blind man with vertigo couldn't get lost here. He says that a walk across town does not even give a man time to get lost in his own thoughts. I guess that is why he sometimes goes walking off into the wilderness on his own – looking to get lost in his thoughts.

Fleur is enjoying the walk. Her coat keeps her plenty warm and she finds a million great things to smell and to pee on. Jacob told me once that he wishes he were a dog so he could pee on everything too. Typical Jacob.

We get to the post office and I leave Fleur outside the door. She curls up in the snow and waits for me, just as Father said she would. I go up to the counter and I recognize the round woman with the sunken eyes who was at the laundromat this morning.

"I need postage for these three letters, please," I say,

handing the letters to the woman.

The woman looks at the envelopes. "That will be forty-five cents for each of these two and one-thirty-seven for the overseas letter. So, your total is two twenty-seven."

I give the woman three loonies and wait for the change.

"Hold on, I've got some mail for you. Let's see, Kidd. Here you go. Oh, and I have one unofficial piece of mail for … Robert Kidd. Someone came in just an hour ago, didn't see who it was, and left it on the counter. Of course, they didn't bother putting a stamp on it. But that's okay."

I thank the woman, slide the mail into my secret pocket, and step outside. Fleur jumps up and puts her front paws on my shoulders and starts licking my face. One would think she hasn't seen me in a year. I push her down playfully and we trot back into the street. I take out the letter addressed to me and look closely at it with questioning eyes. It simply reads *Robert Kidd* on the front in light blue colored pencil, which is really the only address one needs here. On the back is a drawing of a blue, green, and purple squid. Under the squid was written in small print, *the boy who changed.* I place the envelope back into my pocket and savor the mystery. I will open it in my room when I am alone without distractions. It has to be from the girl in the laundromat, but what? Why?

Now, I have found that my father was wrong, for I had just got lost in my thoughts.

Suddenly, I notice that something has changed. Fleur, who usually walks at my side, even rubbing up against my leg, steps in front of me and stops. I nearly fall over her. She produces a low growl. I look up, and standing ten meters in front of us is a man in a parka with a fur-lined hood pulled over his head. He is not moving, but staring right at me. He wears sunglasses, as many people do to tone down the blinding snow that is everywhere. His face is discolored, his nose bent as if broken, and as he opens his mouth to share a grim smile filled with malice, I note that he is short a couple of teeth.

"I'm going to fuck you up, boy. And then I'm going to put a goddamn ax through your daddy's head. I'll make you all wish you never left your fucking Isles."

Fleur lowers her head and bares her teeth. I am sure she will lunge on the man and rip his throat out. My fear walks hand in hand with a growing hate-filled anger. I consider letting Fleur's leash go so she can do her job. The man backs up a few steps with a fearful glance at Fleur. Billy Cloud says, "Next time I'll fill your clothes with stones before throwing you in." He turns and walks off with a notable limp, laughing an alcohol-tinted laugh. But before he is gone, he turns back and slurs, "If you tell your daddy you saw me, I'll kill your bitch-dog within a day."

Fleur looks up at me, whining. I stoop down and grab her around the neck and bury my tear-filled face in her heavy fur. I would run the rest of the way home, but I don't trust my shaking legs. We walk the last five minutes to the house, go inside, and I take off my layers. I hang up my coats, set the mail on the kitchen table, stick my letter in my shirt, and go up to my room. I get to the top of the stairs and look into Father's room on the left. I see him lying in bed taking a nap. In my room, I expect to see Jacob, but there is no sign of him. I plop onto the bed and close my eyes. Fleur jumps up with me. She won't do that with Jacob here, but when we're alone she lies down next to me with a little groan as she settles in.

As I slowly relax, I reach into my shirt and bring out the letter. I hold the sealed envelope, turn it around, sniff it, study the fish drawing with the strange caption, and only when I can no longer wait, I open the envelope. Inside, I find a small note and a smashed flower. I examine the flower – a dried and faded aster from days gone by. I let the flower lie in the palm of my hand. I pick up the note. It reads:

hey kidd
you might be the strangest boy i have met
i wonder how have you changed
i don't think you bite
i do think i might have changed since i met you
i might have changed into a purple aster
i could be the flower in your hand right now
come meet me at the docks at noon
i am there every sunday
-beck

My encounter with the scary man is instantly forgotten.

21

Beck

November 19

I grab my book from my room and go downstairs to sit near Father on the sofa. I look at my watch: half past eleven. What if he won't let me go? I guess I can always wait until next Sunday. I have rehearsed my lines, but my courage is waning, seemingly sinking deeper with each breath I take. If I were Jacob, I would simply sneak out with the deceitful line that I was just going outside to throw rocks. I am not Jacob. I am truthful. If I were to lie, my voice, my body language, my eyes, everything would give me away. I look at my watch again. Eleven thirty-four.

"You've looked at your watch half a dozen times since you sat down. Are you trying to catch the hour hand moving, or have you a date?"

I look up awkwardly at Father, my face burning red. How could he know? I pick at the corner of my book cover, looking down. Then I look up again and ask, "Can I take Fleur out to sit on the boat? I'm getting a little bored and Fleur has been asking to go out and play." None of this was really a lie, but I don't know if Father will allow it.

Father looks at me for a short time, sighs, and says, "Aye son, a lad your age will be getting restless. I was the same when I was young. My friends and I, we would run off to the Cuween chamber cairn some ten kilometers outside Kirkwall. Of course, I was a little older and my brother William had a car to drive us around. We would go looking for the *Hogboon* – a mound dweller spirit who guarded the land, so it was said. Well now, go on then. Keep the dog close by your side, mind you: there are worse things than *Hogboons* around here. The sun should have warmed up the cabin by now, so it should not be so cold inside." He gives me a wink of approval, and I take that as permission to leave.

The day is cold and quiet. There are a lot of people walking along the road. Many are on their way home from church, some on their way to visit family for Sunday lunch, and still others are on their own busy errands. I keep an eye out for the beat-up Billy Cloud, though I feel safe with Fleur by my side. A couple of snowmobiles pass along the road, cutting through the quiet winter day, but they soon arrive at their destination and give way to the stillness once again. I grip my book in my gloved hand, knowing that I will be glad to have it should Beck not show up. Inside the book I have concealed the letter she sent me. I wonder why she wants to know me, who she is, how she could be so brave to write me a letter. What if it wasn't her who wrote the letter? Who else could it be? Could Billy Cloud have come up with this plot? Maybe this isn't such a good idea.

Too late for second thoughts. I am at the boat docks. There are a few people milling around, mostly men working on their boats or unloading them from a morning trip from some other village. No sign of Beck. I am a little relieved. I find that I am sweating. I head straight to the *Bonnie Marie* and climb aboard with Fleur at my heels. There is a light breeze coming off the water, making for an uncomfortable chill in the air. I open the door to the small cabin and my dog and I step inside. Father was right about the sun warming up the cabin. The windows were set so that it was like a functional greenhouse. I fold down one of the small narrow beds and sit comfortably while keeping watch out the window. In time, I open my book and get out the envelope containing the letter. Again, I study the drawing of the squid.

Why a squid? A coincidence? I'd think it more likely that one would draw a fish, or a whale, or possibly an octopus, but certainly not a squid. Was she the one who threw the frozen washed-up squid at my window? No, she would have tied a note to it. I slip the letter back into the middle of the book and open to the page that I last left off reading. I am reading *Jurassic Park*, by Michael Crichton. Jacob would like this book; it's all about bringing dinosaurs back to life. That is, of course, if he could ever be bothered to read. He is not much interested in learning.

Just as I start getting into my story, Fleur jumps up and bangs her hundred pounds of body weight onto the door, giving out an odd, strangled bark. On the other side of the door, a startled scream is cut short. I look out onto the deck and I see Beck standing outside the cabin door. I call Fleur down and let her know what a good dog she is. Beck opens the door, apparently oblivious to the possibility of the dog eating her.

"Oh my God. I didn't know you had a dog! It's beautiful. What's his or her name?" Without hesitation, Beck squats down to the floor with open arms. Fleur shyly walks up to her and hunkers down and licks her face.

"Her name is Fleur. It's French for flower. She sure likes you. I thought I was the only one she would even let touch her." I watch in disbelief, or maybe in amusement.

Beck says, without looking away from Fleur, "I know, right? I have a weird way with animals. It's like they all know we have the same souls. My grandmother says it's my gift." She looks up at me and adds, "It's not like some juju tribal mysticism or anything. It's like some people are just animal people. More in touch with the universe, you know?" Fleur gets up and comes back to my side, tail wagging and nose poking into me. "I can tell you have a way of relating with animals too."

I think back to when we were in Nain and the big white dog with a black head that saw something in me as well. I reply, "I don't know, I haven't been around many animals. Except maybe crabs and mussels, and they aren't really much on conversation." Beck laughs. I smile. Beck lets herself into the cabin and shuts the door behind her to keep in the heat. "How did you know I was in here?"

She laughs, "Really? Everyone knows this is your boat. It's kind of funny-looking, you know. Just like you and your dad. I mean, not that you're funny-looking – just different. Like you're not Innu or Inuit or First Nation or Indian or whatever. You're like Vikings who showed up a thousand years too late. Sorry, not much left to plunder, unless you have a taste for slum houses, bibles, and buckets of shit. Otherwise, the Canadian government beat you to the goods."

I am at a loss for words. Not so sure where to start, I say, "My father built this boat. Well, kind of. He took an old fishing boat and hybridized it. It's not a real pretty boat, but it took him across the North Atlantic and it provides him with a living. It's named after my mother, who died a few years ago."

Now it is Beck's turn to be quiet.

Finally, she says, "Do you mind me hanging out here? I mean, I just don't have many friends. It's not that I *can't* make friends, it's more like I don't *want* to. I mean, I just can't relate to most of the kids here. But you're different. I think you might be an animal, like me."

I ask, "How old are you?"

"Thirteen. And a half. I'm tall for my age. People usually think I'm older. My mom says it's better to grow up than to grow out. She knows, she's round."

I say, "Well, I guess I'm kind of small for my age. I'm twelve, but people think I'm like four." Beck laughs, and I beam. "My father is pretty tall and big-muscled. He says I have my mother's build, but any day now I will shoot up to six feet."

We sit in the cabin next to each other on the bunk, staring out the window toward the water. Beck says, "Why don't you go to school? I mean, there is nothing wrong with that, but kids tell stories about your family. They think your dad kills people, that you're afraid to go outside, and that your little brother was adopted or something. Not that I listen to or care about what they all say, I mean, if you heard the stories they tell about me – *the weird Eskimo girl*."

I think about what she said. And I reply, "I never talk

to any other kids. Father won't let me. And I don't think you're weird. I like hanging out with you." I blush from my own honesty. "I guess my father might not like it if he knew we were talking. It's kind of a secret."

Two hours pass quickly. I look at my watch and tell Beck I need to get back home. "I guess I'll see you another time? Maybe next Sunday?"

"Hmm. Maybe that's too long. I'll see you before then. I'll surprise you." She stands up, rubs Fleur around the neck and whispers into her ear. She turns to me as I stand up, gives me a big smile that melts my insides, and she says, "I like you, Robert Kidd." And without thinking, she reaches over to me, kisses me quickly on the cheek, and runs out the door. I watch her, stunned, as she jumps over the gunwale, and quickly makes her way down the dock in a step that reminds me of an autumn leaf blowing in the breeze.

22

Gasoline Fire

November 22

"Hey Robert, it's time to die again." Billy Cloud was standing in the road laughing at me. I look around me and Fleur is lying on the road, a dark rivulet of blood pouring from her head. I return my gaze to the man, who is no longer a man but a boy, wearing a red hoodie, with a slingshot hanging from his hand. The boy smiles at me with such innocence and says, "Well, it looks like that is one bird who won't be bothering me again." Tears run down my cheeks as I stoop down to touch Fleur. On her exposed belly I see a tattoo I had never before noticed. It is an image of a raven in solid black, the size of my hand. The man-boy who stands in front of me says tauntingly, "How about that, Scotty? It looks like your old Eskimo Dog was nothing but a stupid Bird Dog." He lets out a raucous laugh that makes him sound as if he has a mouth filled with sand. The boy, who turns out to be older than I had thought, for he has the beginnings of a beard, holds up a plastic container of gasoline and drinks it all. Again, that innocent smile comes across his face. He pulls a cigarette from his pocket, puts it in his mouth, and produces a Zippo lighter from his sleeve, *my Zippo lighter*. As he lights the flame, he looks into me and says, "Everyone knows, there's only one way off this fucking rock, Scotty." He lights the cigarette, sucks in the burning embers, and bursts into flames.

I wake up screaming. Fleur jumps up on me, licking my face and whining. Jacob is asleep next to me. I lean over, open the top drawer to my bedside table, and feel around for my Zippo. I find it and pop open the lid and light it up. I hold it up to the lantern by my side and pass the flame on to the wick. I lie back in the dimly lit room, my heart racing, a chill running through me and sweat on my forehead. I feel drained. The wall clock reads two thirty. I grab Fleur to make sure she is alive. The dream felt so real. I look under Fleur's belly – no tattoo. Of course not: it was a dream. A very real dream.

I sit up in bed, unwilling to return to sleep. I am burning up. I listen to the wind outside, the sounds of Father in the next room talking to himself in unpleasant tones, the rhythmic breathing of Jacob beside me. I take a sip of water and let out a whimper. A couple minutes pass and my bedroom door creaks slowly open. The hulk of my father's body fills the frame. He enters the room and kneels down by the side of my bed.

"What are you up to, Robert? I heard you cry out and I saw your light on." He looks concerned.

I look at him, "I had a terrible dream."

"Aye, I'd say you did, that. You don't look so well." He puts his hand to my forehead, "You're on fire with fever.

That explains your dreams. That plastic patch over the broken pane just doesn't cut it; I hope the shop gets the new glass soon or you'll be catching your death with these temperatures. Let me get you something to drink and bring down your body heat." With that he leaves the room and I hear his footsteps clomping down the stairs and into the kitchen.

He comes back into my room and hands me a thermos of hot drink. "Drink this and swallow this Tylenol. Whenever you wake up during the night or in the morning, drink more."

"What is it?" I ask.

"Your mother's recipe: black tea steeped with dried elderberries, peppermint, lemon juice, honey, and a small bit of apricot brandy. Your mother always made sure we had these ingredients on hand. Now try to get some sleep."

"I don't want to sleep. I dreamed a man killed Fleur and then caught on fire and burned himself up. What if he comes back in my dreams?"

Father stares quietly at me for a moment, then says softly, "Robert, that man was a monster. Monsters become bigger and stronger when we fear them. If you see him again, stand up to him and yell in his face, 'I am not afraid of you, monster. Go away before I destroy you!' And you must believe in your heart that you *can* destroy the monster."

* * *

It's morning. Jacob is up and gone. The new day's sun is streaming into my window, creating yellow trapezoids on the bed and wall. A day like this usually greets me with happiness, but this day brings only pain. I feel terrible. I am still on fire and my bones hurt. I reach over for the thermos of my mother's recipe and take a sip of the still warm liquid. My head is filled with the black beating of raven wings. My stomach is rolling like the surf. Slowly, the night comes back to me. The dream. Father's visit to my room. The fever-induced feeling of anguish – physical and emotional. I try to get out of bed, but nearly fall on the floor. My legs are like squid legs, like *kraken* legs, meant for the water. I lie back down and keep the blankets cocooned over me. I hear the front door quickly open and close, accompanied by a quick polite knock that did not wait for a response. Fleur gives a perfunctory woof and lays her head back down on the floor. A conversation drifts up the stairway and into my partially open door.

"Dave, what brings you around?" Father's voice booms.

"Hey John, these are some hard times in this village, eh?" I hear Dave's footfalls meander into the kitchen. "Another suicide last night. A kid, maybe twenty or so, Josh something-or-other, probably high as a kite, dumped gasoline on himself and lit the match."

My Father abruptly gasps and pauses for a moment to think before asking, "Are you sure somebody else didn't light that match?"

"What is it, John?"

My father says, in a voice that was nearly swallowed before it came out, "Did anyone see it happen? I mean, when was he found?"

"I heard he left a friend's house sometime, I don't know, very late. He wasn't found until this morning, so I doubt anyone saw him. Though, I would be surprised if no one heard him. He must have screamed out in tremendous pain, burning as he did. His face and chest were burned pretty badly. You know, if he was breathing the shit in, I imagine his lungs would have ignited as well, eh? What is it? Did you know him?"

"No, I don't guess so. It's just troubling, that's all."

"Well, listen John, I gotta run. Just thought I'd pop in right quick."

I hear the two men walk to the front door, open it, and finish off their conversation just outside. "Hey Dave, why don't you stop over tomorrow. We'll have dinner. Say one-ish?"

"Sure John, I'd like that. It would be good to see the boys." Dave's voice trails off down the front drive.

Ten minutes pass and Father comes up the steps into my room. He brings some hot soup and a thermometer. The soup he sets on my desk, and the thermometer he sticks into my mouth. We stare at each other without speaking. Each of us thinking the same thing. Neither of us wanting to voice it.

"Thirty-nine. Still running high." Father takes the thermometer from my mouth and says, "In bed for the day. You should be feeling better tonight. Jacob won't be bothering you. I sent him off to your grandmother's for the day. All I need is for him to be sick as well."

23

Mr. Dave Comes to Dinner

November 23

Lunch has become dinner as the days shorten. Today is a 1:30 p.m. meal. It is Wednesday and we had our lessons before noon. Father had us reading maps and charting out distances in nautical miles as if we would be boating from here to Miami, Florida. We are to figure out how far we could get each day, establish which port we could stay the night in, and determine what date we might arrive if we left Davis Inlet on the first of May. He brought out some of his old maps for us to use. Father says this is the kind of education we could actually use in life, as opposed to the textbook learning we did with Mrs. Sally. I liked it because it allowed me to dream of great adventures and foreign lands – even though it was just the US, but it was still so different to go to the tropical part of the world. Jacob had a harder time with the math part (which was most of it), but I helped him with it when he let me.

I am excited about dinner today. I was afraid Father would make me stay in bed all day, but I seemed to have exceeded his expectations (*exceed expectations* – a phrase I once read and vowed to use) in my recovery. Well, I'm not one hundred percent, but I have made like I am. Mr. Dave will be coming to eat with us. I've not seen him in a month. He intrigues me. He treats me like an adult, and Jacob like a kid. I wonder where he draws the line between the two? I don't always understand what it is that he and Father are talking about when they get together, or maybe I just get bored with it after a while so I kind of stop listening. But when he comes to dinner he is always certain to include both Jacob and me in the conversation. Father says Mr. Dave is not always appropriate, but he invites him over because he says that Mr. Dave lives by himself and is lonely most of the time. Father says Mr. Dave drinks too much when he is by himself and may one day get so drunk that he might pass out, throw up, and choke on it. I asked Father if that is a real thing, and he said something about John Bonham, the drummer for Led Zeppelin. I didn't know who that was, so the reference was lost on me.

Father prepares the fish and gets the potatoes boiling, while I make a squash casserole like Mrs. Sally once taught me. Father said Mr. Dave usually just opens a can of Chunky Soup, a box of mac-n-cheese, or a can of Spaghetti-Os for meals. It was good for him to eat real food. Also, Father had to buy some beer. Every once in a while he will have a pint of beer. Just one. Every once in a while. While we prepare the food, Jacob is in charge of setting the table and picking up the house a bit.

All the while, Fleur lays on the floor with one loyal

eye on me, and one distrustful eye on Jacob. I am not sure what my dog feels about Father. I think she is okay with him, but he makes her nervous at night. Suddenly, Fleur jumps up, wagging her tail, and runs to the door. The door opens up (why bother knocking when you're expected?) and in walks Mr. Dave. Fleur jumps up on him, whining and trying to lick his face. Mr. Dave had known the dog for a couple years before bringing her to me, and Fleur loved him, though he often claims that the dog simply likes to taste him for a future meal.

As Mr. Dave finishes his dog-greeting ritual, he passes by Jacob, roughing up the top of his thick-haired head. He gives my father a big handshake and hands him a loaf of fresh baked bread from the local, and only, bakery. He offers me his hand, which envelopes my own, as he gives me a measured, firm shake. My father offers Mr. Dave some hot tea "for a cold-as-shit day," which is accepted with gratitude. Jacob places the food dishes onto the table, and we all sit down.

We don't actually say *church* prayers before meals in our house, because we are not religious. Mr. Dave on the other hand, he is religious, and every time he comes to eat with us, he says a prayer first. Father says he is religious because he needs it. I guess it's because he drinks all the time, goes out late, hangs out in the bar and generally, according to Mrs. Sally, lives a sinful life. Like I said, there are no secrets here. Mr. Dave bows his head and asks God to shine his light on these good people who take care of him, and to give guidance to Jacob and me as we grow into fine young men. Then he looks up, winks, and says thanks for the good fish. It's funny that he talks to an invisible god. I guess it's no stranger than me talking to a dog that doesn't speak English.

As we eat, the conversation is like a symphony. My father seems to be conducting it, and Mr. Dave is like the star first violinist. Jacob and I are mostly lost somewhere back in the woodwind section. Father mentions something about the colder than usual winter we are having, and Mr. Dave takes the topic on a long solo, carrying the melody on about the season predictions, the recent temperature trends, the effects on the fisheries and the local marine mammals, and the price of oil heating. Just as the subject is running itself out, Father changes the direction toward the recent suicides in the village. Again, Mr. Dave carries the orchestral flow masterfully through the social problems that are plaguing this community, and the influx of gasoline sniffing. Just as I sit at the edge of my seat thinking the music might open up the question of the man on the street yesterday, or worse, my mother's death, the leader once again waves his baton and shifts the mood into a lighter conversation of the diminishing choices of fine ales in all of Labrador, and with that comes the pouring of the beer.

This is the cue for me and Jacob to clear the table and get ready for the setting sun. That means getting a late-night snack and drink together and putting our books and other activity items by our bedside. Jacob runs upstairs and I fiddle around in the kitchen a little while longer, trying to decide what I might want to snack on at six this evening. I find it difficult to prepare for a future meal when I am stuffed from the meal I just ate. I feel like I will never be hungry again. As I gather some things together, my father and Mr. Dave start in on their strictly grown-up talk. At this point I become invisible. It is an unspoken rule that I do not get involved in this discussion.

"So," Mr. Dave says as he leans into the table staring at Father, "are you still planning the Great Escape?"

My father answers, "Aye, I've about saved up enough money for when we get there. I figure I can still sell off my fishing gear for the rest. I have enough spare engine parts stashed away to avoid any unforeseen problems on the sea – at least as far as the engine goes, and I had Leah and Norm tend to any repairs the sail might need."

"When are you thinking?"

"Likely late June. Give the ice time to clear up north, give me time to rig up the old sail to the *Bonnie Marie*, and give me time to teach my boys to be proper deck hands."

A moment of silence, and Mr. Dave says, "Well, I understand your reasons, but I think it's dangerous. And maybe a little more than foolish. I've no doubt you could teach those boys how to sail, but they are far from strong men. The currents of the Davis Strait will be bad enough, but hurricane season will be in full swing. You'll need to be going far to the north to avoid any tropical storms, making your journey that much longer. And I know you took that boat on the crossing once, but it should have been a one-way trip. Besides, the currents were with you. I saw how you rigged up that mast for the sail; I'd say it was dodgy at best."

"What are you getting at, Dave?"

"What I'm saying is I don't want the sea to take you and your boys like it took Marie! What I'm saying is that if you are still bound and determined to drown the lot of you come June, then let me come with you as your hand. You're going to need the help, and I've got nothing keeping me here on this godforsaken rock. John, do this for me. I'm going to die here, drunk and frozen in the street."

Father is quiet for a long minute. That's how he is. He thinks before speaking. Finally, "Aye, Dave, I hear what you're saying. Let me chew on that offer. And if I do take you on, and if you are a pain in my arse, which I suspect you will be, I may just drop you off in Greenland and you can live out the rest of your sorry days in Nuuk. Should you make it to Kirkwall, we may lose you to the Scapa Whisky Distillery. Or the Highland Park Distillery. Or any other number of whisky makers in the area, for that matter."

"Well then, here's to Kirkwall. How about another pint, John?"

"You know I only have one. But help yourself, you God-fearing lush."

With another hour or so left until sunset, I take Fleur out before going upstairs. Fleur loves it out here in the cold winter. She runs circles around me hoping for some play time. I throw a rubber ball that I found on the shore a couple of days ago. Her new favorite toy. I wonder how Fleur will like Scotland. I guess it will be just about as cold as it is here, but the city of Kirkwall will be like a new world. This time next year we will be living there. I can barely get my head round it. I look across the water and imagine I can see the UK from here. Father says one day Scotland will leave the UK to be their own country again, "And we'll be all the better for it," he says. Father prefers to be left alone in far flung corners of the world. I told him that maybe we should live in Patagonia or Madagascar. He replied, "Och son, you're tearing the tartan from my heart with those words."

24

Stones on the Window

November 30

It's early morning, and I lie in bed listening to Jacob downstairs talking to Father about boats and fishing. I guess Jacob wants to work on a fishing boat when he's old enough. Father tells Jacob that he believes he would make a fine boat hand, and eventually, he could captain his own boat. Maybe even take over the *Bonnie Marie*. That would be good for him. I, on the other hand, have absolutely no desire to make the sea my life. The tales of the sea told by my father are far too frightening for me. Still, there is a certain charm in Father's voice as he sits with Jacob and tells his stories. And as he does, Jacob requests a song of the sea from Father, who is always happy to oblige. I hear him clearing his deep amber voice to deliver his ditty of the old country. Although I cannot physically see him, I can picture in my head the look of dreams that draws across his face as he begins his song.

In early morn, set sail did we
Frae our home in Cromarty Firth
The winds were fierce, our spirits free
We sailed for all we're worth

A storm on portside come sae fast,
"Sail on" the captain said
"We've rum to sell, and coin to win"
We round Duncansby Head

And it's,
Hey dee diddly
Hey dee diddly
Hey dee diddly di
Upon the sea we did set sail
The storm was drawing nigh

Me mates and I braced for the worst
The storm sae fast did come
"We'll soon go doon," the captain cursed
"We're sure to lose our rum"

Lighten the load, keep us afloat
The water's rollin' in
The anchors flew right aff the boat
But tossing rum is sin

Hey dee diddly
Hey dee diddly
Hey dee diddly di
Such fools were we, so young and brave
"We'll meet our end," we cried

We have no choice, the first mate said
The kegs do weigh us doon
Throw them off or join the dead
It's not our day to drown

I look to the kegs, then to the storm
The sea'll gie me my due
A brilliant plan I quickly formed
Grab up your cups and queue

Throw out the rum, but not just yet
For Scotland, drink shall we
Fill yourselves up, all you can take
Piss out your rum to sea

Hey dee diddly
Hey dee diddly
Hey dee diddly di
Now the North Sea is eighty proof
So, look for the incoming tide

I look up at the wall clock. Half past ten in the morning. How can I still be in bed? I get up and begin to get my long underwear on as I listen to the commotion downstairs. My father yells up the stairs to me, "Robert, I am taking Jacob to run some errands with me. You might think about getting out of bed sometime. When we get back, we'll start today's studies." The door shuts and all is quiet.

As I get dressed, Fleur lies on the floor looking up at me expectantly. I reach down and give her a scratching and tell her we'll go out in a sec. I hear some pings on the window. I look out and more pings. Someone is throwing small pebbles at the window – testing out the new pane Father put in yesterday? Down below, I see Beck wrapped in layers of insulation. She has a handful of pebbles ready to launch. I hold up a wait-a-minute finger, throw on my sweater, and run down the steps with Fleur at my heels nearly tripping me up. Hanging on a hook by the front door is my parka with hat and mittens in the pockets. I walk out the back door while struggling with the coat and step into the morning.

"What are you doing out here?" I ask.

Beck looks at me with a menacing smile, "I told you I'd be around." She reaches down to pet the ecstatic Fleur. "I saw your brother and dad leave. Invite me into the house and show me your room."

I look around to make sure no one is looking. "Hurry in, I don't know how long they'll be gone." I look over at Fleur who is doing her morning pee, which reminds me that I have to do the same. I bring the two of them into the living room and excuse myself to use our hybrid indoor-outdoor bathroom. When I come out, Beck looks curiously at the bathroom.

"You have indoor plumbing? Everyone I know just has buckets. I've never seen a real toilet here. I mean, we had one where we used to live, that was before my mom and I moved back here to be with my grandparents." Beck continued to look over the toilet, the sink, and the bathtub. I tell her how we pipe the water in off the creek coming off the cliff in front of our house. The water is freezing, but we always keep some hot water going on top of the stove. I explained how the compost toilet worked and that it never even smells bad.

Beck looks at the living room area, the kitchen, "Where's *your* room?"

I lead her upstairs with Fleur pushing us aside as if the stairs belonged only to four-footed beasts. At the top of the stairs, we turn to the door on the right. "Me and Jacob share it. The dinosaur stuff is his. That's his desk, this one is mine. I do my schoolwork here. Jacob mostly draws in his sketchbook."

Beck looks through Jacob's drawings, makes a grimacing face, and says, "Your little brother is kind of a sick kid." I have not actually looked at his drawings in a long time. I close in next to Beck as she flips through the pages. Most are filled with monsters and blood. Beck stops at a page that clearly depicts Fleur as a giant tooth-filled wolf, or *Witiko*, with blood dripping from her teeth and dismembered bodies of black-haired children thrown around. Another depicts a scene in the ocean with sharks eating dogs, the sharks in turn are being bitten in half by our father. One picture depicts Jacob dressed in white fur alongside a polar bear killing sled dogs with scribbles of red blood covering the dogs. Other pages are filled with equally terrifying images. Jacob draws like one would expect from an eight-year-old, but the likenesses he captures of Fleur, Father, me, and himself are immediately recognizable. There are a lot of drawings of dinosaurs and a collection of boat drawings, mostly the *Bonnie Marie*. Many boat drawings look like Jacob was trying to illustrate Father's songs, with *krakens* and whales and storms.

"We should close the book up before he finds out we've been looking through it," I say, as if he could return any second, which he could, though I don't really expect them to get home for an hour. Father takes his time when he walks into the village.

Beck goes to the window. "Nice view of the water. I'll

bet you can see all the moods of the sea from here."

We sit on the edge of the bed looking out the window at the ravens that are hopping along the beach, searching for morsels that the seagulls may have missed. "So, where did you live before you and your mother came here?" I ask.

"We moved to St. John's when I was just a baby. It was just me and my mom. We lived there for a dozen years before coming back up to this glamorous place."

"So, do you remember your father at all?" I ask.

"All I remember was pooing my diapers. I never even saw a picture of him. My mom never mentions him. I think she threw away anything that reminded her of him."

We continue to watch the ravens out the window as they carry on with their business. The biggest one grabs a crab that tried to make a run for the next hiding rock, and it throws it up into the air and catches it in its beak. It does this a few times, playing a fun game at the crab's expense. Finally, the raven ends its cruel game, drops the crab onto a rock, and pecks open its carapace for a meaty meal. As Beck watches this, she says, "I don't know if I should feel bad for the crab, or happy for the hungry raven."

Just as she says this, the raven looks up at the window, as if it heard her, and it stares at us, calling out its raucous song. Beck remarks that the raven can't see us through the window. She said that it would just see the reflection of the sky. Now, the bird hops once, twice, and the third time it finds the breeze it is looking for to catch its wings. It flies into the wind, which is strong enough to make the bird go straight up from its eating spot. It turns to gain speed, circling around, and catches another current that brings it straight toward us. We watch, expecting the raven to veer up at the last moment and soar over the house. Instead, it flies directly at us, hitting the window right in front of our faces. We both let out a scream of surprise, roll back on the edge of the bed, and fall onto the floor.

"Jesus Christ! I think I crapped myself," Beck says, lying on her side on the floor. "That thing came right at us. It was aiming for us. I'm surprised it wasn't killed. Or I don't know, maybe it was."

I look up from the floor at the window, which now looks like a spider web. Father had just repaired the old broken glass – no doubt he will not be happy. I get up, open the window, and look down. The raven lies on the ground, the wind blowing about a feathered wing, making it look as if it is waving at us. Beck and I look at each other and sit back down on the floor, leaning against the side of the bed. My heart is racing, and I feel a little dizzy. I sit for a couple of minutes before saying, "I know that raven."

Beck looks at me, "You mean you've seen it out there before."

"No; well, yes," I answer slowly, "I know it because it knew me. It called my name once, and it showed me … things on the beach." Beck looks at me with questions in her eyes. "No, I mean, I was on the beach down there and it was almost like it wanted to show me things. At least I thought it did. It hopped around and kept kind of talking to me. You know how they can make so many different sounds, almost like a parrot? It's because of the great plasticity in their speech, or song, structure. I read that in a *National Geographic* once. At one point I almost thought it was calling my name. *Robert, Robert*, it cackled."

Beck nodded slowly and looked curiously at me. "I remember hearing about how smart ravens are," she pauses. "I was right about you. You *are* an animal person. C'mon, let's go get it."

We get up from the floor again. I shut the window gently, so glass doesn't fall out, and we run downstairs with our coats in hand. We go outside to where the bird was, and it is gone. I look at Beck, "I guess it was just stunned and flew away."

"That's weird," says Beck. We stand there looking at nothing but rocky ground.

Beck looks intensely into my eyes and says, "You are definitely the strangest and most exciting boy I have ever met. You died once. You *changed*. You talk to birds. Your dad is either a psycho-killer or he attracts bad luck. Your brother has a sick imagination. You're sort of a hermit. And you are Scottish. What more could there be?"

I look at her with a most serious demeanor, "You'd be surprised."

Fleur starts whining and looking around in her skittish way. "My father and brother must be coming. You need to sneak out of here." Beck grabs my arms, looks at me with … I don't know what, an urgency? This time I don't even think. I simply give her a quick kiss on the mouth. She smiles her delicious smile and comes back for seconds.

"You know," Beck says as she is leaving, "if you need to get in touch with me, I'm at the laundromat every Saturday morning. I get bored and spend my time reading the little postings on the community bulletin board." And she slips away.

25

Edgar

December 4

Jacob leaves the house early this morning, soon after sunrise – 8:30 a.m., shortly after Father left to pick up the new windowpane. Father would be back shortly. I lie in bed thinking about having to get up, take the dog out, and feed the wood stove. I watch out the window as Jacob goes into the backyard and then around the side. I guess he's on his way to meet up with the boys down the street. I really don't think they are nice kids. And I don't think that Jacob is a nice kid when he hangs out with them. And I don't think that Father is happy about Jacob. I fear that one day Jacob will go just a little too far and make Father just a little too angry. And then what? A monster will emerge from him, that's what I fear. The thought of my father's ranting and roaring in the night gives me a shiver. This scenario has been playing through my head since the first time I saw Jacob out with those boys. And this morning, perhaps a new feeling starts to rise from within me. An anger which I can barely settle. Mrs. Sally once told me that when a person reaches puberty, hormones trigger new and strange emotions that take over and are hard to control or to understand. I don't think that is where these feelings are coming from. I think they are coming from the seawater that remains forever in my lungs.

I jump out of bed and make my way downstairs to put some more wood in the stove. Father got it going earlier, but not enough to keep it going all day. I see a half dozen small wood splits on the log rack, which will do for now, but I'll need more soon. I might need to split some of the thicker logs first. I place the pot on top of the stove to make some hot chocolate and throw on my boots and coat to get a couple more pieces of wood. I open the back door to a greeting of frozen air. Fleur runs past my feet and dances in the backyard while I walk around the corner to the wood pile.

Something catches my eye. A small critter tucked away between the logs and the rock foundation of the house. Fleur notices it as well and runs over and sticks her nose into the hiding spot. She quickly lets out a little yip and jumps back. Apparently, she was bitten on the nose as a warning. I stoop down, allowing Fleur to whine to herself behind me, and I stick my thick-gloved hand into the hiding spot to see what might be in there. A black raven hops onto my glove, unafraid. It turns its head sideways and upside-down, as if it wasn't quite strung tightly enough, and settles on a side-tilting position to look up at me. The bird appears hurt in some way. I sit on the cold ground and bring the raven in closer to my body. It makes no attempt to get away. I stand up, stick the bird into my coat to keep it warm, and head toward the door. I really can't tell one raven from another, but I feel like this is the same one that hit my window yesterday. It looks like something broke, like its neck or its brain, when it hit the window or when it fell to the rocks below. I take the raven into the house with no real plan, but I am quite sure it will freeze or starve outside.

Now what? I put the bird into a large cardboard box that we have lying around just outside the back door, and I take it up to my room. I place a bowl of water and some grapes in the box. The raven must be starving because it eats six grapes right away. It wasn't really interested in the water. I guess it was eating snow outside. Fleur keeps sniffing at the box and listening to the raven's feet scratch at the cardboard as it paces in circles in its new home. The bird hops up onto the top lip of the box, nearly tipping it over, and looks around the room. It looks at me and bobs its head before turning it sideways again, giving it the appearance of a crazy, or maybe a curious, person. It flaps its wings and hops off the box to the floor, this time successfully knocking the box over, sending the water, bowl, and remaining grapes flying across the floor. The raven seems to laugh and coo, while Fleur lays down staring at the bird with her haunches ready to spring, whining and looking up at me for advice on what to do about this new stranger in the room. I go about picking up the box, refilling the water bowl, and hunting down the escaped grapes. I put a large rock that I have on my desk into the box to help keep it weighted down. I return to the bird, put out my hand, and reach under the raven's breast and belly, spreading my fingers to go around its legs, and I lift it up. The bird still shows no fear of me or Fleur.

What am I going to do with this thing? Jacob will probably be afraid of it, like he is afraid of my dog. Father will tell me *Let it go outside where it will live or die, it's nature's way*. I can't hide it in here: it's only a matter of time before it will start making its loud calls. I can't let it die. As if it knew what I was thinking, the raven makes a soft sound, jumps up onto my shoulder, and rubs its head against my cheek.

After a couple of hours, Father stops in to have a quick bite and to check on us boys. He is not happy to find that Jacob isn't home. I shrug my shoulders and tell him that Jacob was gone when I woke up. I can't tell from my father's face whether he is angry with Jacob or resigned to the fact that my brother will not easily be reined in. For better or worse, I take the moment to tell Father about the bird. Rather than actually telling him, I take him up to my room and let him see for himself. I explain how I found it in the wood pile, and it did not look like it could care for itself, and it looked like it might die, and I couldn't just leave it there. He looks at the bird. He looks at me. And he forms a little private smile.

"You're like your mum, she had a way with animals too. She got so she wouldn't even eat any kind of animal. Not even fish. What kind of a fisherman has a wife who won't eat fish, I ask you?" He pauses, swallows hard, and continues on. "Och, I don't suppose there would be any harm in you keeping the bird for a time. Though mind you, your dog may find the bird has some good nutritional value one day. And there'll be no tears for the bird. Though I don't reckon it'll live long, with the way it hangs its head."

Father helps me construct a perch out of scrap wood for the raven to sit on in the corner of the living room where I usually sit with Fleur. I line the floor under the perch with old paper grocery bags. All the while, Fleur cannot take her eyes off the raven. I call the raven Edgar, after Edgar Allen Poe's poem – "Nevermore." I don't know if it's a girl or a boy, but it doesn't really matter.

***

Having eaten lunch, I ask Father if I can walk with him to the boat and then come back, just to let Fleur get out for a bit. He says it sounds like a good idea and that I am a good person for Fleur to get attached to. "And it would be good for you to stretch your legs as well," he says.

We get to the boat and Father starts working. I dally for a little while and tell him I'll be heading back home. "If you run into Jacob, you tell him his father says to get back in the house," Father calls out as I am turning around. I tell him I'll look out for him. What I didn't tell Father was that I would be making a quick stop on my way back home.

I stand staring at the bulletin board in the laundromat:

"Learn French – call Lisa and start private classes today – 709-260-7582."

"Yamaha Snowmobile for sale – ask for Chris at The Garage."

"AA classes …"

"Babysitter …"

"Pregnant?"

There are a dozen other messages, and still more business cards. I look around and assess that no one is watching, and quickly put my own message up, using a thumbtack that was left by a previous post. Earlier today,

I spent time making a little business card of my own. On the front, I simply drew a raven. On the back side I wrote, *come by when you can, I have a surprise*. And then I drew a crude-looking squid. Anyone else looking at that note would pass right over it. Hopefully, Beck will take it in.

I step outside where Fleur is lying in the snow, waiting on me. I grab her leash and make my way back home trying to be as inconspicuous as possible. I don't want word to get back to my father that someone saw me coming out of the laundromat. It is bad enough for him that he needs to worry about Jacob. At least he can believe he has one son who will mind him.

26

Freezing Children

December 7

It's dark in the room. Well, not really dark: the moon is scattering patches of light to create negative shapes of shadow. Father is speaking to me with hushed urgency, his face close to my own. He asks me to join him and to bring my dog with me. I look at my watch: 2:10 a.m. I am confused. The spider webs of sleep still fill my head. And why is my father telling me to step on the floor at night? I hear him rushing about getting my shoes and coat together. "Shh, don't wake your brother. And grab your lighter. You'll need it for the lantern."

"But Father, it's night … the floor … I'd be touching the floor …" I babble incoherently. My father cuts me off briskly, "Never you mind about that, son; we have greater monsters to fight tonight".

At that I tentatively get up, surprised at the actual lack of consequence at stepping on the floor in the middle of the night; I throw on some pants and a sweatshirt, get the lighter from my drawer, and flick it on to give me a flame to see by. On the top of the landing to the stairs, my father hands me our small kerosene lantern, which I light. Father tells me that as long as I have my flame burning, I will be safe. I sit on the top step and put on my shoes. I slip on my coat and make my way downstairs. Once at the bottom, I ask, "Where are we going?"

"There are three kids missing tonight. One of the fathers asked me to help in his search. They were last seen running through the street, making a ruckus like kids do, about five hours ago. Their parents are afraid they will freeze to death out there. And freeze they will: it's minus twenty tonight. Get your dog. I think she'll be of help – we'll need her nose. I tried to get her out there, but she won't go with me. You are her master and, apparently, she is loyal only to you."

I put on my balaclava, some snow pants, and my mittens. I have never been out at night, and I am more than a little nervous. We step out into the crisp, frigid air. I keep Father on one side of me and Fleur on the other. My lantern I hold out in front of me to ward off my nightmares. The full moon and the snow work together to light the world of darkness. There are things out here, breathing, watching. I can feel them. Though I am warm under my layers, I feel a shiver working through my blood. Instinctively, I reach down for Fleur.

We crunch on the frozen snow beneath our feet, making our way to the center of town. Once there, we join a group of nine or ten men and women – the search party. There is some discussion on how to proceed most efficiently. Eyes dart around the circle in concern. While most people are assigned a section of the village to search in, Father and I are simply given a couple of articles of clothing, which I assume belong to one or more of the missing kids, and we are told to let the dog be our guide. "I know that dog," said one woman. "It belonged to Lois who turned it into a killer. I don't know that we want it out here with us."

I take hold of the t-shirt and the pair of pants that were given us, and I let Fleur get a good smell of them. Father takes the clothes and places them back in the plastic bag, saying we might need them again to refresh her memory. Immediately, Fleur starts to walk in big circles, sniffing the air for the treasures that dogs find in the wind. Everyone else has left to search their assigned territory. Fleur moves north about twenty meters, turns to the west, and slowly makes her way on a zig-zag trail that only she can see. I feel her excitement and urgency through the tension in her leash. I imagined it would take maybe five minutes to find the kids, but this hide and seek game is taking much longer than I thought. Father says that she is probably losing the scent-trail every time the wind shifts. We are led through yards, around houses and sheds, into the pine woods and back out, and down dead-end paths. Father's large flashlight helps us see in the moon shadows. My lantern doesn't throw off much light except in my immediate vicinity. It is more to keep us safe.

Eventually, Fleur takes us up to an old home, long and narrow, like a single-wide trailer, and starts whining at the door. *We found them.* Father looks in the window with his light and sees nothing. He tells me to stay put and that he is going to take a look inside. He spends a short time jiggling the doorknob until it finally permits him entrance, and he disappears into the dark, cavernous home. Suddenly, Fleur picks up another scent on the air and pulls hard at the leash, dragging me behind, struggling to keep my feet beneath me. I call out, "Father! Fleur, slow down." She pulls me around the house and down three lots to the end of the line of houses and into a stretch of dried old weeds and boulders. We go far enough from the edge of the village that I lose the house lights. The shapes of the town are memories. I trip over a rock and lose Fleur as I fall down into the weeds. I have enough layers on that I am well-padded for the fall.

I have lost the dog, the lantern shattered, the flame extinguished in the snow, and I am alone.

Outside.

At night.

I sit in the scrubby piece of land with sudden panic. I hear the distant voices of people, or perhaps it is but the wind. There is nothing but wilderness around me, though I could not be far from the village. I'm paralyzed in fear. I call out to Fleur and to my father. Nothing. Nothing but panic. I have to move. *Move Robert, move.* I can't move, the water is surrounding me. *There is no water, Robert. You are not drowning in the sea. You are somewhere worse.* The darkness engulfs me, the wilderness screams. I take off my mitten to reach deep into my layers of clothing and pull out my lighter. My hands are shaking from fear and cold. I try to flip the lighter open, and I drop it into the snow. In desperation, I throw the snow around chaotically trying to find the Zippo.

Now I hear something coming through the nearby brush. I freeze. The noise comes closer. I am touching the floor at night. Something is coming for me. I try to call out for Fleur, but my voice fails me. I am alone.

I recall my father's words, *As long as you have your flame burning, you will be safe.* Without moving, I run my eyes over the ground around me. I hear the thing that is quickly approaching me as it makes a strange gurgling sound, followed by a low guttural growling. The growling turns gradually into a loud roaring. *Concentrate, Robert. Find the lighter.* A shadow comes over me. The hair on my neck is standing on end. I am pouring sweat. *Find the lighter.* Whatever it is that is stalking me, it's right behind me. It speaks my name. Like the raven. "*Robert.*" I see a flash of reflected moonlight in the snow before me. "*Robert, come with me to the sea.*" I think of the song that I heard on the local (and only) radio station – "*Come with me, to the sea. The sea of love.*"

I reach for the bright reflection of moonlight. My silver lighter. I feel something brush against my back. I scream as I flip open the Zippo and spin the steel wheel, sending a flame out into the night. I turn around wildly.

There is nothing.

I hear a strange but familiar howling far off. In a minute, Fleur runs up to me with her leash trailing behind her. I grab the leash, as she pulls with more urgency. She continues to howl and whine. She takes me just a short way farther into the woods to a small shed, half as big as our own shed. Fleur jumps up at the door whining and scratching it. I grab the handle, pull my thumb down on the latch, and pull it open slowly. I am afraid of what I might find inside. I hold my lighter out in front of me. Illuminated against the back wall of the shed are three bodies. I step back in surprise. I turn and shout, "I found them. I found the kids. Father!" Fleur is prancing around my legs with worried whimpers.

I call out again. This time I hear my father in the distance yelling back that he is coming. I turn back to the three kids. They are not moving. Or barely moving. They lay on one another like fallen dominoes. The one on the far left does not move at all, he just stares straight ahead. The other two, each leaning on the body to their left, are also staring straight ahead at my flame, but they are shivering uncontrollably. I see them moving, yet I am sure they are all dead. Zombies. I scream again, a loud, clear demonstration of fear. Father shows up, followed by a couple others, and they crowd around the kids. I step back with Fleur and watch. The doorway to the shed is stuffed with grown-ups all trying to get to the children. I hear them talking, but I cannot catch a word. Slowly the shed spits the people back out, and the final three men to emerge each carry a child in his arms. A man is crying and talking too loudly. A woman wraps her arms around one man and the boy he carries, who must be her son.

A hand is placed on my shoulder from behind me. I jump. "Come on son, this has not turned out well. Let's go home." We walk past the hushed voices, the tears of relief, and the tears of distress. We walk over the frozen world that is accompanied by the wind's soft song of loneliness. Fleur stays close to my side. Father carries his flashlight. In my hand I hold my lighter on the ready to ignite.

No words are spoken until we reach the house, where Father says, "Go get some sleep." I shed my boots, coats, hat, snow pants, and fear, and slowly make my way up the stairs. Once in my room, I do not sleep in the bed with Jacob, but light a candle and I lay a couple heavy quilts on the floor and sleep with my arm around Fleur. *No dreams tonight*, I beg to the darkness.

27

The Arctic Air

December 8

Nobody moves today, not even Edgar and Fleur. We all sit in the living room, Father in his chair, Jacob sprawled out on the sofa, and I sit on a cushion on the floor reading. It is minus fifteen outside, and that is about all we will see for the day. This is the warmest room in the house. The events of the previous night sit heavily in the air. Father told us what I already knew: that one boy in the shed had frozen to death. The other two, the dead boy's sister and another boy, were not far behind. Father said that another thirty minutes and they would have been dead as well. I asked who made them sleep in the shed, and Father said it was the Canadian Government with a little help from British Petroleum. I didn't understand until he explained that the government stuck us here in this place of misery, and BP provided us with our only escape. The three kids had been huffing gasoline until they had no brain cells left. That's what Beck calls it – *huffing*. Father said the two kids who didn't freeze to death were in pretty bad shape. Jacob doesn't really know what happened last night, but I know he knows a little about huffing. I am haunted by the image of the three kids huddled in a stupor, their blank eyes staring straight ahead at the doorway as if surprised to learn of its existence. How could sniffing in gasoline be so promising, so intoxicatingly seductive as to make freezing to death a viable option for a good time? A shiver runs through me. Mr. Dave told me the gasoline sniffing had become an epidemic not only in Davis Inlet, but a number of small fishing villages along the Labrador coast. I told him that I thought an epidemic was more to do with a disease. He replied that this was a disease – a social disease. I am beginning to understand what he meant.

Fleur is looking at me with a worried face. "Do you need to go out?" I ask her. I throw on my biggest coat, which is hanging by the back door, and we slip out quickly so as not to let the heat out. My face freezes instantly as I watch Fleur taking her time to find the perfect pee spot. She seems unaware of the cold. In fact, it seems to energize her. I walk around to the wood pile on the side of the house to get a couple of logs for the wood stove. Tucked partly under one of the top logs I find a plastic bag with a note inside. I give it a quick look and see a rough drawing of a squid on the outside of the folded note. With fingers that are quickly going numb, I stick the note in my pants pocket, grab four medium-sized logs, call for Fleur, and we quickly slip back into the house.

Father watches me intently as I stoke up the fire and feed it a little wooden snack. He says, "You're quite the fire tender. I think I'll keep you around."

I am slightly embarrassed by the compliment. Then Father adds, "You were extremely brave last night. And the way you worked with Fleur was, well … the folks in town were all talking about you and your rescue dog this morning."

Brave. No, I was scared out of my head. Mr. Dave once told me that a person has to be afraid in order to be brave. He said bravery is the act of great strength in the face of fear. Maybe I am brave because I have plenty of fears. I give Father a secret smile, and I give Fleur a wide-open smile as I wrestle her to the ground to get some of her energy out. She grabs my entire arm in her mouth, and with the most delicate grip shakes the arm around like a chew toy.

I settle back into my cushion on the floor and discreetly pull out the note retrieved from the wood pile. I remove it from its protective plastic bag. I look at the squid drawing on the outside of the note. This time the squid is in orange and red with yellow highlights. Inside, the note simply reads, *Tomorrow Noon Boat.* Clear enough for me, but cryptic to anyone else who might inadvertently come across it.

Tomorrow is Saturday. Hmm. It may be a little bit busy out on the docks.

I consider Beck outside on this frigid morning, delivering the note to my woodpile. She's a tough girl. She's not afraid to go outside when the sun is down, but she says she doesn't go out after dark because her mother says there are bad men in town who aren't really bad, but when they get to drinking, they turn into monsters. I told her I understood how that is – monsters. She must have stopped by before going to school this morning. I think she said she only goes half days during these coldest months of the year. Makes sense, with the short daylight hours. She knows I am in charge of the fire here at home, so naturally I would be the one to find the note. She's smart. I like that about her.

Today, Father gives Jacob and me a school assignment. Jacob has to draw a picture of anything he wants, and then he needs to write a two-page story about it. My assignment is to write a paper on the moon's gravity and how it affects life here in Davis Inlet. We have a set of encyclopedias and a lot of science books that I can use for my research. Mrs. Sally once told me that we have more books than anyone else in the Inlet. Father said that there is something called *the internet* where all the information you ever wanted is on your tv screen, and that one day we won't even have books. He said that last year the big cities like Ottawa, Toronto, and Montreal all got *the internet* and they connect to a *world wide web*. I am not really sure what he was talking about. He also said that one day, all houses will have computers in them. But, he added, it will be years before we see that out here in this barren hinterland. A place where there are no roads in or out is doomed to be forever trying to catch up with the rest of the world.

This day is moving slowly. It doesn't bother me, but I can see Jacob getting restless. And if Jacob is getting bad, my father is worse. I sense that Father would rather be out working on something, anything, to move about and occupy his hands. "Boys," he announces suddenly, "tomorrow should be a bit balmier. Who's up for joining me out at the docks?"

Jacob, who likes to go out fishing, is not a fan of "going to the docks," where he knows he will just be put to work, says, "I'd rather stay home. It's cold outside by the boats."

"I'll go," I say. "Fleur likes hanging out on the *Bonnie Marie*." And so, my first obstacle to seeing Beck is overcome.

Father looks at Jacob and says, "Jacob, you'll be coming too, lad." Father's look says it all. He does not trust Jacob to be on his own. I wonder if I am going to have to be Jacob's babysitter on the boat while Father does his work. All of a sudden, tomorrow's trip does not sound so promising. I can feel Jacob sinking further into the sofa cushions, trying to disappear.

28

The Slingshot

December 9

"Let's go, boys." Our father's voice booms through the house. We throw on our winter dress, which is to say, our fall-winter-spring dress, I grab Fleur and wave goodbye to Edgar, Jacob grabs his slingshot and his sketch book, and Father grabs a backpack with our lunch in it. Father was right: at least compared to yesterday's arctic temperatures, today is a right balmy minus two Celsius. People are out and about grocery shopping, visiting friends and family, whatever it is people do. As usual, I feel the eyes upon us. The rarely-seen Scotsmen. Me, the dead kid who returned to life with a killer dog who, around me, is as docile as a kitten. My father, the murdering captain, who killed his wife and later killed his crewman, and almost killed the crewman's cousin. And Jacob, the Innu boy who doesn't belong in this family so must have been adopted.

Stories spread quickly in an isolated village of five hundred people, and every story grows and evolves with each telling. Father says it took just two days for the story of a dog that rescued two children from freezing to death to become corrupted into a story of a dog that sniffed out the dead boy and tried to eat him. Let them talk. Let them stare. Let them think we are different. Beck says that is why she likes me, because I'm different. Or did she say I'm strange?

We get to the docks and I look nervously around for Beck. Of course, she would stay out of sight for now. Or she may not even be here. Down the weathered dock we go, and up to the *Bonnie Marie*. Father throws his backpack into the boat and walks along the edge of the dock inspecting every inch of the boat's hull. He caresses the smooth lines and the rough patches equally with his hands and eyes to search for offending bird poo, barnacles at the water line, or any sign of imperfection. There are plenty of imperfections – they were either intentional, acceptable, or on the to-be-fixed list. Mr. Dave would say that Father loves this boat so intensely because it is the only piece of Scotland that he has. We climb into the back of the boat, now cleaned of all the fishing gear, and we have a seat on the side benches. Father goes into the cabin and lights the kerosene heater he keeps in there for such occasions.

Jacob soon gets bored sitting on the boat and wanders down the dock and along the other piers. He has his slingshot with him and is taking random shots at wooden posts and flying gulls. Jacob is still by no means the best shot, but he is improving. I feel sorry for the birds, knowing it will not be long before a well-aimed pebble finds its way home and knocks the bird from its flight pattern and into the sea to become food for the very crabs whose family the gulls have been eating that same day.

I watch him as he continues along, stopping to pick up more small stones and waiting patiently for more birds to land nearby. A raven flies in and lands on a snow-covered post just five meters from Jacob. The raven dips its head down into the snow and brushes it back and forth sideways as if to wash its face. It looks toward Jacob and lets out a raucous call in his direction. A second raven lands on the next post down the short pier and joins in with the calls. I watch as Jacob reaches slowly into his pocket and extracts a pebble. He moves in slow motion, so as not to alert the ravens, and places the stone into the patch of leather on the slingshot. He brings the slingshot up to his eye level. The birds seem to understand what is about to take place.

I stop breathing and watch the tragedy unfold. The ravens flutter up into the air and back down, and up and down again – a pair of stringless yoyos. Jacob is trying to follow their movements with his hands. He pulls back slowly. Concentrating. My hands are clenched, and I find myself willing him to miss.

Just as he is about to release the stone, a figure, a shape really, or maybe a shadow, comes from nowhere and jumps on him, knocking him to the ground, causing him to shoot his weapon harmlessly into the sea. Jacob's attacker lands on top of him. He cries out. The two birds caw and are echoed by a dozen other ravens flapping in a giant blur around Jacob. Fleur lets out a whining growl, jumps over the side of the boat, and runs down the pier toward Jacob. I am sure my dog will rip into the conspiracy of ravens to save Jacob; instead, Fleur, covering the ground in three seconds, stands above Jacob and shows her menacing teeth, daring him to move.

The ravens fly circles around Jacob and Fleur, a flurry of feathers. Finally, they all fly off. In their place I suddenly see Beck, her arms spread out like a large flightless bird, and she calls out, "Fleur!" Immediately, Fleur backs off of Jacob and leaps into Beck's embrace, with tail wagging and sounds of pleasure.

Jacob jumps to his feet, looks confused, yells, "What are you doing, you stupid dog?" I can see anger build up in his face as he raises his slingshot up, aiming at Beck or Fleur. I am not sure which one he sees as more of a threat.

"JACOB, PUT THAT SLINGSHOT DOWN, NOW!" I jump in surprise, as the commanding voice of my father booms out from right behind me. He must have been watching the whole time. Father gets off of the boat, walks down to where Jacob, Beck, and Fleur are, picks up Jacob in one giant arm, and carries him back to the *Bonnie Marie.* He drops him on the floor of the cabin. I have never seen Father so angry. He yells into Jacob's face with a booming voice that is surely being heard by everyone on the island, "YOU DO NOT EVER AIM A WEAPON AT ANOTHER LIVING THING – ANIMAL OR HUMAN! DO YOU HEAR ME?"

Jacob stares at him shaking, tears running down his face.

"I *SAID*, DO YOU HEAR ME?"

His mouth moves, but nothing comes out. His head nods the slightest bit. He does not move from where Father dropped him. Father climbs over the portside, turns to me and says, "Keep your eye on your brother. Do not allow him to leave that cabin."

Father walks off and I turn my gaze to Jacob, who is

curled up on the cabin floor. He stares at me, or through me, with eyes that convey the darkness of an oncoming storm. If he still had his slingshot, I believe he would shoot Father in the head. Such is the hate that has been building up within him.

Father is walking toward Beck. There are once again a dozen ravens flocking around her, bringing up a commotion, landing momentarily and flapping into the air again with their frantic wings. Father raises his arms out to his side and the ravens all take off immediately. He is talking aloud to himself, or the ravens, or Beck. I cannot hear what is being said, just a low tone from my father and the guttural calls of the retreating birds. He picks up the slingshot from where Jacob dropped it, and walks back toward the boat, with Beck following a few steps back. He walks into the cabin, slams the door behind him, stands over Jacob and says in a low voice, "If I ever see you using this slingshot as a weapon, I will throw it forever away into the sea."

Beck waits for him to go back to his work, then steps into the boat and sits next to me. Fleur walks to her and noses her, tail wagging, receiving a scratch on the head and a squeeze around her big body. A raven flies low over our heads, calling out. Father looks up at it and follows up with a suspicious glance our way. He then goes back to work with Mr. Dave and we become invisible to him.

Beck looks at me and says quietly, "Sorry about your brother. It's just that I hate to see anyone hurting another animal. I really don't see where the fun of it is."

I ask, "So, what's with you and the ravens?"

Beck shrugs. "I don't know. They seem to like me. Maybe I used to be a raven or something in my past life.

I don't really believe that, but that's what my mom says."

As she speaks, the wind blows her hair to the side and up in a whirl of flowing black silk, which, for the briefest of moments, appears to me to be the sensuously moving feathers of the darkest raven. Then the illusion is gone, but the spell remains deep in her dark Innu eyes. I feel I could fall into those eyes and never return.

"I have a raven," I blurt out in a whisper. "Remember the one that flew into my window? I found it the next day. I don't think it could survive outside. I mean, it doesn't fly and its head is on kind of sideways."

Beck looks ashamed, and says, "We should have looked for it right away. I guess I just thought it was fine and flew off. I'd love to see your raven." She looks toward my father, completely engrossed in his project. She whispers, "I'm sorry I couldn't make it to your house in the past few days. My mom was sick, the flu or something, or maybe just depressed, and I had to stay with her."

Then her demeanor brightens up and she says, "Let's go touch the water. I'll bet that sea water is colder than ice." We leave the boat, walk down the dock, turn to our left to the rocky gray stones of the shoreline. As always, Fleur sticks to my side. We walk to a place where the water is calmer. Beck squats down, reaches out to the water, and dips her hand in. "Oh my God, that's cold!" She sticks her hand into her coat to warm it up. "I dare you to stick your face in there," she taunts me. "I will if you do." Her devious smile tells me that she knows I won't be able to resist her dare.

"You first," I say. She laughs and shakes her head. The challenge is on. I get into a half push-up position, my knees on the rocks, my hands at the very edge of the water, and my face hovering just above the surface, looking down at ten centimeters of water. I think, *this is going to be so cold. I hate it.* I feel Beck's hand on my head, hear her laughing loudly and uncontrollably, and she pushes my face down into the freezing water. I am overtaken by a shock of icy cold. The water goes up my unsuspecting nose, into my ears, and into my brain. I see a flash of light, and the image of a place much deeper into the ocean. Wrath rushes over me as I am again the *kraken* of my drowning vision. Instinctively, my arms flail in distress so my whole upper body falls flat into the water. It doesn't matter. I stop struggling and allow my arms to undulate in the shallows, or the depths, I am not sure where I am. My world turns blue, and all over again I think, *I am where I belong.* My mouth opens, letting in the water, and I release a loud and terrible noise. All my air is released. I spasm once, and feel my body being pulled up and out of the water. I get a vision of my father watching the *kraken* in the fishing net on the fateful day that Stephen Cloud was dragged into the water. I open my eyes to see that it is Beck pulling me back out of the water. I sit back onto the stones, in shock. And I stare. I feel panicked, as if I had woken suddenly from a nightmare.

"What were you doing?" says Beck. "It was like you were drowning and dreaming at the same time. I mean, where did you go?"

I look at Beck with wide eyes, "I don't know. I was drowning in the deep water again. I was … I was *changing.*" I am scared, confused, and feeling faint as the blood has drained from my face. And now, the cold is making me shiver. My head, neck and chest are all drenched, and the winter air is not being kind. "We should go back to the boat cabin and warm up."

We walk back around to the boat in silence. I can tell

both Beck and Fleur are worried about me. When we go into the small cabin, I see Jacob still sitting there, sulking and staring out the window. I can feel his anger, maybe even hatred, as he looks at us. As he looks at Fleur. Ignoring him, I remove my outer coat and sit in front of the heater to try and dry off the front of my sweater. We sit on either side of the heater staring at each other. Me, looking at the raven girl, and she, looking at the squid boy. Fleur sits at my side, keeping a watchful eye on Jacob.

Father enters the cabin, which is getting more crowded with each body. He opens up his pack with the lunch in it and sits down with us. "Had a bit of an accident, did you, Robert? Figured maybe if you got yourself sick, you wouldn't have to do so much work around the house?" He shows me a slight smile. It's funny that he feels he needs to encourage me to be more adventurous, but he needs to continually rein in Jacob and get him to be more responsible for his actions. "Jacob, will you be joining us for some lunch, or will you be out hunting up some ratty seagulls to eat?" He hands Jacob and I each some chunks of jerky, cheese, and apples. Jacob says nothing, takes some jerky and cheese, and returns to his window. He is always slow to get over his anger, and Father knows this, so he leaves Jacob alone. He makes no motion towards Beck, and I assume that it means he expects me to share my own lunch with her.

As the sun sinks lower and the temperatures with it, it is time to head back home. Beck and I get off the boat first and walk down the dock. Beck turns to me and softly whispers, "Thanks for an interesting afternoon." She places something in the palm of my hand, smiles, and walks towards her own house. I take what she handed me and shove it into my pocket for later. Jacob, Father, and I make our way home, each in our own thoughts.

As we walk back through the frozen world, I can no longer wait. I pull out what Beck secretly gave me. It is a small flat rock, smooth and rounded on the edges from a thousand years of tides. Painted on one side is a squid. On the other side, a raven.

29

Truth or Dare

December 11

Father has gone out this afternoon, taking Jacob with him. He told me I could stay home, but he didn't trust Jacob alone. Not that I couldn't watch Jacob, he told me, but Jacob has not been himself lately. Father says he has to keep my brother busy, or he will find trouble. I don't believe one needs to look far to find it. It's all good by me. I enjoy my time alone. Fleur-and-Edgar-time, I call it. Though today is not necessarily purely that. I am looking out the kitchen window and I see Beck walking along the road in front of the house. She goes down a hundred meters or so, then turns around and comes back the other way. She looks like a person trying to make up her mind to do something or go somewhere.

I open the door and give her a wave. "Hey Beck, where you going?"

"Well, right here I guess," she says with a smile.

"Home alone?" Not really a question, I don't guess. She walks up to the door and looks up at me. This is different. Beck is taller than me by a good inch but standing below the level of the front door threshold, I now stand above her. I like the little juxtaposition.

"You want to come in and see Edgar the raven? No one will be home for a little while. But we have to keep an eye out. And if my father comes home while you're here, you'll need to sneak out the back door." I feel kind of uneasy and dishonest. Father took Jacob with him, but here I am being the bad one. Though, bad for doing what? I can't see what was wrong in letting Beck into the house, but in spite of him not showing any disapproval of her on the boat, I know Father would be displeased.

Beck comes inside, takes off her coat, and she and Fleur go through their ritualistic greeting. Beck looks over at Edgar. She goes up to him and Edgar immediately becomes more animated than he has been all day. He lets out a loud *caw* and follows it up with some awkward head-bobbing. He hops down to his lower perch and back up to the top one. Beck grins at him and releases a laugh, a ray of sunshine on a rainy day. We sit down on the sofa, snuggling up with Fleur, watching Edgar from afar. It feels good, natural, almost like we are a group of little animals in our den, which I guess we are.

Beck asks about Jacob. I start in about Father not trusting Jacob on his own. Beck replies that she really doesn't trust him either. "He has a meanness in him that scares me," she says.

After a bit we sit quietly, and then Beck says, "You wanna play truth-or-dare?" An impish smile comes across her face.

"Um, how do you play?"

"Really? You've never played before? Well, I guess if you never leave your house … I mean, you wouldn't really play truth-or-dare with your brother. So, basically, we take turns asking each other questions. Either you have to answer the question truthfully, or you can choose to do whatever you are dared to do."

"I don't get it," I say. "Why *wouldn't* I answer truthfully?"

Beck looks at me with a bigger smile yet. "Alright, I'll ask first. Do you like me? I mean, as in girlfriend-boyfriend like."

Ah, now I get it. It is like a *revolution* against the way grown-ups speak to each other without saying what they really mean.

I think she already knows the answer, but maybe she doesn't. Am I supposed to ask her the same question? She's waiting for an answer. I take a deep breath. "Yes. I think you're cute and fun and maybe a little scary – in a good way."

With that answer, Beck moves a little closer to me on the sofa. For the first time, I see her blush and actually look a little shy. This surprises me and gives me room for my own question. "Am I the first boy you ever kissed?" Immediately, I want to un-ask the question, because I am not sure I want to know the answer.

All pretense of being shy dissipates with her answer. "You are. And you are the second boy I will kiss." With that, she leans closer yet and gives me a quick kiss on the cheek. Now it is my turn to blush. She reaches down and lightly touches my fingers, looks me in the eyes, and asks me another question.

"How did you change? You know, when you died?" Now I consider taking the dare. What will she think?

I am crazy. I am a liar. I had a dream. She would not believe me. And if she did believe me, she might run. I now realize how much I do not want to lose her friendship.

"Dare."

"Chicken." She looks up at the ceiling for creative inspiration. Her gaze slips to the window overlooking the backyard, and her eyes return to me. Her dark eyes, raven's eyes, stir something inside me. "Okay. Your dare – go outside, take off all your clothes, and then put them back on."

"No way. I'm not doing that."

"You have to. That's how the game is played." She starts laughing, head held back like a bird. Like a raven. "Or you could choose truth."

I sit next to her. Touching her. Not wanting to move from this spot and not wanting to lose this moment. And definitely not wanting to undress outside, in front of her. I close my eyes and breathe to steady myself. I did not realize how the telling of this story might affect me.

"Okay, truth." A deep breath. "I keep trying to forget what happened, but it won't leave me alone. I changed. It changed me. Or maybe the world changed. I find myself getting angry very easily. My moods switch just like that. I don't know what to do with that. I don't really remember being thrown into the water, but I do remember the shock of the ice-cold sea engulfing me. I remember all the colors turned to shades of blue and gray. I became aware of all the living things in the sea around me. I was filled with rage and hate for the world. I still felt a little bit like me, but I also felt like a creature that had been around for a thousand years. My body became fluid. I could barely hang onto this world that we know. It was

like I could feel Robert slipping away. It was more than just a *feeling* that was different. My whole body had actually turned into a monster. A giant, angry, squidly-octopus monster. A *kraken*. Then I was pulled out of the water, and I was instantly myself again. It was a dream, except it wasn't. It didn't evaporate like dreams do. Those feelings are still deep inside me. Does that make sense? You must think I'm some kind of a freak." I look at Beck, waiting for a response. Fearing her reaction.

"I knew it!" A genuinely ecstatic response. "The first time I saw you, I *felt* you. I told you before, I thought you were an animal person. Now I am positive about it." She pauses, as if to remember something, "And those times on the beach, before you knew me–" She stops abruptly. Looks away.

"You mean the laundromat. That's the first time you saw me, right?" Beck continues to avoid my eyes. She says nothing. My eyebrows furrow up in confusion. I can't recall seeing her, ever, before that day. Now it's my turn. "Truth or dare – When was the first time you saw me?"

Beck is having a hard time answering me. She looks around, gets up from the couch, stares out the window into the backyard.

"Well?" I ask. "Would you rather do a dare?"

She continues to look out the window and says, "It was out there in your backyard. Your brother and you were playing in the tide pools. Summer solstice. Do you remember?"

I shake my head, thinking back to that day. "I didn't see anyone that day. Wait, there was that man on the rocks. The one who tried to drown me. He was drunk, or high, and he was yelling bad things at me. And we saw the giant squid arm, and maybe something else in the water. Were you there watching from the road?"

"I was around. You saw me, but I don't think you recognized me. I thought you were very brave, but very frightened. I guess if you are not frightened of something, then facing it would not be an act of bravery, would it?"

Were there other times?"

By now, Beck has turned back from the window and returned to the sofa, sitting close enough to touch me. "And in October. In the same spot. Do you remember the seal woman on the beach? The rotting corpse of the woman who turned out to be nothing more than a seal? And remember the raven that led you to the dead woman?"

I remember the frightening sensation that came over me. Now, realizing that somehow Beck was watching all this and confirming the existence of the dead woman, the sensation is stronger. Goosebumps cover my entire body. "How could you know all this?"

"I was passing nearby. I saw. I visit that beach and a little beyond to escape the other people of the Inlet. No one ever notices me when I keep to the fringes of town. It's like I'm invisible."

"I wish I could be invisible," I say.

Beck continues on, barely whispering, "And then you saw me one month later, you were sitting on the rocks near the boats. You looked very sad."

Suddenly, Edgar starts screaming out loudly and jumping up and down. Beck looks over at him and nervously says, "I have to go. Look for me when you think I'm not around or when you're alone. There is a good chance I'll be there." With that, she abruptly gets up and runs out the door.

30

My Mother's Mother

December 13

"So, John wanted to get rid of you for a couple days, did he?" My grandmother, Alice, gives me a wink. I've always called her Alice. She says that she doesn't like being called Grandmother, it makes her sound far older than she is. I guess she's a young grandmother at forty-eight. Father says that it is a sign of disrespect to call her Alice, but I think it would be more disrespectful to call her something other than what she prefers. So here I am, at Alice's house for a couple of days. I brought Fleur with me because Father says that dog would be howling like a *Witiko* if I left without her. Edgar, I left at home where Father promised to take care of him every day. I think Father has grown fond of that bird.

"Alice? Why did Father want me to stay with you? Jacob said it was so they could have a break from me and my dog." I think about what I said, and I quickly add,

"It's not that I don't want to be here visiting you, it's just that it's been a couple years since I did stay over."

Alice smiles, "Let's just say that you are the closest thing I have to your mother. It's true, Jacob has Marie's face, but you have what is far more important. You have her spirit in you. When I hear stories about you from your father, when I listen to you speak, I am reminded of Marie. Of course, you're not Marie, you're a special soul in your own way. I just hope you can stand being with your Gran Alice for a couple of days."

I arrived an hour ago and stowed my small backpack, with a couple changes of clothes and toothbrush, away into the spare bedroom. The house, like all houses here, is small, with just enough room to live. I like it. It allows us to be together all the time, other than bedtime. And without Jacob, it gives me and Fleur our own room. Fleur makes herself at home. Alice said a proper dog makes itself at home anywhere her owner sleeps.

Father made sure that Alice knew about the sunset/sunrise rule, though I would think everyone knew of this. When he mentioned it, she had a strange look on her face. It is hard for me to explain her expression. Wonder? Surprise? I ask her, "Alice? Why is it that Father worries about the in-bed-at-sunset rule? I mean, I see some people out in the street in the middle of the night, Father himself included, and the monsters don't get to them. I too was up at night once, because Father called me on the rescue team for those three kids who had gone missing, and nothing really happened to me."

Alice closes her eyes for a long moment. I don't think she will answer, but finally she opens her eyes and says, "Your father has many reasons for such a rule. It is all about keeping you and your brother safe. In Jacob's case, well, I have seen him on the street with some of the boys who might invite trouble. They are the young ones who feel they have no future, quit school, breathe in the gasoline for a quick escape from the squalor of this rock. John tries his best to keep that boy off the street and on the path to betterment. To rise above this place." She stops and thinks about what she said. "It is an uphill fight for that one, it is. As for your father, he has demons of his own that run through him. His anguish for the loss of your mother is an intolerable pain in his heart. He blames himself for whatever happened out on that boat. There are people who have heard him roaring and howling from within the walls of your house at night. As I am certain you know all too well. There *is* a monster – it has taken control of John's heart. The more superstitious of the village say that John actually turns into a monster at night. They talk of the *kraken* that lives on his arm. It is all nonsense, as your mother would have attested to. She always said John had the biggest heart in all of Newfoundland. Maybe so, but I always said he was the biggest fool to move here in the first place." She stops talking for a bit to sip some coffee and to refill my hot cider.

"And me? What is he saving me from?"

"You, Robert. He sees you as all that is good and all that is possible in this world. He keeps you at home and within his protective arms because he fears this diseased little village will eat you up and destroy your innocence. You are a special one, like your mother. Maybe you are now at the age that you are just discovering some … different qualities you possess. I believe the real reason your father sent you here to stay with me, though he may not be completely conscious of it, is for me to open your eyes in ways he may not ever be able to."

"What do you mean?" I am filled with a mix of confusion and curiosity.

Alice gets up to start on lunch preparation. "We have some time together ahead of us to further explore this. Now go wash your hands and help me get our lunch together. I hear you are getting pretty handy in the kitchen. That's a good thing. Most men are not good for anything other than throwing a slab of meat on the grill."

* * *

Outside, the sun rides low on the horizon as I take Fleur out for one last walk before bedtime. Sunset will be at 3:28 p.m., just twenty minutes from now. As I watch Fleur sniff around the unfamiliar yard that is nestled between four slapped-together government houses, I think about our morning conversation. Alice likes to talk a lot, but I noticed she never really did answer my question – *What is Father protecting me from at night?* No, she skirted right around that one. With all the other secrets that have been laid bare, how much worse could the secrets of my own life be? Like Alice said, I guess there is time in the next couple of days.

Back inside the house, I gather my necessities for the night. "Goodnight Alice."

Alice shakes her head and smiles, "Goodnight young Robert. I think we will talk tomorrow, and you will not be as young as you are today." With that, I make my way to the back bedroom with my dog at my heels. I lie in bed with a bedside lamp and a book. I watch from my window as the sun takes its final plunge into the hills of mainland Labrador. And I read myself to sleep within two pages.

***

At two in the morning, I jump awake with a startle. I am soaking wet. A dream flies from my memory like seafoam on a wind-driven ocean wave. I was filled with rage. I fell into the sea and drowned. And breathed. And changed. Screaming. A flash of a face, a woman. Beck? No, not Beck, but a stranger. A woman, in her thirties maybe, with Beck's face.

I sit up and put my feet on the floor without thinking. I gasp and quickly pull them up. Fleur is standing in the center of the small room emitting a quiet growl. Her teeth exposed in a warning snarl. "Fleur, it's me." She relaxes her stance and tucks her tail with a slow whine. I reach out to her as she sniffs my wet pajamas. I smell of … seaweed? Of pee? Of *peeweed*, I laugh to myself. But the laugh is filled with nervous fear. Embarrassment creeps into me, and I strip off my clothes, throw them on a chair in the room, and put on a new pair of underwear. The bed is wet as well, so I pull the covers over to the far half of the bed and hope the wetness will dry by morning.

***

With the sunlight kissing the new day, after a marathon sleep I awake to commotion in the backyard. Three large ravens land on the ground just outside my window in search of treasures. Mostly, they are raiding the compost pile to peck up any tasty morsels that Alice would have thrown out there. Though she rarely puts out anything of much value, as she prefers to use all her food scraps for tomorrow's soup. One of the ravens finds a momentary interest in Fleur's poo, but quickly sees it for what it is.

As I watch the ravens, I think about Beck. I won't see her or be able to leave her a note, or receive a note from her, as long as I am here at Alice's. I understand Beck's obsession with ravens, having, like my father, grown fond of Edgar. Edgar and his sideways head. The birds in the yard flap their way into the air and perch on the lower branches of the lone balsam fir in the center of the lot. One of them puffs out its neck and dips its head up and down, spitting out a number of garbled sounds. I listen, imagining that I hear actual words being formed. Suddenly, as clearly as spoken by a person, I hear, for the second time, my name scratched out of a raven's gullet, "*Robert.*" My heart does a funny flip-flop and an icy chill runs through my body. I hadn't imagined it. It is like that first time down on the beach. "*Robert, rah, rah.*" The talking raven flies to the window and flaps wildly as it tries to get a foothold on the outside sill. Finally, it has to give up this fruitless attempt and flutters to the ground along with its more familiar harsh raven calls.

Then I remember the previous night's dreams. I sit at the edge of the bed, afraid to look out at the raven any longer. It continues to call. I press my head against the window and look down to the ground. From this angle I cannot see the raven, but I see something. A triangle? My brows pinch together as I try to comprehend what it is I am looking at. It slowly registers. A triangle composed of a bent arm. The elbow making the apex of the triangle. The arm has no clothing, and the skin is white as snow. I fall back, my legs like rubber, as useless as a fish on land.

"Are you okay in there?" Alice calls from the front room. She opens the bedroom door and Fleur jumps between the two of us. My dog will not let my grandmother near me. "Robert, what is it? You're pale as a ghost. Get some clothes on before you get yourself sick."

I slowly stand up and slip on clean pants and a sweatshirt. "There's someone out there. On the ground." Alice tries to come to the window, but Fleur gives her a warning growl. I motion for Fleur to come onto the bed so Alice can come in. As she steps up to the window, I get this sudden sickening feeling that I imagined the whole thing. Like the seal woman. It's a seal, or a dog. *Please, let it be an animal of some sort.* My heart pounds.

"Oh, dear God," says Alice. She hurries out toward the back door. I find my resolve and follow right behind her. We step outside where we are confronted by a naked woman, contorted and lying face down on the ground, crammed against the side of the house, her skin frosted white as if the blood had been drained out of her. Her hair is frozen against her back. I suddenly feel like throwing up. I run back into the house; the icy numbness in my feet remind me that I neglected even to throw on some shoes before going out. My grandmother follows me in, shaking her head.

"I'd best call the police. Robert, finish getting dressed, and don't go anywhere near that body. And keep your dog inside for now." She picks up the phone and dials as I return to the bedroom to throw on some socks and shoes.

I hear Alice on the phone explaining what had happened. "That's right, naked and frozen. Looks like she was all wet, like she was swimming or something." A long pause ensues, followed by, "No, I don't know how she got here. She must have come into the yard last night and died right there." Another pause. "Well, okay Frank, but hurry up, it's so horrible." She hangs up the phone and paces around the house, unsure of what to do.

"I need to take my dog out to pee. I'll take her out the front door," I tell Alice as I head to the front.

"Yes," says Alice, "I'll go with you to wait for Frank."

It doesn't take five minutes for officer Frank to arrive. I guess that is one of the advantages of living in a small town. He and Alice walk around the side of the house to inspect the body. I take Fleur back into the house, wishing to avoid seeing the dead woman again. Eventually, Frank and Alice come into the house. Alice fixes some coffee, and they sit down at the kitchen table.

Frank says, "I guess I'll have to call the coroner's office. He'll be wanting to see this one. And the chief, she won't be happy. No hurry though, the body won't be going anywhere soon." He sighs, rubs his face as if he'd been up all night, and says, "I'll tell you, Alice, this town is going to shit. It's been two years since those news people came in with their cameras and their reporters, sharing our substance abuse and suicide epidemic with the entire world. And how did that help us? We are just as bad off now as ever. Worse, I think."

Alice sits down with two cups of coffee, and says, "The whole world was laughing at us. As if *we* were responsible for moving our people out here with next to nothing to our names. I told my Marie she should have gone to Scotland with John. Her life would have been better there. But just like everyone else here, her family and community were far more important." Alice shakes her head slowly, holds her cup up to her mouth, but puts it down again. "Is it true what they are saying about moving us?"

Frank leans back and says, "They've been talking about it. I heard they want to pick up this whole village and move us over to Sango Pond. A lot of discussion on it anyway."

I get this picture of them literally picking up all the houses and roads and stores and somehow moving them inland. Of course, I know they really mean to simply build a new town. Maybe this time they will think to put in sewers and running water. A realization sets over me: this must be why Father wants to take us back to Scotland, to get out before everything is gone.

Frank stands up, "I'd better put in some calls. I sure appreciate the coffee. I guess you might want to put on another pot before everyone descends upon your little backyard. Maybe you can sell tickets and make a buck." He gives her a wry smile and picks up the phone.

***

Everyone has come and gone by lunchtime. Photos were taken. The body was removed. Careful inspection of the grounds was undertaken. I stayed mostly in my room calming Fleur from her unease with the parade of strangers coming and going. Throughout the morning, I caught snippets of conversation flowing from Frank, Alice, another policeman, a woman called "The Chief" who I assumed is the tribal chief, and a number of others whose jobs seemed somewhat important. The question of why this woman was naked and wet was the biggest mystery. Did she come from the inlet? Did she come from

the shower? Did she come here on her own or did someone put her here? And who was she? One man said she just moved here earlier this year, maybe had a daughter here years ago who died? Someone else offered that she might have been staying with the Buckthorn family – he heard they had some off-island family visiting.

As to the cause of death? Suicide could never be ruled out, but it seemed unlikely. Substance abuse overdose? More likely. Murder? Possibly, but murder was not common here. And what of the circular bruises on her torso? Perhaps from lying on, or being pushed against, the golf ball-sized stones under her body?

As the men and women did their work, I occasionally looked out past them to see a lone raven perched in the tree. It did not seem concerned with the goings on. It called out, flew off, returned, and peered across the yard and over everyone's head to direct its gaze into my window. It watched me with concern. It did not make any sounds other than normal raven calls. Not even a *Nevermore*. But it looked at me as if to say, *I know what happened here, and so do you.*

I sit back on the bed and grab my good luck tokens that lay on my nightstand – my lighter, and the stone that Beck gave me. I compare the *kraken* on the lighter with the hand-painted squid on the stone. I wonder if Beck meant the squid to be a simple depiction of a *kraken*. She didn't seem surprised to hear me tell my story of becoming a *kraken*. It made sense to her. Everything seems to make sense to her. She is the raven who accepts what is presented to her. I flick the lighter once to produce a flame. I watch it for a while, and Fleur too watches it. Curiosity gets the most of her and she tries to sniff the flame, only to let out a little yip from the unexpected heat. The yip summons Alice into the room. She comes in and Fleur allows her to sit on the bed.

"Strange morning, eh?" A pause, then she adds, "What do you think happened?"

I shrug once, "Who do you think she is?"

"No one seems to know." Alice looks down at my hands and sees my lighter and my stone. "What do you have there?"

I show her my treasures. "The lighter is from my father. He says the *kraken* will always protect me. And the stone, a friend gave it to me."

Alice takes each one in turn and examines them closely. "There's an interesting combination – a *kraken* and a raven." I ask what she means, and she says, "Well, the *kraken* is a symbol of intense strength and fierce rage. It is also a secretive creature that does not like to show itself – figuratively or literally speaking. I feel it is a proper sign for John, your father – he hides his feelings and keeps rage and anguish just below skin level. When I first saw his tattoo, it told me everything about him. Though I don't know if the *kraken* suits *your* personality so much. The raven, on the other hand, is inquisitive, intelligent, wise. They see the world for what it is, and they are not concerned over how others perceive them. You are much more a young raven."

I think this over as I turn the stone around in my hand. "I think my friend Beck is a raven-girl. She talks to ravens, dances with them, and any time I am with her, there is a raven nearby. She is the one who painted that stone."

Alice says, "Beck, short for Rebecca? I don't know her. Does she live here?"

"Yes, she moved up here this past year with her mom.

I think her mom was from here before. Me and Beck sometimes hang out at the boat or …" I drop of my sentence, worried that I'd said too much.

Alice nods her head slowly as if thinking about who she could be. "Listen Robert, I know your father doesn't like you boys talking to other people, but you need to socialize with others. It is good that you found a friend in Beck. I would like to meet her sometime. Not to worry, it will be our secret."

In a village that has no secrets, I think to myself. But I trust Alice. "She says I am an animal person. What do you think that means?"

"You are much like Marie. She could communicate with most any animal. Not really as in *talking* to the animals, more like a matter of matching her spirit with theirs. It is a gift that is possessed by only the greatest medicine-people. When your mother was just a small child and we were staying inland, following the caribou, we could not find Marie. She had toddled out on her own and was missing for an hour, which was an eternity for a mother in search of her three-year-old. We finally came upon her beneath a rock overhang low to the ground. She was laying there with a mother wolf and her two pups. You can imagine, I was scared to death for her. When we approached, the wolf lowered her head and bared her teeth at us as if she were protecting Marie. Much like your dog does when I come to your door. After a minute, or was it an hour, Marie opened her sleepy eyes, saw us, smiled and giggled, crawled out of the shallow den, and walked back over to us. Nobody had ever seen such a thing.

"Marie was charmed. And she was like that with any animal she came upon. But the animal with whom she most clearly shared a common spirit with was the caribou. Kind and gentle, with a need to be near family. Such was the way of your mother, and completely unaware that she was different, in regard to her ways with animals, from other people. I see this same nature in you, Robert. Only, for your mother, this spiritual connection ended when she was inflicted with the atrocity that spread up and down this coast. Alcohol and substance abuse hit Marie hard, and she became a different person. She was fortunate to have been able to pass her animal nature off to one of her sons. You need to take this gift seriously and respect it. It has been passed through our people for as long as we have been a people. You took the outer shell from your father, a Scotsman for sure, but you have the heart of the Innu." Alice stops to think. "I can't say where this will all take you. Like anything in life, you will find it is a long journey to see where your heart will lead. I will tell you what I told your mother: keep your eyes open, and answers will reveal themselves in good time. Well, that sounds like something I once read in a fortune cookie." Alice takes a deep breath, "Quite a lot to hear, I know. You can always come talk to me if you need some direction. I have a feeling that you will do alright with this world."

"Alice, what about Jacob? He says he's a polar bear. What does that mean?"

Alice thinks for a moment. "A polar bear must survive against all odds in an arctic landscape. Determination, perseverance, and strength to keep others at bay. I suppose Jacob will need all these attributes to stand up in a world that tests him."

* * *

I've spent most the day thinking about what my grandmother told me. She put on a coat of assuredness to Beck's words. I am an animal person. I have the spirit of an animal. But what animal? Alice says a raven. Beck says a squid. And I fear it is the *kraken*. I live in dreams of rage and fear. My worst dreams are met by dead bodies. Fleur seems to think I have the heart of a dog.

What does Father think? He thinks I had best get all my schoolwork done while I am here, so I should rest my preoccupying thoughts and open my mathematics book.

31

Fleur's Fury

December 15

Two nights at Alice's and it is time to go back home. Alice has prepared a big breakfast, *to hold you over till the next time you visit, Robert.* I could see that she was sad to see me go. I guess she is lonely here. I guess she misses my mother. I would not be truthful if I were to say that I won't miss our time together. There is a warmth in Alice's house that has a different flavor from my own house. The aroma of winter soup constantly hangs in the air. The scent of bed covers that have hung out in the short December sun to dry. The thick, soft area rugs that are scattered on the otherwise cold floors. And the array of photographs that are pasted on every wall throughout the house – we have no more than three pictures in our place. I am comforted by the omnipresence of Alice, always within reaching distance. I am ashamed to say it, but it has been quite nice to have time away from Jacob

– to be the only focus of this family of two.

I pack my bag with my few belongings, put on all my winter layers, gather up Fleur, and I hug Alice goodbye. That's it! That's what's missing at home! Large, engulfing hugs. Just before I step outside to walk home, Alice grabs me by the shoulders, gazes intensely at me and says, "Remember, should you ever need to talk about what we spoke of yesterday, please stop by your old Gran Alice's and we will talk further. And as for the dead woman in the backyard, I'll make sure John learns of more details as they are known, and he can pass them on to you."

I nod in a way that I hope looks grown-up, and I step out into winter. The skies are gray. The day is fierce. The stabbing knives of cold try their best to breach my layers of warmth. My face freezes instantly, but I am not bothered. I am alive. The screaming wind in my ears is the soundtrack to my hometown. This is Labrador, and I am part of it. For some reason I feel more alive today than I remember feeling in a long time. The events of the past day have given me new inspiration and new fears – the open discussion of the animal spirits, the mix of the dream, the body, and the raven, have all raised my perceptions of this place. And of course, I am looking forward to seeing Beck soon. And now, this one-mile trek through these frigid streets is welcoming to me. I look around and see no one out here today. All souls tucked away in the warmth of their cozy homes. Loaves of bread in their ovens. A fire in their wood stoves. A stark contrast to the unforgiving harshness of winter out here. Fleur's thick fur is sticking out everywhere, giving the effect of a pin cushion as the wind pelts her from behind. The dog doesn't seem to mind. As always, she is invigorated by this weather.

I approach our house, and something seems off. I stop at the end of the driveway and try to put my finger on it. Fire. Or rather, the lack of it. There is no scent of a warm fireplace, no smoke sifting from the stove pipe. It looks almost deserted. Father would never let the fire die in the winter. Maybe he and Jacob slept in. Maybe they aren't at home. *Or maybe they were touching the floor at night.* I stand and stare at the cold house, suddenly afraid. Fleur stands by me, filled with anxiety as well, whining and sitting down, standing up, sitting down. There is definitely something off. Fleur's whining turns into a low growl. Stepping out from around the side of the house and stopping in front of our entranceway, just ten meters in front of me, is a man.

Billy Cloud.

"Good morning, Robert. How's our Bobby Boy today?"

I say nothing.

"Ol' Johnny took your brother out to do some camping at some old hunting cabin for a couple of days. Guess he's going to teach him to be a man or something. Crazy-ass Scotsman to go out in this weather. He told me to watch over you while he was out." The man was listing to the left. I couldn't move. "Well, come on in the house, son; it's colder than a mermaid's pussy out here." The man opens our front door and steps inside. He holds the door, signaling for me to follow. Fleur is increasingly upset. She tugs on her leash one way and then the other. "Come on Bobby, it's not getting any warmer out there." The man is now half yelling. I feel the strength of Fleur's tense body as she struggles against my grip.

A pair of ravens land on the driveway between the doorway and myself. They begin dancing in circles, calling out. *Robert. Robert.* One by one, more ravens join in. They call out, louder and louder. Soon, a dozen large birds are flapping their wings in front of me.

"I said, get in here Bobby Boy, your father has entrusted me to your care, Goddammit." The rage-filled man takes three slow steps toward me.

There are now at least twenty ravens blocking my vision of the house, flying about in a frenzy. *Robert. Rah, rah, Robert*, they call out. Wings brush my face, and the sounds of the frenzied calls are disorienting. The angry man is now within a meter of me.

And another voice. It is Beck's, but it's inside my head. "The man is a monster. Face him." I release Fleur's leash as a hand grabs me and pulls me forward. Screams. Snarls. My own arms wrap around the force of the man who is now falling on me. I am suffocating under the weight of his body, the thickness of the ravens, the powerful heaving muscles of Fleur, and the voices smothering my own thoughts. I am drowning. Now, I am filled with rage. I yell out, my own savagery mixing with the screams of the man. Mixing with Fleur's fury. Almost inseparable. I cannot breathe. Something is pressed against my mouth. I bite down. Warmth spreads over my face and down my neck.

A blink of time passes. "Get up, Robert. You have to get up." I feel so cold. I am lying on the ground with Beck looking down at me. Fleur is licking my face and whining. Beck continues, "Robert, are you okay? We have to get rid of him."

"What?" It takes me a second to return to the moment. "Where did *you* come from?" A rush of panic, "The man!" I suddenly feel as if I am Dorothy from *The Wizard of Oz* and none of this is real.

"It's okay. He jumped on you and Fleur attacked him. He's dead, Robert." I look beside me at the body of Billy Cloud, dressed in a hooded jacket covered in the blood that seeped out through the layers of clothes that concealed the multiple dog bites on his torso. There is a strange bite mark of sorts on his neck that is still pouring out blood. How much blood could a body hold, I wonder. His face is still recognizable, but barely. I look at my own coat, splattered in blood. I don't think it is my blood.

I look helplessly at Beck, "What do we do?"

"Look," she says, "we need to get this man out of here. Hide him. If people find out that Fleur killed him, they will shoot her."

"But she was only trying to save me," I plead.

"Doesn't matter. They'll shoot her. Now, we have to move fast before anyone comes by, or before your father comes home."

I think to myself, *where to hide a body? The body of a monster.*

The sea.

Monster beach would be not only fitting, but the clearest path in which to drag him. I grab his wrists and pull. The man is heavy. I can pull him just a few inches at a time and find I have to rest. After two meters, I am sweating. I can't do it. Fleur is pacing, filled with energy ready to burst. An idea blossoms in my head. I run around the house to the tool shed. I get some old ropes that are hanging on the wall.

When I get back with the ropes, I find that Beck has disappeared.

I go to the body and tie two slipknots around the man's chest, just under his armpits. One rope, I tie to my own waist, and the other I tie to Fleur's harness. I recall that Fleur was initially raised to be a sled dog and I hope she still remembers how it all works. I hold on to her leash to help guide her along with me. Together we are able to pull the body to the side of our land and away from the road toward the secluded beach.

The ice on the rocks makes it hard to keep balance and get a grip, but at the same time it makes for an easier slide for the body. Within twenty minutes, we have created a blood-spotted trail from our driveway to the beach. I stand at the shore and I am struck with a bad thought. I will have to drag the man into the icy waters until he can float away. The good news, if there is any good news in this predicament, is that the tide is about to turn, and with it will go Billy Cloud. Both Fleur and I very reluctantly step into the sea. Once the man is in a foot of water, I untie my dog, as she will not be of much use in the deeper water when she has to swim. I find I can now easily tow the man out. I get up to my waist before untying myself, and I shove the man and his ropes out as hard as I can into the sea. I am so cold I could scream, but I force myself to wait before getting out. I must make sure the tide takes its secrets out to rest.

I run back to the front yard to try to make snow balls out of the bloody snow left behind and I throw this snow far off toward the beach. Just as I am getting the site as cleaned up as possible, the gray skies above whisper softly to me in a flurry of giant snowflakes to cover up the remains of the incident. I run inside the house and strip off my clothes. I see that the blood on my coat, as well as the dog's coat, had washed off in the sea. I did read somewhere that blood stains come off with cold water. I throw on a dry pair of pants and a sweater, run back downstairs, and get out my Zippo to start a fire in the wood stove. Fleur and I sit on the floor in front of the stove and wait for the heat to relieve and relax us. And now I have time to reflect on what happened, and I can't stop crying hysterically.

Alice's words come back to me. *You are much more a young raven. You are transforming. I think it is time to tell you about yourself. I told you yesterday that you are a special boy and I felt I needed to open your eyes to help you understand. Your friend Beck is very perceptive. You are an animal person. Just look at you with your dog. Dave tried and tried to find a home for that dog, but it wouldn't accept anyone. Finally, your father agreed to let you take the dog on as a challenge to both of you. And there you are, no challenge at all. Robert, you are of the animal world.*

Two hours pass. I have not moved. I hear the front door open and, for a horrific moment, I am sure it is Billy Cloud returning from his death. But no, in come Father and Jacob. Both shake off the snow that has been falling heavily. Both look angry. Father shouts out, "And don't let me see you doon here till morning, lad." Jacob stomps up the stairs with eyes that could burn holes through the world. Father carries his cooler into the kitchen, comes back out into the living room, and sees me.

"Robert. I didn't know you were sitting there. I see you warmed up the house for us and put some water on to heat up. You're a good lad, you are. I'm sorry we're back so late. We were at the boat and I had a little problem with a vanishing wee lad. Good time for you, eh?"

He knows. Everybody knows. How could they not? I look down, unable to meet his gaze. "I, I thought, I mean, you were on the boat? I thought you went camping with Jacob at some hunting cabin."

My father looks questioningly at me. "Now where

would you get that idea? Did Alice tell you that? I swear, that woman gets some crazy notions in her head. Who would go camping in this weather?" I shrug, grateful for the misdirection. "I trust you had a nice time with your grandmother?"

"There was a dead lady in the backyard yesterday morning. No one knows who she was or what happened," I blurt out.

"Oh aye, so I've heard," my father answers. "A right bit of a mystery, it is. They say she had no alcohol or drugs in her blood. Considering the circumstances, I am willing to put my money on murder victim." He pauses, rubs his hand through his beard, and says, "This village has gone bad. It was built on a cursed rock if you ask me. The sooner we get off this rock, the better." Father turns and goes upstairs to change. I can feel Jacob brooding more and more heavily the farther up the stairs Father gets.

32

Jacob's Story

December 15

It's three o'clock. Time to take Fleur out one last time before heading to bed. I step out into the backyard with my heart pounding. Firstly, I am afraid I will see Billy Cloud's bloody body washed up on our shoreline. Secondly, I am hopeful that I might see some sign of Beck. I scan the water's edge and feel the relief pour over me when there is no body. I walk around to the wood pile, pick up a couple small logs in hopes of finding a note that isn't there. I am anxious being outside, and Fleur senses it. She goes to the door to signal that it is time to go inside. I open the door and she runs past me and upstairs to our bed. I stop at Edgar's perch to make sure he has enough food. He watches me with his head nearly upside-down. He emits a soft cooing sound and I reach up and scratch deep into his neck feathers.

"Two minutes, boys." My father's voice booms out

to warn us of the oncoming sunset. I run up the stairs, gather some things, and jump into bed. Jacob is slumped into the corner of the bed, hugging a pillow, and looking like an approaching storm cloud on the horizon.

"I hate him," says Jacob. "I wish he were dead instead of our mother."

I don't know how to respond, filled as I am with the day's events and their horrid impressions of panic and terror, so I sit quietly on the foot end of the bed and calm myself by picking through a small bowl of stones I have collected on the beach. I look closely at each stone that belongs to this collection. Each one is gray, like my world, with one or more thread-thin white lines wrapping around it. Beck told me once that these were wishing stones. She said to *hold one tightly in your hand, hold your hand to your heart, and concentrate on what you want most.* At first glance, each of the six stones are the same. But as one looks more closely, one realizes that they are vastly different. Which stone is Jacob, and which stone is me? I put the stones down and light my lantern on my bedside table as the room fades to darkness.

Abruptly, Jacob speaks, "I'm going to run away. Me and two other boys decided we should go on an adventure. Get away from this stupid place. Get away from Father. He's a monster, Robert. And he'll end up killing us both. He'll eat us one night, or he'll lock us in this house until we starve." Jacob is speaking with a strange darkness in his eyes. "My friend, Gary, says he knows the guy that runs the ferry, and we could maybe get down as far as St. John's. We could catch the early morning ferry and leave before anyone knows we're gone."

"Well, when are you thinking of leaving?" I ask. "I don't think it's a very good idea, especially in the winter."

"Shut up. What do you know?" He is getting angry now. I've never heard Jacob say shut up to anyone. Mrs. Sally told us it was a bad word. Jacob gives me a suspicious look like he wished he hadn't told me his secret. "You better not tell Father what I told you." Is he pleading with me, or is he threatening me? I can't tell.

"I won't," I say in a quiet, disapproving voice. And it is true: I won't tell on him. He's eight. He's making it all up. He'll forget about it tomorrow. I let some time go by before asking why Father is so mad at him.

"I told you, he's a monster. I just wanted to play with my friends. It isn't fair, Robert, all the other kids get to go out and play together. Why do we have to stay home all the time?" Tears of frustration start leaking from his eyes. He rolls over and hides his face in his pillow. I watch his chunky little body heaving with each breath. Then he gives out a muffled yell, "I HATE HIM!" At that exact same time, I hear another loud guttural yell. That of my father from somewhere within the house. Fleur gives out a howl. From downstairs come Edgar's full-out calls. The house is alive with madness. I lie down with my pillow over my ears and wait for the night to crawl on by us.

33

Father's Eye

December 16

I have become invisible. Which kind of suits me, seeing as I have a hard time pretending everything is alright when I can't stop the thoughts running through my head: *A man died because of me. I killed him. Billy Cloud is dead because of me.*

Jacob ignores me, preferring the company of his sketchbook. Father overlooks me as he keeps his attention on Jacob, waiting for his youngest son to step out of line so he can put him back on course. I am left on my own to entertain myself. The house is filled with the weight of our presence. No one has ventured out since I returned from Gran Alice's. At the same time, the house has been void of happiness, laughter, or warmth. I miss Mrs. Sally, and the cheerfulness she brought. I go on about my day helping with the meals, keeping up with the wood stove, reading, and finding solace in my animals. *You are an animal person.*

I have been working with Fleur on some, I guess they are tricks, but in a non-traditional sense. My mother's spirit was aligned with the caribou; what if I possess the spirit of the wolf, or dog? I recall the encounter with the white dog during our summer trip to Nain. That dog was not comfortable with Jacob, but with me it acted like we were litter mates. Maybe it just liked the way I smelled. Fleur feels a closeness to me, as if we were of one mind. Alice told me that Fleur would not take kindly to anyone before she met me. I have been thinking it might be time to see what limits Fleur and I have. Two animals, one spirit.

I wait until Fleur is sleeping in her spot near Edgar's perch, and I quietly make my way upstairs to my room. Rather than enter the room where Jacob sits in his dark cloud of poison, I sit quietly on top of the stairs. I close my eyes and I think about Fleur. In my mind I try to call her up to me. I am sure she can feel me calling. After five minutes of concentrating, I open my eyes and find that there is no dog. So, I go down to the kitchen and find a small scrap of leftover caribou in the fridge. I get it out, thinking about Fleur, and she immediately shows up by my side. I reward her with the meat. Now, I look at her as I stand above her, and I think to myself, *sit.* As soon as I think it, Fleur sits and looks at me expectantly. I give her another bite of meat. I put the scraps of meat away, save for one last treat. Fleur is watching me intently. I tell her with my mind to sit again. She sits and waits with hope in her eyes. I show her the flat of my hand – the sign for *stay* that I had taught her when I first got her. I walk into the living room, sit back on the sofa, and I send my mental messages to my dog to come to me.

Within ten seconds, she walks in from the kitchen, jumps onto the sofa, and starts sniffing and whining. I hand her the treat and scratch her ears. She is totally reading my mind. I am getting excited thinking of the possibilities.

We lay on the sofa for a short time before she gets up and wanders back to her sleep spot and curls up under Edgar's ever-watchful gaze. Again, I quietly sneak up to the top of the stairs and call Fleur in my mind. I hear movement downstairs. I am sure that Fleur is about to come to me, and then my father's bedroom door opens up, he comes out, steps around me, and walks down the stairs, breaking my concentration. He goes into the kitchen, opens the refrigerator, and immediately Fleur half runs into the kitchen in hopes of a snack. My heart sinks. Of course, she wasn't reading my mind. Fleur is just a dog, always on the ready for food offers.

I was hopeful I was a dog spirit person, but no, deep within me, in my subconscious? My soul? My – I don't know the word I'm looking for, but I can feel I am not a dog or wolf. I am a *kraken*, like my father.

A little disheartened, I grab my coat and hat and go to the back door. Fleur runs over to me, not reading my mind, but knowing my movements mean *outside time*. "I'm taking my dog out," I shout to my father. No answer. None expected. I watch Fleur as she runs out to the ever-present grayness of our world. The sea is calm, barely lapping at the shore. *You know my secrets*, I hear my mind say to the sea. The tide is down, exposing the seaweed and barnacle-covered rocks. I watch Fleur going up to her choice rocks to mark her territory. I let her be as I turn the corner to gather an armload of wood for the stove.

I go to the wood pile and pick up a couple pieces, and

something catches my peripheral vision. I look up and my heart freezes. Standing at the side of the yard is Billy Cloud, and he does not look good. Instantly, Fleur is by my side. Panic runs through my body. I feel ice circulate through my veins.

I blink the cold out of my eyes.

And he is gone.

In his stead stands Beck. She is smiling, and says, "God, Robert, you look like you've seen a ghost. Are you alright?"

I lean against the wood pile feeling rubber-legged. Hallucinations. Fleur felt it too. One mind, shared? No, two perceptive souls. I find my voice. "What are you doing out here? Have you been standing by, waiting for me to come out all morning?"

"How's Edgar?"

"What? Oh, he's doing well."

"I worry about him," she says.

"I have so much to tell you from the last couple of days. I was at Alice's and some strange woman turned up naked and frozen stiff in the yard – right under my bedroom window. And then Alice started telling me about spirits and animals, just like *you* said."

I step back from the wood pile, slip on the ice, and the next thing I know I am on the ground with Fleur licking my face and whining. I look up, "Well, that was a strange dizzy feeling. What have you …" Beck is gone. As if she was never there. I notice something on the ground where she was standing. I get up, go over to the spot, and pick up a small bundle of dried plants. The roots are still attached with a flourish of dried leaves. Cut separately and stuck in the bundle are dried flower heads. The brown bouquet is cut to about twelve centimeters, and tied with an old string to make a bunch about as thick as my wrist. Did Beck drop this, or was it already here?

"Robert, do you need a hand?" My father comes around the house looking inquisitive. I look at him, I look at the spot where Beck was, or wasn't, and I look back at Father, who is still looking solid. "You've been out here quite a while. I thought maybe you've run off like your brother. But of course, you wouldn't. The two of you are apples and oranges. Come on, I'll help you with the wood." I still feel a little dizzy, and the cold is seeping into my clothing. I pick up the logs I'd dropped while Father grabs a couple more from the stack. I am careful not to crush the dried plants that I have slipped into my coat, and I make my way into the house.

Inside, I stack the wood in the rack before going to the kitchen for a hot drink. I set the dried plants on the table in front of me to get a better look. I don't really know a lot about different kinds of plants, but I like the display. It's like a bundle of herbs left behind by a medicine woman. I decide to tie it to the top perch of Edgar's growing collection of perches. It hangs down a short bit so the bird can play with it and bat it with his beak, which is exactly what he does.

Father watches me watching the bird. "I continue to be impressed that you have kept this bird alive. Most wild things don't do well when confined." He watches a little longer and says, "Listen Robert, this is important." He places his giant hand on my shoulder and gives me a hard stare, "I need to take care of some business in town, and I've asked Mrs. Sally to come watch you, and mostly Jacob, for an hour or two. Jacob is not to leave this house. He is not to go outside one single step. Mrs. Sally has been told this as well. I'll be leaving as soon as she gets here. I know I can trust you, son, to be responsible for your younger brother. And I know how much you care for Mrs. Sally. It will be good for you both to have some time together."

Within an hour, Mrs. Sally arrives. Within ten minutes, it feels like she never left. Father was right: it is good to share some time with her. She is at the stove warming up some leftover chili that she brought with her. I sit at the table telling her of the past month's adventures. Jacob has not shown his face; he is hiding from the world in our room. Mrs. Sally is particularly curious about the woman in Alice's backyard. "You're sure she wasn't a misplaced harbor seal?" she asks, and we both roll our eyes at the last body episode I had.

"You know," Mrs. Sally confided, "they found out who the woman was that you found when you were at your grandmother's. She used to live here years ago. She had a cursed life, they say. Her father used to beat her horribly, both her parents were alcoholics, she left school at a young age, which seems to be the norm here, and soon she found herself with child. Her husband or boyfriend, whatever he was, was in a snowmobile accident and froze to death. She ended up taking her infant daughter down to St. John's to start a new life. People don't learn, you can't outrun a cursed life. The bad luck will follow you because it is inside of you like a devil. Her daughter – what was her name? – disappeared when she was a young teen. She was never found. So, the woman moved back to the inlet to give up on life. What *was* her daughter's name?"

A cold chill runs through me. I suddenly know the answer. I am afraid to say it. My mouth goes dry, and I force out, "Beck?"

"No, it was a longer name. A pretty name as I recall."

I breathe again. I was being stupid. Of course it wasn't Beck. We talk some more as we share the chili and some warm bread. I tell Mrs. Sally about Edgar, and she is curious to see a raven up close. Especially a tame one. We go over to his perch where he sits with his head on sideways, cooing at me. He takes a couple pokes at the hanging herbs and returns his attention to us. Mrs. Sally is completely taken by Edgar. She slowly reaches her hand out and allows him to give her love bites before stepping onto her wrist. Mrs. Sally is beaming with excitement. I am beaming with pride for my bird. "You know, the raven is said to be a transformer, a guide to transformations. The raven spirit can shift from bird to human and back to bird. I have been told of ravens changing into human form to interact with us and help to take our lives in directions that are needed for us. There are countless tales concerning the raven, I think they are mostly just for fun, but I also feel there is some truth in the old stories. The raven is a sneaky little trickster. I wouldn't be surprised if this bird of yours is simply tricking you into taking care of it for these cold winter days. Edgar is a beautiful bird all the same. Though I think you may have misnamed it. Notice its size? Edgar is a girl bird."

"Oh. I guess she will have to just be a girl Edgar," I say with a silly grin.

After some initial introduction time, Edgar jumps back onto his perch and returns to his, or *her*, new favorite herbal toy. I watch as she breaks off a small bit of the dried leaves and eats it.

"What is that?" Mrs. Sally grabs hold of the bundled plants and takes a close look. "Did you put this together?"

I shake my head. "I found it lying in the yard, like someone dropped it or it just blew there. I liked the smell of it."

"I'm sure you did. These are healing herbs. The pineapple weed, this one with the thin bunchy leaves and the now faded round flower heads, is a nice aromatic plant to ease your stress. The other plant which is broken up because it would be too big to make a small bundle with, is the primrose. Notice the longer thin leaves and the petaled yellow flowers. This also is a strong healing plant – the roots, leaves, and flowers. My mother used to use this for every ailment known." She looks at the bird and back at the herbs. "Come with me." We return to the kitchen, where she takes a small cutting from the herbs, a little bit of root, a bit of leaves, and a couple flowers, and she crumples them up in her hands to make a powder. The roots she uses a knife to cut up. She puts them in a small bowl, pours boiling water from the kettle over them. "We can put this on the floor for your bird to drink or to pick at, as she pleases. Who knows? It might help to bring her back to health. I want you to give her a fresh bowl of this tea each day. If your Edgar likes it, I will see if I can get some more of these dried plants for you." The rest of the bundle she hangs back up from the perch for the raven to play with.

A short time passes, and Jacob comes down once, quickly, to use the toilet, and disappears back upstairs without a word. I take a bowl of chili up to him, at Mrs. Sally's request, which he accepts at his desk while he continues to scribble in his sketch book. "Aren't you going to go down and say hi to Mrs. Sally?" I ask.

"No," is his only reply.

I look at the scowl that has become a permanent fixture on his face and ask, "Have you been painting in your sketchbook?"

"What? Why?" he asks.

"I don't know, you have some blue paint on the side of your nose. You look like you might be turning into a Smurf." My attempt to humor him fails, as he wipes the paint from his face and turns away.

I return to the sofa to read. Father comes in after an hour and a half of *taking care of business*. He speaks with Mrs. Sally softly in the kitchen for a while, then goes upstairs to change his shoes and remove his layers. Mrs. Sally packs up her things and comes into the living room. "I'll be leaving, Robert. Your father has asked me to come in for a couple of hours a day once again, with the problems he's having with Jacob and all. Anyway, it will be good to spend more time with you boys once more. And, Robert, you keep watch over Edgar and see if she doesn't get a little stronger with her herbal medicines. And don't let your dog drink all of the bird's tea."

I get up, go over to Mrs. Sally, and give her a hug. "Thanks for helping out." She is surprised by my show of affection. She smiles and tells me she is always around if I need her.

As she opens the front door to leave, she stops suddenly, snaps her fingers, and says, "*Rebecca.* that was the girl's name. So, yes, maybe Beck." And out she goes, happy to have not lost her memory.

I let her words sink in for a moment. I return to the sofa, sit down, and allow my mind to swirl.

From behind me, on the perch, I hear, "*Robert. Rah, rah, Robert.*"

34

Notes

December 17

I am in a panic. I did not sleep well. I lay in bed all night watching the silhouettes of clouds slowly breaking up and wisping away under the starry sky. There is no moon, it had set just after sunset, chasing the sun into the darkness, with no one to remark on it as both sun and moon had been secretly playing in a shroud of thick clouds. My thoughts have been swimming and continue to do so with the words *Rebecca … So, yes, maybe Beck*, reverberating through my head. Words don't die, they keep moving and bouncing. Energy cannot be destroyed. And people, do they truly die? Or does their spirit continue to move and bounce around? Rebecca and Beck are two different names and two different people. Of course, they are. It is the only possibility.

I get out some paper and a pen and start writing notes. One, I will tack up at the laundromat. Another will go into the wood pile. And yet another, I will post on a random piling at the docks. I can use the excuse of going to the grocery store. While I'm there, I might as well put a note on the message board at the entrance. Each note has a squid drawing and reads the same:

Must see you asap

It's not the best squid drawing, but I think she'll get the idea. And what if I don't hear from her? I can't even think in that direction. I grab my boots, mittens, coat, and hat, I call Fleur, and make for the door. "Father, I'm taking Fleur down to the grocer's. I'm out of dog food. Can I have some money for a bag?"

Father is in the kitchen, doing Father stuff. He looks up, "Well, I guess you'll be needing some money. You can't buy dog food on your good looks." He winks and hands me a ten. "And don't be long, lad. You've got your studies to keep up with."

I make my way down the street with Fleur on a leash and the notes in my pocket. The day is blindingly bright in my eyes. The temperatures have dropped with the clearing of the clouds. I keep Fleur close to me and walk without looking up. I do not want to see anybody if I can help it. I am filled with so many emotions this morning: fear of a secret behind Beck, fear and guilt from the killing of Billy Cloud, a lack of confidence in my new responsibilities of keeping Jacob secured in the house, and maybe some pride in my new official title of Animal Person – whatever that really means. I stop first at the docks and find a post with a small nail to stick my note on. It looks so obvious to me, but I feel most people will walk on by it as if it were nothing more than trash on the ground.

The laundromat has a couple of people in here, but they are busy folding their clothes and don't notice me pinning my second note on the bulletin board. Now, I hurry over to the grocery store, leave Fleur at the door, and run inside. I look around and find I can tack my third note up on the message board without being seen. I go down the aisle, grab a large bag of cheap dog food, and carry it to the checkout counter.

The lady at the counter looks at me, "That's a lot of dog food for a little guy."

"It's actually for my dog. I won't be eating it."

The cashier laughs, "My mistake, young man. Don't you have that big white dog? I don't know how you tamed it. That thing nearly killed its last owner and *did* kill a couple of good sled dogs. You haven't had any problems with it? I mean, biting anyone?"

Images of Billy Cloud fly through my head. I need to blink a couple times, breathe in deeply, and say, "No, she's a real gentle dog."

The lady shrugs, "Just stories, I guess." She hands me my change. I throw the dog food bag over my shoulder and go back outside. Fleur is waiting dutifully for me. I pick up her leash and make my way back down the street toward home.

35

Healing

December 18

"The bird is getting stronger already. See how she holds her head up. She doesn't look like a drunken sailor anymore. I've never seen such wonders. And she appears to be trying to use her wing more as she hops around." Mrs. Sally looks incredulously at the bird, and then over to me. "Such magic you have with animals. Your grandmother was right, I think. You *are* an animal person."

I smile at the compliment, "But you're the one that made the tea for her."

"I just used what you knew to be the right herbs for the healing. Think of me as your lovely assistant." Mrs. Sally does a little curtsy and laughs.

I am glad she is back with us, even if just for an hour or two each day. This house has felt like it had been smothered by twenty feet of snow. The air stale, the warmth sucked right out. We have all been suffocating.

Now, at least some laughter has been creeping back in.

Edgar looks at me with her deep brown eyes and coos softly. She takes a giant hop and flaps her wings to gain some lift, and lands on my shoulder. I walk her over to the kitchen with me where I sit down at the table to work more on my Canadian History studies. I wish Beck could come by to see how she's getting along. *Still* no word from her. I have been making more trips than necessary to the wood pile to look for replies to my notes. Nothing.

I had a haunting dream last night. It has been creeping around the edges of my mind all morning. I was flying with Edgar and his conspiracy of ravens; actually, a flock of ravens is also called an *unkindness*. Better than a *murder*, but not as cool as *conspiracy*. So, there I was, floating along with the soaring ravens, when I realized we were not flying, but we were underwater, swimming. We kept swimming deeper and the water kept getting darker. I could see a dull shape hovering in the water ahead of me, neither sinking nor floating, but it seemed to find equilibrium at whatever depth we had gone to. The ravens that had joined me flew around the shape and pulled it to me. When they dispersed I could see it was a figure. It slowly rotated in place with the sea current until its face was before my own. I found myself staring into Beck's wide-open eyes. She opened her mouth and said, "Rah-rah-Robert." Then all of the air escaped her lungs and she sank deeper. I woke up screaming. I was still wet from the sea. Again, I had to change clothes and hang my wet ones on my nearby desk chair. I have learned as of late to keep a spare pair within reach.

Mrs. Sally takes me out of my blank stare, "Will you do me a favor and ask Jacob to come down here? It's time to do some lessons with him. You might want to move your own work upstairs or in the living room so we don't disturb you."

I put Edgar back onto his perch, close up my books, and take them upstairs with me. "Jacob, Mrs. Sally wants you downstairs to get a lesson. I think it's mathematics."

Jacob avoids looking at me. He grunts something unintelligible and leaves the room. I don't know what is up with him. He has been this way since he and Father came back from the boat on the day of my own return from Alice's. Jacob's sketch book, which he has buried himself in as of late, is sitting on his desktop. I go to the door, and I can hear Mrs. Sally tutoring Jacob in his maths. I close the door and grab the sketchbook. I flip it to the most recent drawing. My jaw drops open, and I sit down. The picture depicts Father with gnashing teeth and eight arms. His eyes are red and shooting out lasers (I think). Next to him is a picture of (maybe) Jacob. He is holding a gun with fire coming out of it, and there is a speech bubble above him saying, "FUCK YOU. YOUR NOT MY FATHER. NOW DIE!!!"

My hands are shaking. I never knew anybody who talked like that. Maybe Billy Cloud, but he was always drunk. I flipped back to the previous page to see another depiction of Father with pointed teeth and eight arms. This time he is standing next to a smaller version of himself. Under the small monster was scribbled "SCOTTY MINI-MONSTER." Fleur, with the same big sharp teeth, sits between the two figures saying, "WE EAT PEEPLE". There is a lot of scribbling in black pencil in the sky around the three monsters. Another drawing – this one is a depiction of Fleur with blood coming from her eyes and baring teeth that look more like shark teeth. In front of the dog stand Jacob and a polar bear, each with large claws, knives, and sharp teeth. Below this drawing, the scribbled words: DOG-FUCK OF DETH MUST DIE. I flip through the book and it is filled with drawings of monsters, curse words, statements such as *I will kill you*, and half-Jacob half- polar bear creature carrying a knife or a gun. All of the drawings are in black pencil with red pencil for the blood spouting from bodies and mouths.

I look around, go to the door to make sure he isn't coming back, put the book back on the desktop just as I found it, and begin to rummage through his desk drawers. I am afraid I might find a knife, or maybe a gun. I see a lot of the things I figured I would find: pencils, random papers, a calculator, old cards, Hot Wheels cars, small plastic toys. Somewhat troubling is his collection of dinosaurs – all the carnivores have their heads cut off. But what makes me even more unsettled is Jacob's secret treasure given him by the man back in Nain, left on the desktop – the incisor of a polar bear. I look closely at it and wonder what it was that the man said to him about it. Perhaps he told him it had secret powers. Like Mrs. Sally said – strength and perseverance. In the bottom drawer or the desk, I find an extra piece of wood lining the bottom. A makeshift secret compartment, about three centimeters deep. I pull up the false bottom, and inside I find a zip-lock baggie. The inside is blue with a rag of sorts. I unzip it and find that the contents are just as they appeared – the bag contains a rag soaked in blue spray-paint. The odor immediately goes to my head, and I quickly close the baggie and put it back in the drawer. I hear Jacob coming up the steps and I sit at my desk as if I had been studying the whole time during his absence.

He comes into the room, grabs his sketchbook, gives me a distrustful look, which I guess I deserve, and sits back on the bed with nothing to say. He is not an easy person to be around. I pick up my book and go back down to the kitchen.

Mrs. Sally sits across from me and says, "What happened to our Jacob? He used to be filled with laughter and he would light up the room when he was here. Now he is a different person. It is as if his soul was taken from him."

"Mrs. Sally?" I hated to tell on my younger brother, but I can't stop myself. "I think Jacob has been huffing paint and gasoline with his friends again. Sometimes he smells that way," I look down and continue, "He has a baggie in his desk drawer with a rag covered in wet spray paint." I have betrayed him. I have just drawn a line between Jacob and myself that says, *we will never be the same again.*

Mrs. Sally gasps, and lets out a long sigh. "I'll talk to John. Don't worry, Jacob will never know that you were the one who told me this. In fact, your father already strongly suspects as much."

We sit in a long silence. Finally, I ask, "Do you remember that lady who died in Alice's backyard? The one you said had a daughter who died?"

"Yes. Is there something bothering you about it? Seeing a dead person can be a heavy experience."

"It's not that. I was just wondering about what her last name was. And maybe if you know more about her daughter, Rebecca?"

Mrs. Sally says, "The woman was called Mary Ravenswood. I knew her as I know everyone in this village. It's a small, isolated place we live in. As for the daughter, it is a bit of a mystery. And like all mysteries, there is not a shortage of stories that get passed around. I know that Mary was not close to her mother, but she was all she had. Occasionally she would write to her. In one particular letter, her mother shared it with me after church one day, Mary described how her daughter was at a seaside cliff just north of St. John's standing at the edge of a dreadful drop. Suddenly, a bunch of ravens – or were they crows? – came down by the dozens and surrounded her, a black cloak of moving feathers. Mary wrote that the birds took off for the sky, leaving no trace of Rebecca. She just vanished. It was assumed that Mary had lost her mind. It was also assumed that the girl fell or jumped off the cliff into the all-consuming sea below. When Mary returned here to the Davis Inlet, she kept to herself, speaking to no one. Well, in a sense she spoke to no one. She was often seen speaking to and laughing with Rebecca, who, of course, was not actually there. So, I suppose you can say she was speaking to no one."

A chill runs through me. I return to my studies.

36

Dog and Bird

December 19

Screams of terror come from the stairway. Father and I are just coming inside from gathering some logs to fend off yet another frigid day. Father runs to the stairway and I follow at his heels. Jacob is screaming, my dog is snarling. Fleur is on the step below Jacob with his lower leg in her mouth, dragging him down the steps. Father wraps his large arms around the dog's chest and, with his hands, pries her jaws open, allowing Jacob to scramble up to the top step whimpering. Father drops the dog and gives her a mighty kick down the steps, placing his own body between Jacob and Fleur. Fleur lands at my feet, where she sits leaning against my leg with her hair on end and a growl in her throat. She is shaking, so I stoop down and put my arm around her to calm her down. Father rolls up Jacob's pant leg and examines his skin. He looks at Jacob's face, and he looks back at the leg.

"She didn't break the skin," he says. "Tell me what happened."

Jacob is sobbing and his words come out ragged, "I don't know. The dog just came up and started biting me for no reason."

I am suddenly scared. Billy Cloud floats in front of me. I know what Fleur is capable of when she needs to protect me. But I wasn't in need of protection. I wasn't even in the house.

Father comes down the stairs, telling Jacob not to move from where he is. He looks at me, and he looks at Fleur. His brow is furrowed as if he is trying to figure it out. "Robert, what did you do to your hand? It's got blood on it."

"What?" I look at my hand and ask myself the same question, *What did I do to it?* I got some blood on Fleur as well. Wait, the blood is coming from Fleur. I look closely at my dog, and see a hole, no, *two* small holes in her. A small wound on her shoulder and another on the left side of her forehead. Father sees the wounds and looks up at Jacob, who grabs something from the floor at the top of the stairs and slides it behind his back. My father, who often reminds us that he had not just fallen off the back of the potato truck, watches Jacob's movements.

"What have you got there, son?" he says with a new intonation in his voice. Jacob says nothing. "Why don't you give me whatever you have behind your back?" I watch as he turns from a concerned and worried father into a growing monster filling with rage. Jacob looks at Father with wide frightened eyes but does not move. Father takes one giant step up the three stairs that separate the two of them, and grabs Jacob's small body in his giant arms, picks him up, and carries him into our room.

As they disappear, Jacob drops something from his grip. His slingshot.

Dog-fuck of deth must die.

Fleur was not attacking Jacob, but defending herself, and by proxy, defending me. I hear Father's roar as it rises in volume. Jacob screams in terror. I cannot stay here and witness this coming chain of events. Still wearing my coat and boots, I grab Fleur's leash and take her outside to escape. I am no longer certain which of the two facing off upstairs is the true monster. Jacob's epic play battles of Tyrannosaurus Rex versus Triceratops plays through my mind.

I walk Fleur around the backyard, along the side, and to the road in the front. Looking down the road, I see nothing but winter, a frozen world gritting its teeth in wait of a new spring. I am overcome with a sudden need for the spring thaw. In two days' time, we will have the shortest day of the year. The new moon will watch us from its hiding, and from that day on, the days will start to stretch out. I will count the days till the snow melts and the first tundra flowers greet the sun.

I walk Fleur along the final path of Billy Cloud toward monster beach. An especially low tide invites the sea bottom to rise up to this day. We walk over the small rocks, onto the barnacles, and through the stranded, slumped seaweed with its resident crabs darting in and out of their shelter, carefully balancing a search for food with an avoidance of prolonged exposure to the subzero air. Broken sheets of frozen seawater lie scattered on the rocks as the tides break and refreeze the surface ice on the water. With no waves to speak of, I am able to walk up to the edge of the water without fear of wet feet. Under that ice lies a body, or two, or three, or even a hundred from the past centuries – or decades -- seeing how people seem to die like flies in these quarters of the world. Some have been dragged into the water, others have gone in of their own volition. *Volition.* I miss Mrs. Sally's vocabulary lessons. I hope she brings them back. My expanding collection of words is like a door to a new world. I could be a Writer. Or a Speaker. An *Orator.*

Above me, a pair of gulls scream out, no doubt scouring the tidal bed from above. A raven lands on a nearby piece of driftwood but says nothing. It watches me carefully. It has something in its mouth. It flies into the air, circles around once, and drops a stone on me.

"Ow. Watch it!"

The raven lands again, a little farther away. Again, it jumps up, takes wing, and deposits another rock on my head.

"What?! Hey! Stop it!"

This odd behavior continues until I manage to catch one of the rocks, cradle it in my palm, and take aim to give the bird back its own medicine. But as I look at the raven, I get a chill as the image of Jacob aiming his slingshot at Fleur dances in front of me.

Cruelty. I will have none of it. Instead, I allow my fingers to explore the smooth sides of the flat, rounded stone in my hand. I look at it closely and notice the thin, white random line that crosses the surface. I look down at the ground at the other rocks that the raven dropped. Every one of them, the same. Thin white lines of quartz running through them. *They're wishing rocks. Hold one tightly in your hand, hold your hand to your heart, and concentrate on what you want most.*

I look around, "Beck?"

"Rah Robert." The raven calls, and then gives out its

usual jagged call.

A trickster. A transformer. A guide to transformations. I look on at the bird. In a quiet, strained voice, I say to it, "Beck, is that you?" I feel foolish. I gather up the stones that the raven offered me, and I fill my pocket. One stone I keep in my hand, hold it close to my heart, close my eyes. And I make my wish.

37

The Broken and the Whole

December 20

Jacob is broken. Edgar is whole again.

These long nights are killing me. I feel the brewing storm that is Jacob in my bed next to me. He no longer speaks. Yesterday's encounter with our father seems to have destroyed him. He should be thankful that Father didn't transform into a monster and eat him. He should be thankful that Father has never laid a hand on us in anger. But what I heard yesterday coming from this room … I too would be broken, had I been at the receiving end of Father's rage. I believe it was all that Father could do not to expose the *kraken* that lurks inside him.

Jacob is shut down. He will not look at me. He will not talk to me. He will not eat. He will not move from his corner of the bed.

The sun is just rising, thank goodness, because I have to get up and leave the room. Fleur had to sleep downstairs to keep her at safe distance from Jacob. I am not sure what either would do to the other. All morning I have been listening to Edgar calling out in an uncharacteristic manner. Perhaps she and Fleur had things to say to each other. I make my way down the steps and I am immediately smacked in the head with what feels like a wadded-up rag. I regain my composure only to be hit from the other side. What is going on? I look to my left, and flying around the living room, somewhat awkwardly, is Edgar. She is hopping from one perch to another, taking flight to the back of the sofa, and back to the kitchen. Fleur is plastering herself as close to the floor as possible, not sure what to make of the raven.

"Well, thank God you're up," says Mrs. Sally from the back corner of the kitchen.

I jump, just as surprised that she is here as I was that Edgar was flopping into my head.

"I'm sorry, Robert. I didn't mean to startle you. Your father asked me to come in early this morning. He mumbled something about your brother. I take it they aren't getting on so well. Anyways, I came into the house and Edgar is going nuts, flying everywhere, running into everything. It looks like she finally made her transformation. Either that, or she has indeed been having us on all this time. You know Robert, the strangest of animal souls seem to end up in your care." Mrs. Sally stands in the kitchen doorway, drying off her hands from preparing breakfast. Her long black hair is tied back in a braid, which she does when she has no time to wash it. "I suppose you're going to have to offer Edgar her freedom soon. She may not take it, but a wild thing needs to be able to be wild. Maybe move her perch outside during the day. If she wants to come inside at night, then so be it."

I eat some oatmeal, eggs, and potatoes, down some tea, and move to the living room to see Edgar. She is restless and still flying around driving Fleur a little crazy. I grab Edgar's set of perches and take them out the back door. I set them up close to the side of the house just under the eaves to protect Edgar from the weather. Edgar and Fleur both follow me out the door. Edgar takes flight around the backyard and lands on a boulder. She calls out a couple of times, looks around as if surprised to find herself back outside, and flies over to me and lands on her perch. I bring out her food bowl and her special herbal tea and leave her to herself.

The house seems empty without the raven. She has only been here for two or three weeks, but I have got used to her. I refill my tea, stoke up the fire which Father must have started up early this morning, and sit back on the sofa. I'll give the sun a couple of hours to warm this day up before taking Fleur out for a good walk. We will head to the docks in hopes of seeing Beck. I fear she is gone forever, and I can barely stand it. Tomorrow is the solstice. We should be celebrating, but I don't know that this will be a year of celebration. Father will be here all day. Mrs. Sally may not. I do not foresee Jacob celebrating anything. And Beck has vanished. Maybe it is good that I am an *animal person*. It seems that animals are all I will have to celebrate with.

* * *

The one o'clock hour comes, and the day will get no warmer. I dress accordingly and grab the leash. Fleur is at my side immediately. We walk down the street toward the *Bonnie Marie*. I see one of Jacob's friends on the way. The taller one.

"Hey Scotty," he yells to me, "where's your brother? Did the monster finally eat him?" He laughs.

I ignore him. I didn't think he would be so intimidating on his own, but he easily steps up to the position of fearless bully.

The boy calls out again, "What, are you running from me? Scared of a little Eskimo? Hey, I'd come over and kick your ass back to Scotty-land if you didn't have your dog with you."

I pull Fleur closer to my side. She feels my anxiousness and tenses up in response. I continue down to the docks. My eyes are constantly sweeping the area in hopes of catching sight of Beck. Nothing. I go to the boat where Father is sitting in the cabin talking with Mr. Dave. Father signals me to come and join them. On the table, they have a map spread out before them.

"Robert," my father says, "we were just charting out some possible routes to Scotland. You're a smart lad, any ideas?"

I would normally be a little shy about saying anything, but with Mr. Dave's presence I find I am relaxed. I am suddenly very happy that he will be traveling with us. I look closely at the map at hand and remark, "Nanortalik. That would be the best town in Greenland to aim for. But we will have to go a bit north to make compensations for the currents that will fight us the whole way. I think we should stay close to the coast as much as possible and stop at the southernmost point of Greenland. I heard they have a sandy swimming beach there."

Mr. Dave raises an eyebrow, "Maybe you should consider a life as a sailor." He looks at Father, "He must be from Labrador, if he thinks a beach in Greenland would be in any way desirable." The two men laugh.

After a short time in the comparatively warm cabin speaking of possibilities, Father gets up and says, "I'll see you in a couple days, Dave. I need to walk this young man home and see about an early dinner. You're welcome to join us if you wish."

"Thanks, John, but I have a date with a sweet girl this evening. And if I don't shower and clean up first, it may be my last date with her. I tell you what, I need to mind my step, I'm running out of available women in this village." He smiles and goes off on his own way.

38

Winter Solstice

December 21

The sun will set just at 3:30 p.m. and will not bother to get up until 8:00 a.m. or later. These are the hardest nights to stay in bed. As usual, I will have to put some snacks, a glass of water, and a book on the nightstand, and a bucket on the side of our bed for when I wake in the middle of the night to pee. One of our assignments with Mrs. Sally was to make a chart with the sunrise and sunset times for each day of the year. Jacob is no good with numbers or time yet, so I had to do most of the work. We hung the poster we made on the wall of our bedroom next to our clock. This was important, since on cloudy days we could not tell where the sun was.

Tonight will be the winter solstice. The longest night of the year. During the shortened day we usually celebrate the soon-to-be shortening darkness by running around the backyard in the snow and wearing ourselves out. We periodically go inside to warm up at the ever-present fire in the wood-burning stove. We stay active all day so that we are able to sleep through the eternal night. There are no lessons today and Mrs. Sally is not visiting to help us celebrate. It seems as if I have enough energy to run a hundred kilometers through the snow with Fleur. Jacob, on the other hand, has been getting more tired and tearful throughout this day. Father bids him to leave our bedroom and join in today's celebration, but he is worse than his usual self and sits motionless on the sofa. It is half past two and my father goes to Jacob and puts his hand on his forehead. "You're burning up," my father says. He gets a thermometer from our bathroom medicine cabinet and takes Jacob's temperature. "Nearly forty degrees," he says quietly. My father's eyes narrow with worry. This makes me scared. I know that normal body heat is thirty-seven degrees Celsius. That is what Mrs. Sally taught us last year. Jacob is sitting in front of the wood stove, wrapped in blankets and shivering. Sweat is covering his face. He speaks and mumbles, but makes little sense.

My father says Jacob needs to go to bed and that I might as well go too, as the sun will soon be setting. We crawl into bed and even though the room is warm from the rising heat of the downstairs stove, Jacob worms deep into the quilts and whimpers. I am plenty warm and stay on top of the covers for now, though I know that the fire will grow cold by morning and I will have to burrow in close to Jacob. In his current state, I don't think he will object. Our father says that he will leave our door open and says his goodnights. He looks at me and puts on his most serious face, "Robert, do not let Jacob get out of that bed tonight. This is the longest night of the year, and the most dangerous."

Throughout the evening and late into the night, Jacob cries and murmurs and shouts out in his weak voice. He calls for our mother and seems to be speaking to her. By midnight, the bed is moist from his sweating body. He complains of aching arms and legs. His head hurts. He calls to our father, but he is in his own room in his bed, making his animal noises. This night will never end. I turn on my bedside lamp and light my lantern and read for a while.

At four in the morning, with another four hours to go, Jacob sits up, screaming. He tries to get out of the bed, so I roll over on top of him to stop him from struggling. The light of my lantern, which I left burning just in case, shines on his sweat-covered face. I hold him down tight. Jacob shouts out, "She's out there! Our mother!" I lay on top of him, speaking softly into his ears. Telling him to go back to sleep, for it was only a dream. I hear our father yelling out in the next room.

And now, I hear the other noise. A soft, scraping sound, mixed with whispers. It is coming from outside the house. I freeze. I don't dare make a stir. I cover Jacob's mouth. "Shhh." I hear the front door shake. The soft, almost inaudible voice of a woman can be heard. No, it is Edgar. No, it is our mother. No, it is the wind. Now the wind blows and the windows rattle with the force. My body turns to ice. I cannot move.

Again, Jacob cries out. "It's our mother. She's calling us. She's stuck outside with the *kraken*. We have to let her in." He pleads with me through his fever-induced hallucinations. Only they are not hallucinations, for I hear them too. I hold strong to Jacob and we stay that way, tangled together, his fevered body wrapped up in my own cool body. Two brothers in a room lit by one candle. In a night that cries for the light of a moon that is lost in the sun. Two brothers lost in a small village at the edge of the sea. Our father's rumblings, as always, continue in the next room. And eventually, fitfully, we fall asleep.

***

I awaken at a quarter to eight. Eighteen minutes until sunrise. We made it. The longest night. *Perhaps it was nothing but dreams*, I tell myself. And now, each night shall get shorter, and everything will be normal again. I roll over to wake up Jacob from his fever-filled slumber.

His side of the bed is empty.

39

Just the Two of Us

May 3, 1996

This house is an empty shell. It has been five months of empty nights and hollow days. There are no words bouncing around the walls. There is nothing but guilt, and holes in our hearts. Father no longer says a word. The people of the town stare and whisper on those rare occasions that we are out. Jacob has never been found. Missing now since forever ago. Missing now since just minutes ago. Missing since the winter solstice. We spent every hour of the days and nights following his disappearance hunting for clues of his whereabouts. Fleur and I had sniffed out every square foot of Davis Inlet. Every house and outbuilding. Every bit of shoreline and wilderness on this rock. Father and his friends dragged the Inlet waters with fishing nets, coming up with nothing more than fish, seaweed, trash, and the carcasses of long-dead sea mammals. We talked to every resident of this village and turned up with empty hopes. After a week, I knew he was dead. If he tried to run away, he did so on his own and there would be no way off this island over an ice-choked waterway. January's ravaging ice winds were topped only by the relentless arctic blizzards of February.

The first day of Jacob's vanishing, December 22, Father searched through Jacob's belongings for clues to his whereabouts. I took Jacob's sketchbook and hid it in my own belongings to spare Father the pain of Jacob's tortured mind. As always, the town's people whispered stories and accusations concerning the murder of the Innu boy who lived with a white family. A boy whose mother was murdered just a few years earlier. The whispers spoke of a large brutish Scotsman who was a monster in his own right. Again, they brought up stories of the dog that eats people. Rumors were resurrected concerning the disappearance of Billy Cloud. Even Mrs. Sally was looked on with suspicion by virtue of association. Our lives echoed the somber death grip that winter seems to have had on this world. A particularly harsh winter, they say. Dogs and wolves alike were found frozen on the ground. The older people of the village had been relenting to the season of slumber and watching the end of their lives come drifting in.

And now, on this early day of spring, the second of May, the ice is giving way to the lichen-covered rocks below. The first green leaves are pushing their way through the soil to rejoice in the sun's heat, absent for so long. The migratory birds are returning, and the occasional seal can be seen bobbing along with the current. Father has again returned to life on the sea, coming home each day smelling of seaweed, wet nets, and fish entrails. The memories of Beck still linger in my peripheral mind like sweet dew on the morning buttercups, as the memories of Jacob loom large and hard, pounding waves on a jagged rocky shore. The light spring rains, followed by the sparkling sunlight as it refracts in the lingering raindrops, bring life back to our world, back to our house.

I would have thought it impossible, but we are returning to life as a family. A family of two. Though Mrs. Sally is here for most of the day, and Mr. Dave seems to drop by far more often. And Edgar the bird, for some reason she is still around, but seems to be getting more restless in these lengthening days. She stays away for a couple days at a time as she joins in with the other ravens. Mrs. Sally says it is mating season for all living beings and they all are helpless to heed the call of nature.

Father and Mr. Dave spend a lot of time working on the *Bonnie Marie* to ready her for the voyage. They are replacing whatever old parts that are in need of it, painting the hull, adding drums and compartments to hold what Mr. Dave says is *enough gasoline to blow the whole island into the sea.* Sometimes when I go to help with the cleaning of the boat, I see Father crack a smile, ever so slightly. Mr. Dave says quietly, "Time heals our wounds, and God knows your father has plenty of open wounds in need of some care."

Fleur is now my only friend. I am counting the days until we leave the island. Fifty days. Mrs. Sally will be sad to see us go. Still, she gets excited as she speaks of the future that awaits me. Since last June, she has been making me keep a journal. I now know what to call it – *My Final Year in Davis Inlet*. And then I subtitle it: *(Monsters in Us All)*. This makes Mrs. Sally smile.

40

Departure

June 21

It is fitting that we shall embark on our journey on the summer solstice.

"Put your bag in the cabin, Robert, wherever you plan on sleeping." Father has been yelling out orders all morning. He is a mix of emotions, as am I. We pack up the *Bonnie Marie* intrepidly, filled with anxieties, heavy hearts, high hopes, excitement. It is hard to isolate one feeling from another. They are intertwined like a forest of roots underground.

I am allowed one bag. That is it. I put a couple changes of clothes, rain gear, books, and one or two keepsakes into my dry bag, and close it up tight. In my pockets, always, I keep my special rock and my lighter. I take my turn at loading vast amounts of sea rations and gallons of fuel onto the boat. Father goes over the equipment in the cabin one final time, sorts through the charts, checks all the ropes securing the cargo.

There is only a handful of people on the dock to see us off. To Mrs. Sally and Gran Alice, I give giant hugs amid tears. The others are mostly old men, old to me anyway, who are shaking their heads in wonder. I do not know if their sense of wonder is derived from the beauty of our boat and the bravery we hold within us, or if it is over the folly of this entire expedition. Ravens fly past us, and one smallish raven lands on my head and allows me to reach up and scratch her neck, to the awe of the onlookers. Edgar flies off and rejoins the other ravens. I get Fleur into the back of the boat, and I sit down on the bench with her by my feet.

Father is talking with the other men on the dock. "Aye, we'll be heading a bit north to avoid any hurricane that may try to catch us. At the same time, we surely don't want to go too far north, lest we find ourselves stuck in a sea of icebergs. I don't fancy being the next *Titanic*." Everyone laughs and chuckles.

Finally, goodbyes are said, and we motor away from the docks. I sit and watch as my hometown slowly floats away from me. We pass by our house, our shore, monster beach, Jacob. I squeeze shut my eyes and try to let go of this place. The only place I know. I try to think of our lives ahead in Kirkwall.

We all look to the sunrise and get lost, each in his own thoughts.

"Father," I ask, "Are there any monsters in Scotland?"